P9-CEO-131

The
Nobodies

The
Nobodies

Liza Palmer

FLATIRON
BOOKS
NEW YORK

THE NOBODIES. Copyright © 2019 by Liza Palmer. All rights reserved.
Printed in the United States of America. For information, address
Flatiron Books, 120 Broadway, New York, NY 10271.

www.flatironbooks.com

Designed by Devan Norman

Library of Congress Cataloging-in-Publication Data

Names: Palmer, Liza, author.
Title: The nobodies : a novel / Liza Palmer.
Description: First Edition. | New York : Flatiron Books, 2019.
Identifiers: LCCN 2019012555| ISBN 9781250169846 (hardcover) |
    ISBN 9781250169853 (ebook)
Classification: LCC PS3616.A343 N63 2019 | DDC 813/.6—dc23
LC record available at https://lccn.loc.gov/2019012555

Our books may be purchased in bulk for promotional, educational, or
business use. Please contact your local bookseller or the Macmillan Corporate
and Premium Sales Department at 1-800-221-7945, extension 5442,
or by email at MacmillanSpecialMarkets@macmillan.com.

First Edition: September 2019

10 9 8 7 6 5 4 3 2 1

This book is for my fellow failures.
We're going to be okay.
It's just going to be a different kind of okay.

The
Nobodies

1

[crying emoji]

"This is that rock bottom I'm going to mine for the inspiring commencement speech I'll give at an Ivy League college in a few years. This is that fun, disruptive detour I'll laugh about on various international stages while dispensing my pearls of wisdom to auditoriums full of admirers. This is the temporary crucible of failure in which I will create my greatest work and—"

"Cute top. Vintage?"

"What?" I turn around, interrupted before I can finish the well-practiced pep talk I've been giving myself over the last two weeks.

This very same rousing speech got me through yesterday's interview for a job as a part-time receptionist at a small insurance company in Pasadena. A few days before that, I whispered this speech as I power-stood in the poorly lit ladies' bathroom of a dentist's office in Highland Park that needed a file clerk. And the week before that, I screamed it in a garbage-drenched back alley just before trying to convince a surly biker that I could be the best bar back in the world. He laughed in my face about the bar back job, but then said he did need a go-go dancer for the weekday lunch hour, if I'd be interested in that. When I hesitated, he then scanned my body, flicked his toothpick to the other side of his mouth, and shrugged that I'd only have to show "maybe one titty."

It's nice to know that I've got options going into today's job interview.

"Is your top vintage?" he repeats. I loosen my fingers from around the cold metal bar that's supposed to stop me from launching myself over the side of this rooftop parking garage and face the inquiring gentleman. Chunky mint-green glasses. Floral shirt with shoulder pads. Jodhpurs.

"No, it's just from my closet," I say, touching the fabric of my shirt with newfound disdain.

"You're hilarious." He loops his messenger bag over his head and meticulously flips his collar so it falls perfectly over the argyle-patterned strap. "Have a wonderful day." He pushes his glasses farther up his nose and waits.

"Yeah, you too," I say, feeling downright bullied into reciprocating his obscene level of cheerfulness. I watch him suspiciously as he bounds down the four flights of stairs instead of taking the perfectly good elevator. Once he's gone, I'm finally able to finish my now thoroughly deflated speech.

"—the temporary crucible of failure in which I will create my greatest work and prove her wrong. I'll prove them all wrong."

~~~~~

Bloom. A company of trendy tech people whose parents have no idea what they do for a living. And me.

I pull open the glass doors.

There is no lobby. Bloom's neon blue flower logo takes up an entire wall. I quickly scan for anything familiar. Receptionist? No. Coffee table with old magazines? No. The swell of pride and purpose I once enjoyed as an award-winning journalist? No.

I step forward a few more careful inches. The impossibly cool workforce moves like blood cells, hurtling through the rows upon rows of computers that cut up the barn-like space. I reach into my pocket for my phone, hoping to offer my proximity to technology as a white flag.

I scroll through my group text thread and scan the texts I've gotten in the last five minutes. Reuben's play is opening tonight. We're getting tacos and then caravanning over to the theater. Lynn is asking about the parking situation. Hugo says he *thinks* there's street parking. I pocket my phone before the untold thousands of follow-up texts come flooding in. A conversation about parking in Los Angeles is never a brief one.

"Welcome to Bloom, how are you today?" It's the man from the garage. "Oh, hey. I know you!" His effortless intimacy and exuberance makes me immediately wary. I can feel my phone buzzing in my pocket.

"Hi. I'm—"

"Hi!" Eyes narrowed.

"Hi," I say.

"I'm Caspian."

"Hi."

"Hi!" Do I . . . is it my turn? Caspian continues, "You have lovely skin, what kind of moisturizer do you use?"

"It's this homemade soap my parents make, but it's not just for the face, it's . . ." Why am I still talking? "It's for the whole body."

"Oh, fun. I live with my parents too."

If it weren't for the hyper-efficient numbing I've perfected in the eight months since I got laid off and subsequently had to move back in with my parents, Caspian's comment about our comparable living arrangements would have flattened me. Thank god I'm a mere husk of the person I once was. Every cloud.

Caspian hands me a clipboard. I take it. "So, Ria is running a bit late, but if you fill this out for me, maybe we can wrangle you a glass of cold brew before your interview."

I'd heard about the secrecy at tech companies and look down at the clipboard fully expecting to find a nondisclosure agreement attached. Instead, I find what appears to be a three-question survey about my first impressions of Bloom. Each question is multiple choice, but rather than A, B and C, they've provided (neutral face emoji), (heart eyes emoji), and (crying emoji) to help me express myself.

"How did you know who I was here to see?" I ask.

"I am the all-seeing eye." He pauses for dramatic effect. "I'm just kidding!" He awaits my reply with a troublesome level of eye contact.

"Phew," I offer meekly.

"But I kind of am, though." He lowers his clunky mint-green glasses. "I know everything." He turns his monitor around and points to today's schedule. "You're Joan Dixon. Here to interview for the junior copywriter job with Ria Jones. I got you, girl."

As I scan the survey, Caspian greets every single Bloom employee who walks past his counter with unadulterated joy. The bespectacled IT kid. Exclamations and high fives. The pack of fashion mavens. Peals of laughter and a quick selfie. The blue-haired Amazon carrying a motorcycle helmet. Tight, closed-eye hug.

I circle the (heart eyes emoji) for my parking experience. A (neutral face emoji) for the Bloom lobby and a (crying emoji) for "Initial Human Greeting"—which I can only assume is tech for Caspian.

"You said something about coffee?" I ask, handing the survey back to Caspian.

"Ooh, yes." He unclips the survey, scans it, and sets it into a pile. "Right this way." He hops up onto the counter and spins around, landing in front of me with the grace of an Olympic gymnast. "That took me months to perfect," he says with a wink.

"Is this my 9 A.M.?" A voice from behind us asks. We turn around. Tall and lanky, Ria Jones has on a flannel shirt, vintage wingtips, and pants that could, at best, be categorized as "high-waters." Her dread-locked hair is swept up in an immaculately tied wrap.

"Yes, hi. Joan Dixon," I say, extending my hand. Ria takes it. Firm handshake.

"Ria Jones. Let's get to it then." Ria motions for me to walk into the mosh pit that appears to be the inner workings of Bloom. Ria abruptly stops, turns around. "Which room are we in, Cas?"

"You guys are in Tupac," Caspian says, air-kissing a girl who's wearing a misshapen, plum-colored felted hat.

Ria speaks like she's atop a double-decker bus careening down Hollywood Boulevard. "Bloom was started eighteen months ago by Chris Lawrence and Asher Lyndon, but the legend began over ten years ago in a Caltech dorm room when the then roommates developed the CAM algorithm. CAM, which stands for Collects All Materials, is—"

"So, it's a storage unit. Like, a digital storage unit," I say, absently scanning the conference rooms as we stride past: Freddie, Whitney, Luther, and what looks to be a real corker of a meeting going off in Selena. When I focus back on Ria, she is not amused.

"The CAM algorithm sets Bloom apart. It means we don't use server farms."

"Very interesting," I say, trying to work out the theme of the conference rooms.

"So, yes, CAM is like a digital storage unit, but without the actual hassle of a physical storage unit." I nod, my face twisted in focused concentration that—a-ha, got it! The conference rooms are named after beloved, yet sadly passed, singers. Ria conveniently mistakes my euphoric expression for an understanding of whatever it is she's talking about. Continuing her speech, she checks us in on the tablet just outside our conference room, opens the door to Tupac, and motions for me to go in. I oblige her. "We moved into this office space just last month, so pardon the mess. A tech company that's more company than tech, Chris and Asher started Bloom in order to make it more accessible because we all experience tech differently."

Based upon Ria's nonsensical—yet clearly practiced—dissertation, Bloom's need for copywriters is worse than I thought.

Ria settles herself on an uncomfortably modern gray tweed couch. Cement block walls. Dark wood rafters. Ria screws open the lid of her travel mug and the smell of coffee wafts through the tiny conference room. My seating options are a navy-blue beanbag chair or a persimmon-colored cube adorned with pizza slices. I choose the cube.

"What does Bloom actually do?" I wait. Ria sets her coffee on the cement floor.

"So, you were a journalist?" Ria asks, ignoring my question. She sifts through her messenger bag, pulling a large stack of applications from its depths.

"I am," I say. Ria looks up at me, vaguely curious.

"But that's not what you're applying to do here?"

"No." It dawns on me. "No, you're right. I meant to say that I *was* a journalist." Ria nods. She flips through the papers, finally pulling mine from the heap.

"Right." Ria scans my application.

"Right," I repeat. I wonder if now is when I should let Ria know that I am a highly sought-after applicant, already fielding exciting part-time work loosing one boob at a time for lucky lunchtime diners along the Pico-Fairfax Corridor.

"Let's move on," Ria says, crossing her legs. "You didn't go to college."

"I was able to get an internship at *The LA Times* right out of high school," I say.

"That's impressive."

"Thank you."

"How did you manage that?"

"When I was the editor of my high school newspaper, I broke the story of a city councilwoman who was taking bribes. It was this whole land development deal. Usual politics stuff, but the woman was pristine before this went down."

"How old were you?"

"Seventeen."

"You went on to cover local school board meetings."

"Politics, yes."

"Which Hogwarts house would you be sorted in?"

"I'm sorry?" My voice stutters.

"Which Hogwarts house would you be sorted in?"

I am . . . quiet. Stumped.

"Hm." Ria scribbles something on my application. She's decided something about me.

"Is that important? That I know that?" I ask.

"You've had seven jobs in under a year."

"I'm . . . was a journalist. The work is primarily freelance."

"And would that freelance work continue should you be hired here at Bloom?"

"At the moment, I'm looking for a full-time job to replace the freelancing."

"But—and excuse me if . . . I'm just having a hard time under-standing. Isn't there full-time work within the field of journalism that would better suit someone of your skill, age, and experience?"

(crying emoji)

I try to find the spin. Find the reason I've been unemployed. The exhausting hustle. Walking another box full of my belongings through a crowd of people who are relieved it wasn't them. Getting evicted from the shithole studio apartment that was already a last resort. Having to move back home with my parents. Spending six months writing a story I thought would put me back on top only to be told that it—along with my writing—wasn't compelling enough to "even run on someone's online blog, Joan."

"Joan?" Ria asks. "Why the gap?"

"I've been applying for jobs within the journalism field. I haven't—"

"No one will hire you on full time."

"No."

"Why do you think that is?"

"Why are you asking?"

"To see if you understand where your strengths and weaknesses are."

"For a junior copywriter job?"

"Do you think the job is beneath you?"

"I don't think any job is beneath me."

"You're thirty-six, and, no offense, but most of our junior copy-writers are twenty-two, twenty-three. Fresh out of college." I am quiet. Ria leans down, picks up her coffee. Unscrews the top. She contin-ues, "So, why should I hire you?"

Ria sits back on the couch, takes a long drink of her coffee. I study her as she luxuriates in what is most assuredly some kind of pour-over home brew that has to be prepared in just the right way. Fresh face, no makeup. Pressed jeans with cuffs that had to have been measured, they're so symmetrical. The printed-out applications. Calling Caspian Cas. A 9 A.M. interview.

I take a breath. "The world is changing. Companies like Bloom are the future. I am a serious applicant and want to learn. And the way I learn, as you can see from my application and work history, is by doing. Let me try."

Ria screws the top of her coffee tight and stands. She extends her hand. "Thank you. I will let you know." I take her hand. Firm handshake.

"I'll work hard." I look her right in the eye. She holds my gaze. "Please." An efficient nod. Ria opens the door to the conference room and we walk out.

"Remember to get your parking validated on the way out." She walks me back to the front desk.

"I took the bus, so I don't need validation. But thank you," I say.

"Well, then you're all set," Ria says and leaves without another word.

"You are seen and valued," Caspian says with a wink. His voice dips to a whisper. "Get it? Validated?"

If only it were that easy.

2

To Go

I loved being a journalist.

The habit of sitting down at my computer, notebooks filled with my coded shorthand. Stakeouts and cheap hotel rooms. Catching someone red-handed, unearthing long-buried secrets. Connecting the dots and finding the pattern. And the cruelest cut of all? Losing my chance to do it, but not my need for it. All of that energy still swirled inside me. But, instead of putting it to good use, it just ran around the field looking for nonexistent sheep to herd.

I whittled down my expenses, cut phone lines, television, cable, traded in my car for one I could buy for cash and then sold that car because I couldn't afford the insurance anymore. All this, just so I could keep writing. I wrote listicles and quizzes, pitched think pieces, started a podcast, followed the trending hashtags, wrote "for exposure" hoping it would turn into a steady gig (it never did). And I slowly, quietly, ever so painlessly drowned.

But then I found The Dry Cleaning Story. It had everything: family drama, extortion, infidelity, and a backdrop of a sleepy, upscale neighborhood dry cleaning store.

Over the next six months, I tirelessly researched, wrote, revised the story, belt-tightened, pep-talked, and picked up shifts at my parents' gardening center whenever they had an open slot. I sent countless breezy emails to anyone and everyone for whom I'd ever worked.

Late one night after a particularly furious Googling session of all the breathtakingly mediocre journalists who, as far as I could tell, appeared to be thriving, I decided it was time to go big or go home. I emailed Tavia Keppel with a synopsis of The Dry Cleaning Story and asked for a meeting. Yes, it was a Hail Mary. But I truly believed I finally had a story worthy of a Hail Mary. My email went unanswered for months.

Tavia Keppel's family name can be seen all over on theaters, hospital wings, and libraries around Los Angeles. Her family's history is threaded into the lore of old Hollywood. Grand parties at their mansions, scandals covered (or not covered) in their newspapers, and stars made and unmade in the movies they produced. The Keppel family did it all. I'd caught her eye—or rather my work had—when I was nineteen. She'd read a story I'd done and said I had "natural talent" and wrote for "the ordinary people." Tavia's compliments always had a way of cementing how lucky someone like me was just to be in her orbit.

And then, two weeks ago, Tavia texted: "lunch drinks today. 1115 soho house."

It was my chance.

"Hi, I'm meeting Tavia Keppel." My voice was strong. I was ready. I was excited. It was my time to shine and I knew it.

"For lunch?" The hostess asked, poking at her tablet for the reservation.

"Lunch drinks," I said.

"Lunch drinks?"

"Yes." A beat. "Lunch drinks."

"I have a lunch reservation for two under Mrs. Keppel's name, is
that . . ."

"No."

"Right," the hostess said, replacing the menus. "You're lunch—"

"—drinks. Just drinks." She nodded. We stood in awkward silence.

"Joan!" Tavia said, swanning in. A pair of oversized sunglasses
took up her entire face. Her white-gray hair extended past her shoulders in a long, thick mane. She wore a men's oxford-cloth shirt, but
it was buttoned asymmetrically so it showed off her taut stomach.
Wide-legged tweed pants and oxford shoes finished off the outfit that
was the alpha to my outfit omega. She came in for a hug, which was
more of a side-body pressing than anything else. My cheek got most
of the action.

"It's so great to see you," I said. The hostess turned to grab two
menus when Tavia tugged on my arm and pulled me over to the bar.

"You simply must try their iced tea," she said, raising two deli-
cate fingers to the bartender. She glided onto one of the stools, took
off her sunglasses and set them on the bar. She scanned my outfit.
"So, tell me, are you still looking for work?"

"Aren't journalists always looking for work?" Tavia smiled as the
bartender set down two iced teas in front of us.

"Then please, tell me, what is going on with you?" Tavia asked,
setting her phone on the bar between us. Given this opening, I
launched into The Dry Cleaning pitch, my voice easy and practiced.
I hit my stride, built anticipation, and pulled Tavia in, but just as I
was getting to the climactic reveal—Tavia pulled her phone closer and

absently spun it around in the space between us. Fine. I shifted gears and switched over to another angle, grounding it in something that she could relate to and built out the first moment of the story. Sights and smells. The quiet around the pivotal moment and how, on the surface, this juicy story lurked behind just another small town façade and—Tavia cut me off midsentence, my mouth hanging open as the words "city council" were cruelly bisected, transforming my searing think piece into a zany exposé on a corrupt city cow.

"You know, I always liked that about you."

I jerked my pitch to a halt. "What's that?"

Tavia picked up her phone and swiped it open. She took a long, luxurious drink of her iced tea, her phone still balanced in her hand. I waited.

"You're such a workhorse." Tavia scanned the legion of texts that flooded her phone.

"A workhorse," I repeated. Tavia focused in on one of the texts and read it more carefully. She replied to the text.

"Hm." She looked up at me, awaiting another tidal wave of gratitude. Finding myself utterly speechless, all I could do was smile in reply. We sat in silence. Tavia tapped away on her phone while I indulged myself in quite the existential crisis.

"What do you think of the story? Do you think you can find a home for it?" I asked, my voice forced and choked.

"Which story?"

"The . . . the one I pitched you."

"Oh . . . that's—" She tapped out another text. "A no." She poked and swiped at her phone. "Do you have anything else?" I leaned in, bending lower so she had to look at me—if only just in the background of her phone.

"I really think The Dry Cleaning Story has everything. It's small-town intrigue and—"

"There's no payoff. No third act."

"The store closed down and the family hasn't spoken since, I don't—"

"It's soft, Joan."

"It's a small story that has big emotional stakes and I think if you could—"

"It's boring." Tavia looks up from her phone and locks eyes with me. "It's boring."

"I think it's quiet and elegant, but not—"

"That story reminds me of this house we renovated up in this little beach town in Central California. We funneled hundreds of thousands of dollars into this thing thinking the neighborhood would someday get—you know—better. We'd seen it in *Sunset* magazine, after all. But the neighborhood never got better and our multimillion-dollar mansion is still sticking out like a sore thumb. Such an embarrassment." Tavia waits. "You renovated this story beyond its neighborhood."

"But—"

"The story isn't compelling enough to even run on someone's online blog, Joan." I remember marveling at how utterly serene she looked as she spoke. As if she were sitting on a bench in an art museum admiring a lush oil painting of frolicking children.

"Then . . . what if we use the story as a writing sample and maybe you could find someone who's looking—"

"But it's the writing that's sloppy." Tavia sighed. "You know, I hadn't really thought about this until right this very moment. How old are you now?"

"Thirty-six."

"Thirty-six." We waited while my age stunned Tavia into open-mouthed silence.

"Refill?" The bartender asked. Tavia checked her phone, read a text, and began to gather her belongings.

"My lunch date is here, so I'll be taking mine with me, but maybe you can make hers to go?" Tavia slid down off her stool.

"Why did you ask how old I am?" My voice crumbled under its strained civility.

"Because, even with that homespun work ethic, you're still writing like you did when you were nineteen. There's no"—Tavia melodramatically arced her arm in front of her—"*there* there."

"No *there* there?"

"Yes." The bartender placed a plastic to-go cup in front of me.

"Thank you," I said in a haze.

"Oh, you're so welcome," Tavia answered, thinking my thanks was for her.

"I can revise the story and send you the next version. We can chat later," I said.

"I'm not interested."

"If you could—"

"Don't let this story become your white whale, Joan. I've seen it happen and it's—" Tavia feigned a kind of performative empathy for these poor journalistic Ahabs as she smoothed her long hair to one side, twisting it so it fell in a perfect thick ringlet.

"It's a good story," I said. Tavia didn't pull out her phone. She didn't break eye contact with me. She gave me her full attention.

"No, it's not."

"I'm a good writer," I said.

Just as Tavia was about to answer, the elevator dinged open and Matt Abbott stepped out. My ex-boyfriend. It took a second for it to even register, like when you see your elementary school teacher in the supermarket. No. You don't belong in this place. But then the understanding washed over me, and all at once it felt right that he, of all people, should bear witness to this moment. Tavia turned to greet him with an exuberance I didn't know she had.

I watched as Matt fumbled with his sunglasses, switching them out for his regular black-rimmed glasses. His brown hair stuck up in cowlicks just as it always had. His hooded brown eyes told the tale of no sleep, deadlines, and the blistering schedule I yearned for. The uniform of a wrinkled oxford-cloth shirt with rolled-up sleeves and dark jeans appeared to still be his standard.

I just stood there. I remember smiling, which worries me because I'd never felt less like smiling in my entire life.

"Joan, you remember Matt," Tavia said, bringing him over.

Matt and I seemed to get the same unspoken memo of how to handle that moment: we didn't. Instead, we were polite and acted as though we never loved or broke each other. It's what people do.

"Yeah, sure. Hi," I said.

"Hey," he said. That same raspy voice, like he's been screaming at the top of his lungs for hours. But I know that it's permanent. A bout with colic as a baby left his vocal chords permanently strained. The sadness of knowing that fact, and no longer knowing him, settled in around me.

"Two for lunch," Tavia said to the hostess. My stomach dropped. Matt got lunch.

As the hostess checked Tavia in, they rambled on about some impossible-to-get-into spin class where there's apparently a world-class DJ and it's all the rage and Tavia never misses it and it took all I have not to yell, "Don't let that spin class become your white whale!"

"It's good to see you," Matt said.

"Yeah. You, too." I'd long dreaded bumping into Matt again. Journalism is a small world and he always seemed to do and be better in that world than me. Maybe it was perfect, then, that our reunion would happen the same day that all my hopes over the last eight months were dashed, the anxiety of seeing him eclipsed by my own blinding rage.

"You got lunch?" I couldn't help the grunting simplicity of my words.

"Holy shit, right?"

"This is big," I said. How did I miss whatever story it was that landed Matt this lunch invitation? Had I been that far off my game? "Congratulations." The word broke my heart.

"Thanks," he said.

"They're ready for us, Matt," Tavia said, resting a friendly hand on his upper arm. She flicked her gaze to me. "Oh, Joan—" I perked up. "Did you valet? I'll give the girl your ticket and she'll get you validated." Tavia peeled her hand from Matt's broad shoulder and extended it to me, awaiting a parking ticket I didn't have.

"I took the bus," I said. Tavia's hand recoiled. She wordlessly turned back toward the hostess.

That was my chance.

The hostess told Tavia and Matt to follow her.

That was my chance.

Matt looked back and waved as Tavia dropped her phone into her purse. They began to walk through the restaurant.

That was my chance.

I watched as they were handed menus and set upon by deferential waiters. I turned and walked toward the elevator before they caught me gazing longingly at them. I pressed the button for the bottom floor.

As I hurtled away from the Soho House and lunch drinks and grateful workhorses and white whales, I could hardly keep one thought in my head. I contemplated throwing away the Soho House iced tea, as if to say, I may have needed you, Tavia Keppel, but I certainly did *not* need your handout iced tea. But I did need it. It was hot and the walk to the bus stop was steep. I tugged my phone from my pocket and pulled up my group text thread. My hands were shaking.

I didn't know where to begin to tell my friends about what happened that day. I had big plans to surprise them all with it after Tavia went nuts for the story, a wonderful—long-overdue—celebration marking the end of my drought. What could I say to them now? I set up a meeting with Tavia Keppel and it took her mere moments to pass on that amazing story I was working on just before Matt Abbott walked in and had the career-making meeting I thought I'd be having? And they'd all respond with the obligatory "we hate that guy!" and "she sucks!" texts, but I had no inspiring follow-up tale about how I told them both off and rode off in a blaze of glory.

No, I got rejected and then saw my ex, who's doing better than ever, and all I felt was lonely, left behind, and filled with regret. And a pep talk, however well meaning, would only amplify those feelings.

God, I'm so tired of pep talks.

3

There's Always Nudity

Eight hours after my "interview" with Bloom, Lynn pulls up our driveway and slows to a stop in front of me. I push myself to standing, wipe any front stoop detritus off my butt, and pull the passenger's side door open.

She is wearing her usual uniform of a black shirt, black moto jacket, black pencil pants, and a layer of white fur from her newly acquired, spoiled-rotten longhaired kitten named Phyllis. She loves the kitten, she loves wearing black—we're all waiting to see how this plays out. Our money is on Phyllis.

Lynn and I met when I asked if I could camp out in her little vintage clothing shop across from what I was sure was a gambling den behind the oh-so-modern storefront of a TV repair shop just off Magnolia Boulevard in Burbank. I was right, of course. There's no way they could afford that rent. Lynn's little vintage shop is now an online marketplace creating original pieces and employing twenty people. Not so little anymore.

"Hey, sorry I'm late. I was at the fertility place," she says, backing down my driveway. I look over and wait for her to continue. I've learned, over the three—soon to be four—rounds of fertility treatments that Lynn has endured, to wait for her to elaborate rather than ask a question that may have a heartbreaking answer. "It's nothing bad . . . it's just doing all my blood work for the next round and to see how much weight I've officially gained. Which is always fun."

"How are you feeling?" I ask, wading in.

"Fine. It's fine." We are quiet. I wait. "Please tell me about your day before I get sad about maybe never getting a chance to be someone's mom," Lynn says, her face coloring.

"Okay." My mind reels. Where do I even start telling someone about my day? I don't want to rehash today's disastrous interview at Bloom, nor can I bring myself to tell anyone—not even Lynn—about my truly soul-crushing encounter with Tavia two weeks ago. I'm about to say something dramatic about how lately I've been feeling like I'm at a shitty summer camp and begging my parents to let me come home. Come home to my life, my routines, my people, and my language. I just want to come home. Instead—

"Can I read you that story I've been working on?" I ask, tugging my phone from my pants pocket.

"The Dry Cleaning one?" I nod. "Yeah, sure." Lynn turns down the radio. I poke and swipe at my phone, finally pulling up the now ill-fated email I sent myself attaching a PDF of The Dry Cleaning Story just in case Tavia wanted a copy. "Thank you, this . . . well, I'll just read."

The city muffles around us as I read, stopping and starting as we make our way to Echo Park. I usually get a wonderful sensation when

I choose to read my own work aloud, but today a sort of disoriented hysteria settles deep in my bones. I can't bring myself to look over at Lynn. Is she bored? Was Tavia right? I can hear my pace getting faster and faster as I bring this little intimate experience to its merciful end.

I read the last line. Shut down my phone and let it fall to my lap.

"Do you remember when you came to me with that design for a neon jumpsuit and—"

"You want the truth," Lynn says.

"Best Friend Truth," I say, flipping my phone over and over in my sweaty hands.

"I liked the part about the neighbor. I thought that was really great how you threaded in her story—especially considering how it ended for them." Lynn looks over at me. I nod. "I can hear you working, if that makes sense. Like I can feel you tugging story lines over to meet other story lines that don't necessarily—" Lynn pulls on an invisible story line. "Don't necessarily connect organically."

"It's writerly," I say.

"I don't know what that means." Lynn pulls into the Guisado's parking lot, and I can see that she's immediately regretting her assumption that she'd find an open space.

"Right there," I say, pointing to a tiny spot in the corner of the lot. Lynn inches her car into the spot that we'll probably never be able to get out of and we unlatch our seatbelts.

"Writerly just means that the story doesn't move itself forward, the writer does."

"Good word," Lynn says.

"So, is it?" Lynn beeps her car locked and we get into the growing line outside Guisado's.

"I don't think you knew what the story was about, if that makes sense. I have that happen when I'm designing sometimes. Where I don't have a clear vision, I tend to overdesign."

"Someone said that it was kind of like when you renovate a house beyond its neighborhood," I say.

"Who said that?"

Before I can answer, Hugo weaves through the line and tells us that he's already found a table inside. Lynn and I met Hugo and his boyfriend, Reuben, at a John Williams concert at the Hollywood Bowl a few summers back. Lynn bought tickets for my birthday, and splurged on two of four seats in a Garden Box. As we popped open a nice bottle of red, Hugo and Reuben sat down in the other two seats each dressed as Jedi—complete with lightsabers. By the end of the night we'd exchanged information, followed each other on social media, and slurred that we loved one another and were probably soul mates.

We tell Hugo we'll be in as soon as all these selfish assholes get out of our way and let us get to these tacos already. Hugo apologizes for our language and slides back inside with a wave.

"Who said that?" Lynn asks again. Lynn waits. Ugh.

"Tavia Keppel. She read the story and basically told me—and I'm paraphrasing—that I should quit writing."

"She did not say that."

"She didn't need to." I scan the line, trying to act as casually as I can.

"We've known each other for how long now?"

"About . . ."

"Ten years."

"Ten years? Jesus."

"Started out as work friends. You squatting in my store, staking out the TV repair shop," she says, using giant air quotes around the words "TV repair shop."

"You're doing that building-a-case thing," I say.

"I am merely trying to nail down a set of facts upon which we can agree," she says.

"Your use of perfect grammar terrifies me."

"I know you . . ." Lynn trails off and my entire being goes from super-faux-casual to IF YOU DON'T FINISH YOUR SENTENCE, I MAY DIE.

"Are you kidding me right now?" I ask, my voice jerking and gasping with "super-laid-back" and "breezy" laughter.

"I know you are happiest when you're writing," Lynn finally says.

"That's definitely true," I say, leery of confirming or denying anything.

"We know this last year has been hard," Lynn says as we shuffle forward in line.

"You went from I to We," I say.

"Well, we love you, so . . ." Lynn says, her voice as inconveniently steady and nonjudgmental as ever.

"I know that," I say.

"Do you?"

"Of course I do."

"Then you've got to talk to us."

"About what—" The words choke in my throat while attempting to, once again, exude an air of detached fine-ness.

"How about we start with what you read on the drive over. It's clearly important to you. Are you working on more than just that one story or—" We finally get to the front of the line. Scattered and unable to choose, I end up getting the taco sampler and a large horchata. Lynn orders some quesadillas "for the table" along with an agua fresca and her own taco sampler.

"Yes, all of my hope eggs were in one story basket," I say, my voice a whisper.

"*Were*," Lynn repeats. I am unable to even look at her. The girl behind the counter gives us our total. I pull out my wallet, but— "You'll get the next one," Lynn says, offering her card to the girl. My entire body deflates. "When was this meeting with Tavia Keppel?"

"Two weeks ago." Might as well just unload the rest. "Matt was there too," I say.

"What? How . . . it's unheard of that you'd present me with a perfect example of exactly what I'm talking about," Lynn says, utterly flummoxed.

"I was going to surprise you guys with it once she took the story out, but instead—" I trail off as the girl hands us our drinks and we continue on into the restaurant. Hugo waves us over to a small table just under one of several Dodger-themed pieces of art.

"Joan saw Matt," Lynn says. I give Lynn a pointed look. "Look, you can't be trusted to voluntarily tell people things, so here we are."

"What? Where?" Hugo asks.

"Two weeks ago at Soho House," I sigh.

"There's stuff she's not saying." Hugo points across the table at me. "There's stuff you're not saying."

"Jean-Baptiste?" A waiter calls out, holding a tray filled with food. Hugo raises his hand. The waiter brings his food and Hugo nods and smiles, but doesn't dig in. We sip our drinks.

"And how is Matt?" Hugo asks.

"He's inconveniently great," I say, forcing myself to take a deep breath.

"That's what we want for all of our exes. To thrive and live full lives without us," Lynn says, her voice flat.

"What was it that he said? Right there at the end?" Hugo is reaching into the depths of his mind to access a string of words that have haunted me for the ten months since they were uttered.

"Shit, Joan, why can't you just leave it alone. You ruin—"

". . . fucking everything." Both Lynn and Hugo finish the sentence with me.

"Yeah." I am closing in on myself.

"Araya!" A waiter calls out. Lynn puts up her hand, and he brings over our food. We thank him. And then a silence expands as we each dig in.

"You're every bit as good as he is, though," Lynn says.

"See, I don't think I am. And I'm not saying that to bash myself." Lynn starts to launch into a rant, but I keep talking. "Tavia told me The Dry Cleaning Story was boring, had no third act, and was soft. That there was no *there* there."

"No *there* there?" Lynn asks, her mouth full of steak picado. Both she and Hugo roll their eyes.

"I thought she was full of shit, but then Lynn—even you said it didn't sound like I knew what the story was about."

"In a nice way. I said it in a nice way," Lynn says, looking over at an appalled Hugo.

"No, you . . . you were a good friend." I take a long drink of my horchata. "It's one thing to think you're phoning it in or that something isn't your best work, but I had no idea. I truly thought the story was good." This is me talking to people. Don't I look comfortable? I pick up my mole poblano taco. "This whole time I thought I got laid off because of hard times or it was unfair or whatever, but—" Instead of saying such a gut-wrenching truth out loud, I take a huge, wonderful, drippy bite of my taco. The table is quiet. Everyone is staring. I set the taco down, grab the napkin once again, and clean myself up. "Maybe they fired me because I was bad at my job. Maybe Tavia was right."

"Up to a point," Lynn says, her face lined with concern.

"People are allowed to have slumps," Hugo says.

"No, I get that. I get . . . that. But what if you don't even know you're in a slump? Because I certainly didn't know. That's the scary part. I'm going over all these stories and it's not just The Dry Cleaning Story that was boring and soft . . . This slump could reach back years." I am detaching. I am shutting down. I am so far away as I repeat, "*Years.*"

"We'll figure this out," Hugo says.

"You'll find another story," Lynn says.

"So—" Hugo cuts in before I can launch into my extremely compelling argument against ever finding another story and hope of any kind. That somehow I'm existing in a space with only enough hope to fuel my revenge and prove Tavia wrong. "I have an idea and you guys are going to hate it, but Reuben will love it. Remember that part. That Reuben will love it."

"I don't like where this is going," Lynn says.

"We all know that Reuben's greatest wish is—"

"To be the lead singer of a boy band," Lynn and I say together.

"The theme of his birthday party this year is the 1980s—"

"Oh, no," I say.

"So, what if we learned the dance from New Edition's 'If It Isn't Love' video. You know how he knows the whole thing by heart." We nod. Lynn claps her hands and sweeps her arm across the table in one of the video's signature moves. "And if we start playing the song at the party, he'll get up to do the dance. We know he will. But what if this time, he had the rest of New Edition behind him—minus Ricky Bell, because he's on the end and there's only four of us, not five. Can you imagine a better birthday gift?" Hugo looks each one of us directly in the eye. We all share looks of deep concern.

"No," Lynn and I say in unison.

"The party is—" Lynn says.

"It's not enough time," I say, pulling out my phone and counting it out on my 98-percent-blank calendar.

"Look, we all kind of already know it, so we'll get together before then to practice and it doesn't have to be perfect," Hugo says.

"Yes, it does," Lynn says. Hugo finishes off one of the "for the table" quesadillas. "No way I'm getting up there and not killing it, although I hate—" Lynn tugs at her black cashmere sweater. "I just wish I were in better shape." She smooths the sweater down, over her body. "Poor Josh."

Josh is Lynn's boyfriend of five years. We all hate Josh.

"Poor Josh?" I ask. Lynn believes asking Josh to "tolerate" her fertility treatment weight gain for their future baby is akin to having him help her bury the body of an enemy she's just brutally murdered.

"I know you guys don't like him," Lynn says, throwing up her hands. Hugo and I are quiet. We don't argue with her. "This is our last round anyway, so . . ."

"Why is it your last round?" Hugo asks. His voice is achingly gentle.

"It's too expensive and—" Lynn's voice chokes. Hugo and I immediately lean in. We each grab one of her hands. "I just can't take it anymore."

Hugo and I don't ask about adoption. We don't ask about surrogacy. We don't tell Lynn that this round could be the one that actually takes. We don't tell her that maybe in a few years when she's less stressed, she and Josh will get pregnant when they least expect it. Lynn knows all of that. She doesn't need us to offer solutions she's already thought of. What she needs is to ugly cry and eat some tacos with people who love her.

"Plus, can you imagine Phyllis allowing anything into the house that threatens to take any sliver of attention away from her?" Lynn asks, trying to lighten the mood.

"That kitten is ridiculous," Hugo says, shaking Lynn's hand a little.

"We should probably head over to the theater," Lynn says, moving us along.

We clean up our table, throw our trash away, and Lynn and I spend the next twenty-five minutes trying to eke our way out of the Guisado's parking lot. By the time we've arrived at the theater, there are barely any empty seats.

"There," Lynn says, pointing to Hugo in the front row, his jacket spread over three empty seats.

"I am not sitting in the front row," I say, scanning the theater for any other four empty seats.

"What? Why not?" Lynn asks, waving to a panicked-looking Hugo.

"There's always at least one full-blown sex scene in Reuben's plays and I don't even want to talk about what happened last time. We were too close. The things I saw. The angle—can't unsee that. Can't unhear that."

"There are no other seats. Hugo needs us. Look at him." Hugo wipes his brow with his silk pocket square as he eyes the unmade bed in the center of the stage. We make our way down to him.

"What took you guys so long?" Hugo asks.

"We parked in the lot," Lynn says.

"You never park in the lot," Hugo says, handing us our programs. Wild-haired and utterly captivating, Reuben races down the aisle and sits next to Hugo just as the doors to the theater close. Hugo takes his hand and Reuben pulls him close with a nervous grin. I watch them and melt. And then feel so lonely I can't bear it.

As the lights dim and a woman in a bra and panties and a completely nude man take the stage, I can only turn to Lynn and shake my head.

In the blackened silence of the theater, I wrestle with why I can't tell my friends what I'm feeling. Lately, it's like all my words and emotions are tangled Christmas lights. A seemingly innocuous request to simply talk about what I'm doing pulls with it this snarled mess of shame about not achieving my full potential, or maybe I asked for this or haven't been working as hard as I should be. Or this is simply what happens to people who aren't good enough.

They fail.

4

Turns Out, You Can Go Home Again

"It's a simple question, Mom."

"Have some tea," she says.

She takes the kettle off the old stovetop and pours it into two earthenware mugs. Over the past several weeks, I've sent Lynn, Hugo, and Reuben a series of confessional texts trying to keep up my end of the "you need to talk to us" bargain. Sure, my texts are mostly just weird observations I've made on the bus or repeating whatever prying interview question has flummoxed me that week, such as "Are you well known?" after I told one baby-faced HR person that I used to be a journalist. No, Jason. If I were well known, do you think I'd be applying to work at this insurance company as a file clerk?

"Mom—"

"Coriander, cumin, and fennel. Fresh from the garden. Good for your belly," Mom says, setting the mug down in front of me. "Blow on it, though. It's hot." I thank her and she gives my shoulder a quick squeeze.

My mother can best be described as a "sturdy" woman. It's an attribute we share. We are the hearty, broad-shouldered pioneer stock born from a long line of women who can harvest a crop, raise wild-haired babies, and protect the land from shifty ramblers. Her graying black hair is cut in a sensible bob and she's wearing some version of the same button-down shirt, quilted vest, and black work pants she always wears. With her dark brown eyes and sun-kissed olive skin, looking at her is basically looking at my own future. You know, minus the active lifestyle and decades-long loving marriage.

"Are you and Dad growing marijuana, yes or no?"

"We're farmers, honeybunch. We grow a lot of things," Mom says, putting a loaf of homemade banana bread on the table. I thank her and cut a slice.

"You're evading the question," I say, reaching for the butter as I try to evade the now uncontainable panic as eight months being unemployed slides into nine.

"Honey?" Mom clangs a pot in the sink as she rinses it. "The job interview. How did it go?"

"Mamamamamamamama." My brother's two-year-old daughter, Poppy, races into the kitchen naked as the day she was born. Her brown hair everywhere, and is that—

"Please say that's dirt on your child's face and not—"

My younger brother Billy rushes into the kitchen, tugging off his worn-in baseball cap and making sure not to track in dirt. Billy is six foot six, barrel-chested, big-bellied, with a laugh that can shake a house.

"We were out by the roses, helping Dad. There may have been a dirt-eating incident. Her, not me. I was trying to get her into the bath and she made a break for it." Billy sweeps the giggling girl up into his arms. Poppy runs her tiny, mud-caked hands through Billy's thick beard.

"Momma, you have any of our honey?"

Mom hands him a Mason jar full of fresh honey from our hives. "What's it for?" she asks with an arched eyebrow.

"Yes, okay. It's a bribe," Billy says. Poppy's eyes widen as Billy twists open the jar of honey. "And before you say anything, I'm a weak man who just needs this baby clean by the time Anne comes home from her shift at the grocery store." He gives Poppy a little taste. "I swear I'll mold her character when she's not covered in dirt." Billy gives Poppy another taste of the honey. "So, now you had some honey, you ready to get in that bath now, Pop?" Mom and I share a knowing look. Poppy straightens her body and howls.

"I'm afraid you've been had," Mom says, laughing. Billy sets Poppy down safely and she immediately takes off down the hallway.

"I really thought the honey would work." Billy sighs, following his flash of a daughter.

"I don't know whether to make fun of you or feel sorry for you," I yell at him.

"Revenge is best served cold, Joan," Billy yells as he disappears down the long hallway, Poppy's laughter echoing throughout the house. Mom puts the honey back into the cupboard and turns to me.

"So?" Mom asks, not missing a beat. "The job interview. Was this for the—" She sits down with her cup of tea, and breaks off a chunk of the banana bread.

"The coffee shop. It was fine. I've got another one tomorrow at that florist down on Washington—right on the corner?" Mom nods. "They need someone to clean up and help around the store," I say.

"Something will happen." She brushes a rogue hair behind my ear. "It always does."

I nod and feel my heart pull through my chest toward her hope. "Yep. I know," I lie, offering her a smile.

"Maybe later on tonight, you can look into registering for some classes down at the city college. There was one on being a professional organizer that looked fun. And, you know what? Now that you've mentioned it, I bet they've got some great classes on becoming a florist. Who knows more about plants and flowers than you? Something to think about."

"I'll take a look," I say, my heart breaking as I watch my loved ones ever so slowly lose faith in me. My smile falters.

"Just because you take a few classes doesn't mean you're giving up on being a journalist, hon."

But I'm terrified that's exactly what it will do. Ever since that fateful lunch* (*lunch drinks) with Tavia, I've felt as though I'm dangling off the side of a cliff, gripping journalism's hand. Each week that passes, each job interview, each community college catalog left on my bed, and each unread article is another sweaty finger lost.

"I know." I am shutting down.

"Life is long."

"Yep."

"Something to think about," Mom repeats.

"Okay." Mom looks up from her coffee. "I will think about it."

She smiles. The look of relief on her face breaks my heart.

"I'm making rosemary bread tonight. It's growing like crazy over on the back fence by the . . ." Mom trails off.

"By the marijuana."

"By the greenhouse."

"The greenhouse that's full of marijuana."

"It's just a greenhouse full of wholly uninteresting regular plants, sweetheart. No big story there except that your dad could use some help with the roses. It's almost their second bloom cycle and apparently he's momentarily lost his assistants to bath time."

"I do love deadheading." The small cheesecloth baggie of spices Mom placed in the bottom of my mug floats up and leaks into the hot water. I stand, tucking my wooden chair back under the table.

"Don't leave your mug in your room," Mom says as I continue down the rabbit warren of a hallway, past the bathroom filled with squeals of laughter, Billy's low soothing voice and way too much splashing.

"I won't," I yell, letting out a sharp laugh, thinking how hilarious— is that the right word? Maybe it's less hilarious and more sad, pathetic, or just plain tragic.

As my scoff hangs in the air, I . . . I worry about who I'm becoming. This flat, embittered person who's been emerging over the past eight—no, *nine*—months feels like one of those store-bought plastic Halloween costumes that slowly smothers you throughout what you thought would be a lovely night of trick-or-treating.

I'm losing myself.

But I don't know how to stop. Stop the worrying. Stop the monologuing about how unfair it all is. Stop comparing my life to everyone else's. Stop feeling ashamed that it's come to this. Stop being endlessly offended and insulted that people haven't called me up to the big leagues now that journalism is booming on a global scale. I can't stop being scared. I can't stop turning into someone I don't recognize. And I can't stop running away from the one question I won't ask: Am I a failure?

"Something will happen," I say to myself. "It always does." The second part of that pep talk comes out a bit more like a threat. As if I'm warning myself that something better happen . . . or else. Or else what? Or else I'll disappear completely into this person I don't recognize, and forget I was ever any other way. Waking up one day to find myself an embittered professional organizer who has long forgotten she was once a journalist.

I open up the back door, cross the back deck, and step down into my parents' fairy tale of a backyard. I pick my way through winding pathways, past hidden gazing balls and burbling water features, carefully dipping under fronds of lush green to finally unlatch the back gate and step into the bustling gardening center and nursery my parents have owned for the last forty years. I make my way back to the roses, where Dad is definitely not also growing weed.

I find my father huddled over a rose bush known as the Pilgrim. That same green, broken-in Dixon Gardens baseball cap pulled low over his forever-squinting eyes. Clean-shaven, wire-rimmed glasses, green Dixon Gardens polo shirt with "William" embroidered in yellow, khaki pants, work boots, and a Japanese hori hori knife tucked into a leather sheath connected to his belt.

"Hey, Dad," I say, setting my tea down on a low wall. I pull my phone out of my pocket and take a quick picture of one of the roses, tight yellow petals unfolding like a supernova, impossibly beautiful. And while I've got my phone, couldn't hurt to check some email. Nothing. Anyone call? No. I click off my phone without looking at the picture of the rose.

"You can never capture their beauty. I keep trying to tell you that, Bumble," Dad says, in his gravelly drawl. Bumble. A nickname I earned due to my penchant for getting stung by bees. Mom always said it was because I was so sweet, but then Dad would correct her by saying no, it was more likely because I was loud, clumsy and the mere vibrations of my existence were terrifying to them. So . . . you know. Either or.

"It's what I do, Dad. I document."

"Well, today you're deadheading," he says, pointing over his shoulder. "Start over in Tranquility."

"So, that's where you've been hiding," I say to the Tranquility roses.

I spend the rest of the morning seeking out dead flowers and plucking them from their stems before they undermine the health of the plant, so they'll bloom again. A practice that feels a bit on the nose, considering.

"Before we head back in, your mom wants us to grab a handful of rosemary," Dad says.

"Oh, right. For the bread," I say, absently. I reach back to nab a particularly out-of-reach deadhead.

"Now there's that reporter brain hard at work," Dad says.

"Can one have a reporter's brain even if they're no longer a reporter?" Before I can blurt out some deeply raw yet sarcastic follow-up that's "just a joke," my phone rings in my pocket.

"Well, thank god for that," Dad says, gesturing to the ringing phone. I give him a pointed look, brush my hands on my pants, and swipe the phone on.

"Hello?"

"Joan, this is Ria Jones from Bloom."

"Oh, hey. Hi." I sit back on my haunches, surrounded by dead roses. "Wow, thank you for calling. I didn't—"

Ria cuts in. "I apologize for making you wait almost a month, so I hope you're still available, but we'd like to officially offer you the job of junior copywriter."

"Really?"

"It's a three-month probation. If you're a good fit, we'll make you full time." I am quiet, not quite able to believe the reality of finally receiving The Call.

"Ms. Dixon?"

"Yes?"

"Do you want the job?"

"Yes. I would like the job. A lot." Dad takes off his baseball cap, pushes the swoop of salt-and-pepper hair off his forehead, and replaces the hat. I've come to identify this gesture as "William Dixon is having feelings."

"I think you're a good fit for Bloom."

"Thank you," I say.

"Then we will see you tomorrow."

"Tomorrow?"

"Onboarding starts at 9 A.M."

"Thank you. I really mean it. This is—"

Ria cuts in again. "Welcome to Bloom, Joan."

"Sounds—" Ria hangs up. "Good," I say to no one. I hang up the phone and look over at Dad. "I got it," I say, unable to keep my voice from cracking. "I got a job."

"And you said you weren't a reporter anymore," Dad says, crawling back under a rosebush. As I text Lynn, Hugo, and Reuben the news I don't have the heart to tell Dad that as of tomorrow, I am officially not a journalist anymore. I am a junior copywriter for Bloom.

5

Doris Lessing Is My Nemesis

I slept like shit last night. And it wasn't about nerves, although they're definitely in play now as I try not to vomit on this bus hurtling toward Melrose Avenue. No, at some point in the early morning hours, I decided if I was finally going back to work I also needed to read more classics, organize my finances, catalog my writings, start eating healthier, and probably come up with a new exercise regimen.

So, at four o'clock this morning, after doing a combination of exercises I'd found online to "strengthen my core," I Googled "who won the Nobel for Literature." Scouring my and my parents' bookshelves, I finally settled on Doris Lessing's *The Golden Notebook*. At close to seven hundred pages, I decided this book was exactly what I needed. It exuded greatness. It was impressive. It was intimidating. It was everything I was a bit low on at the moment.

Four hours later, as I sit on the third and final bus on my commute to work, that doorstop of a book, that harbinger of greatness, bucks and jerks on my jiggling knee with cruel hilarity. But instead of cracking the damn book open and starting the process of bettering myself, I've bitten my nails off to the quick. By the time the bus nears my final stop, I'm now chewing on the inside of my cheek so violently that the poor woman next to me must think I'm trying to suck my own face in on itself. When I finally arrive at Bloom, red faced and sweaty, the fifty-pound book has become my nemesis.

I pull open the door to Bloom and find myself, once again, in the lobby that isn't a lobby with seating options that aren't actually seating options starting a job that's not actually a job.

(neutral face emoji)

I look over to the reception desk. No Caspian. No sign of Ria, either. No one to tell me where to go or what to do.

I shift the book to my other arm and choose to stand rather than to sit on one of the expensive, chic blue couches that I'm afraid will make me instantaneously start my period on them. I've also suddenly become more and more aware that the kale, turmeric, and goat's milk yogurt smoothie I made this morning—as my family looked on in horror—was probably not the best choice. I look forward to panicking about a workplace bathroom situation later on today.

As the Bloom workforce begins to arrive, I'm again surprised by the absence of thumping indecipherable music and people with man buns riding around on skateboards and giving one another complicated fist-bumping handshakes. Turns out, in the hustle and bustle of the early morning, Bloom feels more like a public library than a hip start-up. The only sound echoing through the cavernous open-concept barn is the coffee machine clicking and whirring to life as one by one Bloom workers fuel up. Head flicks, quiet "good mornings," and tired smiles. I scan the rows of computers and see a few people already hard at work, headphones on, tapping away in reverent silence. Two coworkers quietly catch up in the back corner, and their hushed conversation wafts freely throughout the space.

The quiet professionalism unnerves me. I want this place to be wacky. I want to roll my eyes, take sneaky photos of millennial hijinx, and laugh with my friends about how much more adult we are. I guess I could make fun of the sleek blue couches, but even they're starting to grow on me.

I cross my arms and am immediately thwarted by the world's hugest book. Sigh. Scan the room. Act like I'm ridiculously interested in the vaulted ceilings. Sigh. Finally, I pull my phone from my pocket and mindlessly try to scroll my nerves away. It's not working. Nothing is working.

It's been such a long time since I've been new at something. I'd rather I discovered that it got easier because I'm a little older. Or, at the very least, I was more mature about the whole thing. But, as I stand here, sweat soaking through my shirt and about to throw this fucking book across the room, I realize not having to try new things was exactly what I liked about getting older.

Wanting to try new things, sure. Reuben drags us to pottery classes and cooking classes and weird exercise classes all the time. But I'm not going to receive a performance review for how I did at Candlelight Yoga.

I've lived in the same area my whole life, done the same job since the day I walked into that first newsroom at seventeen years old. Hell, even my music playlists are filled with songs I know most of the words to.

Bloom is brand new in every way. And as I step in deeper—as I *have* to step in deeper—I live in fear that all my anxieties will suddenly be on public view and the values of the company, the pace, the expectations of their employees, the work itself, and the culture will remain about as clear to me as if they were in hieroglyphics. And that this raw, off-balance, emotional shitstorm I'm living in will become just another day at the office.

All of the first-day-at-school sensations flood my nerve endings. Each second drags on with a lovely combination of battling hysterias: everyone is looking at me but I'm completely invisible.

What would it have been like to stand in this lobby as a journalist for *The LA Times* . . . no, *The New York Times*? Observing the surroundings, recording little asides in my voice recorder. Noticing details. Going over my notes and reviewing interview questions. Assessing the workforce, maybe trying to get a quote from one or two particularly emblematic Bloomers—a name I'd coin for the Bloom workforce. The story would go on to win a Pulitzer—an arch, unflinching look at the tech industry, the wide-eyed child army of drones and the boy kings who rule them. The book I'd write as a follow-up (multiple offers, sold at auction) would be made into a gripping indie film ("A modern-day *All the President's Men!*").

"Jesus," I say aloud to no one. I sound so delusional.

It didn't sound delusional at seventeen. Oh, you're going to college and then maybe law school? Fun. Me? Pulitzer. *New York Times*. Book deals. Nellie Bly. Martha Gellhorn. Sky's the limit, they'd say. They could see it. I could see it.

We were all going to do big things.

Clearly in some kind of fugue state, I make eye contact and attempt a breezy smile with each person who walks through those front doors. The replies range from civil to confused to patronizing to downright surly. After a guy in neon sunglasses returns my expectant smile with a snide sniff, I have to force myself to take a deep breath.

"I don't think we've met." He's wearing an untucked blue gingham button-down shirt, low-slung khaki pants, and Vans. Disheveled, light brown hair and, as he takes off his sunglasses, a face that is disarmingly youthful.

"Joan Dixon." I tuck a chunk of rogue sweaty hair behind my ear, shove *The Golden Notebook* under my arm, and extend my hand.

"I'm Chris Lawrence," he says, waiting for his name to register. A slight lip curl flickers, but disappears just as quickly as it takes me a second too long to realize I'm shaking hands with one of the cofounders of Bloom himself.

"Lovely company you've got here."

"Oh." Chris scrapes his hand through his already messy hair, sputtering a half laugh. "Just once I want to introduce myself to someone and have them not know who I am." What an odd thing to say. Chris clears his throat. "So, what is it that I can help you with?" That constantly scanning gaze is now fixed on me. Unblinking. Solemn. Clenched jaw.

"Today is my first day at Bloom," I finally say.

"Well, welcome . . ." Chris trails off. The lag tugs at the bottom of my stomach as I realize he's forgotten my name.

"Joan." Chris nods and smiles.

"Well, welcome, Joan. Hopefully you can—"

Thwack. Chris lurches forward. "We've got a meeting in Scooby Doo in five, Chrissy." Asher Lyndon. The other cofounder of Bloom. His overtly tousled black hair, pressed dark jeans, "vintage" Journey concert T-shirt, and distressed leather jacket reminds me of when your friend's divorced dad bought a new hip and cool wardrobe to get "back out there" and now insists you call him Brian, because "his father is Mr. Patterson."

Asher doesn't acknowledge me in any way. "Git along, little doggie," Asher yells to Chris as he continues on without looking back. I look from a disappearing Asher to a now stooped Chris.

Chris and I stand in Asher's wake. I cut into the silence with one final question.

"What was it you were going to say? Before? Hopefully, I could—"

"Right. Hopefully, you'll add some much-needed age and wisdom to our team."

"Ah, good. Yes. Perfect," I say, my face flushed.

"It was a compliment," he says. Chris pulls his phone out of his pocket.

"Welcome to Bloom, Joan." He swipes his phone open and continues after Asher, eyes downcast.

6

No Such Thing as a Stupid Question

I give it a wide berth. I'm not ready to approach. Bloom employees weave around me, undeterred. My breath quickens. My mouth waters. My fingers twitch.

"You in line?" An Asian man with long black hair awaits my response. "You in line for coffee?"

"Oh, yeah," I say, shuffling behind the girl closest to me. She looks over her shoulder with a sustained glare of disdain. Her poorly dyed blond hair is wet from the shower. She's wearing mirrored sunglasses, which just makes it easier to see the sad bewilderment in my own eyes.

"I haven't had enough coffee to figure out how to stand in a line yet," I say to her, my voice unrecognizably sweet. The guy behind me laughs. I look back at him and envy how at home he looks. The chasm between his demeanor and mine could not be wider.

How quickly I slip back into old habits. All of a sudden, I'm fifteen again and walking into high school, using bland civility to slide under everyone's radar.

I used to fantasize about going back to high school, armed with everything I learned in the years since. Kicking the door open, slinging blistering one-liners, and finally earning the respect and awe of my classmates. No longer would I need to weaponize my niceness so even the most sadistic mean girl would think I was far too banal to target. And yet, here I am, seconds away from yelping, "Working hard or hardly working!" to any po-faced millennial who glances my way.

This is going super.

But then the rest of the world falls away and it's just me and it. Eyes darting around the monolith with a growing panic. This is what I came here for.

Me versus The Bloom Coffee Machine.

It's as big as a vending machine. Swirling colorful graphics of coffee pouring and bags of espresso beans spilling into awaiting burlap sacks. Steam rising from crisp white mugs. And one by one Bloom workers step up to the machine, place their mug onto the drip tray, press an arcane maze of buttons—their fingers moving across the keypad like a dragonfly skittering across the water—and out pours everything from fresh steaming coffee to lattes with steamed milk, thick hot chocolate, hot tea, and spicy chai.

"Where's your mug?" the blond woman asks. She waits as I struggle to answer the world's simplest question. "Hello?" She whips off her mirrored sunglasses and locks eyes with me. "Do you even have a mug?"

"I . . . no, I don't. So sorry." I start to get out of line. That's it. My face is hot. I want to go home. I want to go home and make coffee in the normal way people make coffee. I could just eat the grounds if someone would tell me where they are? I scan the open shelving. They only have espresso beans. Of course they do.

"Hey, wait—" The man with the long black hair gestures for me to stay right where I am. He looks from me to the blonde. She steps closer to him, flips her wet hair over her shoulder, and smiles. She's just about to say something when he steps forward, ignoring her completely. She angrily jerks her eyes from him over to me, shoves her mirrored sunglasses back on her face, and turns around.

The man pulls a basic white mug with the Bloom logo from one of the shelves and presents it to me like a prize in a game show. A whimpering burst of relieved laughter shoots out of my throat. Sweet Jesus, I am hanging on by an emotional thread.

I reach for the mug, but he pulls it back. Can't he see how fragile I am? Dear god, I just want my coffee. He sets the mug down on the edge of the counter in a line of other mugs.

I scan the counter. In my delirium, I failed to notice the little coffee cup line right in front of me. He sets his mug just behind mine. I smile at him so openly it's downright erotic. He smiles back and steps in line behind me. I look at my coffee mug, now happily standing in line.

"Thanks," I say, gesturing to the mug.

"Not a problem." We fall into silence. I steal a glance at the man who helped me. His beard and mustache are tidy, as are his worn-in jeans and black T-shirt. Intricate tattoos lace up his lean arms.

"It's my first day," I say, my voice choked and gravelly. He leans down. I say it again. "It's my first day."

"Cool, cool." He swipes his hands on his faded jeans and extends a hand. "Thornton Yu." I take his hand.

"Joan Dixon."

"Oh, hey. Wait a minute. You're my new junior copywriter." We shift our coffee mugs closer. "I'm your manager."

"That's great!" My mind is a riot. This man—*my new manager*—couldn't be more than twenty-four, mayyyybe twenty-five? But he's kind and helped me and didn't make me feel like an idiot. I'm relieved, but also horrified?

"You're up," Thornton says, gesturing to my mug. I'm next. I gulp and nervously scan the growing line behind me. Everyone waiting. Watching. Judging. Why are you guys not staring at your phones or taking selfies? *Look away!* I want to shout.

I pull my coffee mug from the line and place it on the coffee machine's drip tray.

"Do you"—Thornton reaches for my book—"want me to hold that?"

"Oh . . . *oh*. Sure," I say, handing him the book. He takes it with ease. "Thank you." He nods.

I turn back to the machine and spin my mug around so the handle is toward the front. "Come on, Joan," I mutter to myself, lifting my hand to touch the Main Menu. The pictures of steaming coffee and spilling beans disappear and in its place appear three buttons: Coffee. Hot Beverages. Gourmet Drinks.

Okay. Let's keep it basic. I push Coffee. That wasn't so hard. I bend down a bit and wait for the coffee to pour into my mug. I have this vision of not placing the mug just right and the stream of coffee spilling all over the concrete floors. A long pause. No whirring or clunking. Nothing is happening. I stand back up and look at the Main Menu. Where there once were three buttons, there are now five new buttons.

"Crissakes," I say, quickly reading the new offerings. These five buttons are all different types of coffees. Not lattes or mochas, which I expect await me under the Gourmet Drinks button—or are they just Hot Beverages? We may never know. No, these new five buttons each describe an actual coffee bean.

This is the worst Choose Your Own Adventure game in the world.

I scan the offerings. What the fuck is a Coffee 50-50 and shouldn't Hot Water be under Hot Beverages? I sneak a quick glance back at the line. It's grown by three people. Okay, concentrate. I choose something called the SOM: Sip of the Month. I bend down, once again making sure my mug is well placed on the drip tray. Nothing. I stand back up. And where there were once those five buttons there are now three new buttons. Another quick glance back at the line.

"Do you need some help?" Thornton asks.

"Nope. I've got it," I say. Thornton nods, smiling.

I steady my breathing and turn back around. These three buttons are sizes. Would I like a small, medium, or large coffee? I want a large. I need a large. But, not knowing what their definitions of these things are, I choose the medium. Confident I'm finally at the end now, I bend down once again, shift my mug around on the drip tray and . . . nothing.

What the fuck?

I stand back up and where there were three buttons there are now five new buttons. I'm supposed to pick which strength I'd like my coffee. Would I like my coffee mild, regular, or strong? Also? You know what, while I'm here on this, the thousandth screen, would I like to add milk or do something they call "whip the coffee"?

"Lotta options!" I yelp to no one.

I punch the Strong button with a single-minded fury that shocks even me. And this time, instead of bending over once again, I stand and await the next inevitable screen because apparently this is some kind of Sisyphean exercise to see just how pathetic and obsessed those in search of caffeine can become. And sure enough, there is another screen and more buttons. The machine is telling me to place my cup on the drip tray and press Go.

In an exhausted flourish, I push the bright green Go button. The machine whirrs to life with clunks and spilling beans. The words "Your Drink Is Being Prepared" burst across the screen along with a little blue line that slowly progresses as, I imagine, my drink does.

"I knew you could do it," Thornton says. I look back at him. He shifts the book under his other arm and lifts his hand in the air. Dear lord, he wants a high five. I whip my hand up and wave it easy-peasy in his general direction and feel, with perfect clarity, my fingers brush the side of his forearm as I lurch forward.

"Lack of caffeine," I say, laughing too hard. I quickly turn back to the coffee machine before he can respond. I know me. Whatever comfort he'd give would just feel patronizing.

Finally, hot black coffee streams out of the machine and into my awaiting mug. I pull my mug from the drip tray and let the coffee within warm my hands. I inhale the smell and almost tear up. Standing there, holding a mug that's half full of strong Sip of the Month coffee, something wonderful happens. A long-lost feeling swells from deep inside. Something I haven't felt in a very long time.

Pride.

"Hey, Joan." I look up. Thornton. "Hold up." He pulls his mug from the drip tray and strides over. He hands me back my book.

"It's good?" he asks.

"Won the Nobel," I say.

"I'll have to check it out." Thornton and I stand in the main walkway. Holding our coffees. Quiet. "So, when does your onboarding start?"

"Thirty or so minutes?"

"I want to show you where you're sitting," he says, gesturing up a small flight of stairs in the back of the building. "Our team's got an ideal setup. Out of the main area. Less noise. Less traffic. No one bothers us." I shift *The Golden Notebook* to the other arm and settle in next to him as he glides through the main workspace of Bloom.

"Oh, good. You're a fast walker," I say, struggling to keep up. He immediately slows. I try to change the subject and make him focus on anything but me being slightly out of breath. "This whole open floor plan thing . . ." I trail off with a whipped arm around the now bustling main area.

Thornton shrugs.

"What?" I ask. Thornton's shoulders lower and he leans in.

"I think they believe it's conducive to collaboration."

"But . . ." I lead.

"Without actual walls or offices, people have to express that they're busy and don't want to be disturbed with their bodies." He stops, scans the main area. I look around. Huddled workers, headphones, hardened faces that communicate to keep walking. "Plus, without an office door to close—if you have someone who believes they have sole ownership and a right to someone else's time?" Thornton flicks his gaze to a spindly man looming over a woman at her desk. Her entire demeanor screams that she is in the middle of something—ear buds are in, her eyes are fixed on the email she's now unable to focus on—and yet he weeble-wobbles over her, completely oblivious. "Everyone is just as siloed and in their own little worlds, except the walls are . . ." He trails off, thinking.

"Invisible," I finish.

"And ineffective."

"Sounds like the bullpen back when I worked in newsrooms. But they relished being cutthroat," I say.

"That's right. Ria told me you used to be a journalist," Thornton says. Used to be. It's fine. Drink your coffee, Joan. Smell the coffee. Inhale the pride of that accomplishment and don't let the fact that he put your journalism career firmly in your past spiral you back down into a bottomless pit of shame. "Can't wait for you to meet the rest of

the team." My stomach drops. Thornton eyes my coffee. "How is it?"
I take a sip.

"Delicious," I say, resenting how good it is.

"Straight black coffee, huh?" Thornton asks.

"It's all I could manage technologically and emotionally," I say.
He laughs. We climb the stairs, Thornton taking the steps two at a
time.

"I don't want to spill my coffee," I say, lying as I move at a much
slower pace. We both notice that my mug is half full—or medium
full according to The Coffee Monolith. "I'm actually shocked more
people don't fall going up and down stairs."

Oh, good. Yes, let's elaborate on this hysterical train of thought.

"Like how most people get in car accidents five miles from their
house." Thornton looks at me.

I am quiet. "Oh. *Oh!* Okay . . . More people should fall going up
and down stairs because it's a thing people do all the time just like
getting into car accidents right around their own houses. I get it."

"There you go," Thornton says, smiling. He holds up his hand,
awaiting another high five. Okay. I've got it this time. I can do this.
Since he is four steps further up the staircase than me I hurry up to
meet him, my hand outstretched to meet his.

Everything slows down, my hand floating through the air in
search of a celebratory high five that will never come. Instead, I find
myself lunging up the stairs, my outstretched hand slapping a wooden
stair with desperate exuberance. My other hand is no help, it's full of
coffee and impossibly giant books. Thornton reaches down to help
me up.

"Nope—"

"You've got it," Thornton finishes. He graciously steps away from
the top of the stairs as I right myself. As I walk up the rest of the stairs,

I'm certain the cold slap of my hand on that wooden stair will be my recurring nightmare in the coming weeks.

"I think we've both learned a valuable lesson here," I say, as I reach the top of the stairs.

"And what's that?" he says.

"That high fives should be left to the professionals."

"Look at the elbow next time."

"What?"

"The key to a perfect high five—look at the elbow." It takes everything I have not to look at my own elbow.

The small loft space is bisected by beams and sloping ceilings. Strands of Christmas lights twinkle. There's a bright yellow Wiffle ball bat in the corner of the room surrounded by a pile of neon-green Wiffle balls. Nerf bullets litter the ground, evidence of some long-ago battle. A set of Legos are scattered across a low table and what looks to be half of the *Millennium Falcon*. All that's missing are a set of cubbies for my emergency set of clothes, should I have an accident, and a rug with the alphabet on it.

"I'm over in the corner and you're here next to Hani," Thornton says. Thornton leans down in front of who I'm assuming is Hani and waves his hand in front of her face. She jerks back and then laughs. She bolts upright, immediately pulled down by her headphones. A trill of giggles as she becomes tangled in her headphones and finally—

"Hani Khadra, this is Joan Dixon. The new junior copywriter," Thornton says, setting his coffee on his desk. "Joan, meet the rest of our team." Hani shoots her hand out and shakes mine.

"Boy, can we use some extra hands around here. Thornton's been trying to get another copywriter for months and, well, you're a sight for sore eyes." Hani looks even younger than Thornton. She's wearing a gray headscarf, an oversized jean jacket, and black skinny jeans with Air Jordans.

"Happy to be here," I say.

"Happy to have you here!" Hani stands with her arms akimbo, open faced and smiling, her dark brown skin crinkling at the corners of her eyes.

"So, is this me?" I ask, pointing to a stark white desk next to Hani's.

"Yep, your laptop is there, along with a monitor, wireless mouse if you need it, your first day folder, plus some Bloom swag. And feel free to bring in anything from home to decorate your desk," Thornton says.

"Oh, I've made it a habit not to fill my desk with personal stuff. That way, when my last day comes, I can just leave and not, you know, pathetically walk through the office with a box filled with my now tragic knickknacks." Thornton's eyes flick from me to Hani. I look over at Hani's desk and it's overrun with action figures, strips of photos from various photo booths, stuffed animals, a bouquet of blue flags, each with a white star in the middle, a set of Nerf guns, a pair of Captain Marvel walkie-talkies, and countless items of swag from various movies. Her office chair has a hockey jersey over top of it, as well as a black hoodie strewn over that. "But, that's just me."

In the silence that follows—and it is a long one—I start and stop way too many apologies.

- "Hani, you are young and filled with wonder, fill your desk with things that bring you gladness and pay no attention to the jaded monster."
- "I've been down a dark road, Hani, you wide-eyed beacon of light, please don't let yourself be corrupted by the likes of me."
- "Hello, Hani, you earnest angel, I am your cautionary tale come to life. Save yourself!"
- "Hani. I'm an asshole. Feel free to ignore me."

"Welp, it's great to have you," Hani says.

"Thanks," I say, stifling the urge to lunge into her for a long, apologetic hug.

"I don't think we can do much until you're onboarded. But why don't you pull up a chair and I can at least walk you through some of the basics of what we do up here," Thornton says. I roll my office chair over to his desk and watch as Thornton interacts with a computer in ways I never thought possible. Shortcuts, multiple windows, swiping away whole documents while simultaneously shifting his coffee mug to the other side of his desk and pulling his phone from his pocket and setting it gently on his desk, next to his wallet, sunglasses, and keys.

"I'm already terrified," I say, clutching my coffee.

"Yes, good. Then my elaborate plan has worked," he says, minimizing his music player and another window full of his legion of text messages. Thornton pulls up an interoffice messaging system, scrolls through a list of names, stops on Hani's, and quickly types: Turn around.

I look from Thornton's computer over to Hani's back and wait for someone who's mere inches away to read an electronic message that's basically the equivalent of a friendly tap on the shoulder. Hani turns around in her chair, flipping her headphones up onto her forehead like a black-banded visor, the earphones fanning out as if they're open car doors.

"Well, well, well, well—" she says in a low mysterious drawl sounding as if she's just unmasked a murderer.

"I wanted to show Joan some examples of the kind of work she can expect to do. Can you pull up that—"

"The Holicray party email," Hani finishes. Thornton nods solemnly. Hani whips off her headphones, unplugs her laptop, and scoots over to Thornton's desk.

"Everything you know about being a copywriter is going to have very little to do with what that job actually looks like here at Bloom," Thornton says, tapping away at Hani's computer.

"It's kinda like when I used to play Gin Rummy with my mom during summer vacation and then I played it again with a friend a few years back only to find out that none of the rules Mom taught me were real. She'd made the whole thing up," Hani says.

"We generate most of the written content for press releases and marketing materials, and we wrote all of the copy on the Bloom website," Thornton continues.

"You wrote everything on the website. That was before my time," Hani says to Thornton.

"That all sounds pretty standard," I say.

"Yeah, standard pretty much flew out the window right away. I spent my first weeks here writing a complete style guide for the website only to have Asher write back, 'tl:dr,'" Thornton says.

"I don't know what that means," I say.

"Too long; didn't read," Hani says.

"Jesus," I say. Thornton nods wearily.

"So, now we just jump in on everything from Instagram captions and tweets, to various and sundry shout-outs, and edit"—Thornton finally turns Hani's computer so I can read the document—"Holicray emails."

Asher Lyndon's Holicray email is a solid six paragraphs of tight prose and zero punctuation. I manage to get through the first paragraph in which Asher waxes rhapsodic about the several holiday parties he's unable to remember due to "too much raging" only to crawl through three more paragraphs where he goes on in way too much detail about "this one time in Ibiza" where "some wild shit happened yo." By the time I stagger through to the final paragraph, the actual details of the Bloom holiday party are so muddled and arcane that I don't know whether to RSVP or hose off.

"Who was this email being sent to?" I ask, pushing Hani's computer away.

"The entire company, the board—" Thornton says.

"Everyone," Hani adds, tapping away on her computer. She pushes her computer back to me.

"We got it down to this," Thornton says. I hesitate, but am relieved to find that Thornton and Hani's edited version of Asher's Holicray email is just a series of informational bullet points and fun holiday GIFs.

"And he was okay with you—"

"No, not really," Thornton says.

"Chris is the—" Hani scans the loft space furtively and continues in a whisper. "Chris is—" And in an apparent abundance of caution, Hani simply raises her index finger and mouths the words, "number one." Then, with a wide smile, Hani scoots back over to her desk, puts on her headphones, and begins tapping away again.

"It can get awkward, but Chris looks to us as a final defense. It's why he brought me in."

"You knew Chris from before?"

Thornton nods. Something on Thornton's screen catches his eye. A furrowed brow and then—

"I'll let you get back to work," I say. I stand.

"Let me know when you're heading out to onboarding."

I nod.

Hani and Thornton quickly settle into their morning routines. Hani takes a sip of an elaborate iced coffee drink that was clearly made here. Someday, I must unlock the magical mysteries that machine holds.

I roll my chair back over to my desk and sit. The chair is comfortable. I situate the height and roll closer to my desk. *My* desk. It's nice to have a desk again. More than nice. I sip my coffee. Black coffee and a desk. Now this is familiar. I take a deep breath. I take another sip.

The laptop is new. Newer than any computer I've worked on in recent years. The whole thing probably weighs only a couple of pounds. I don't even know where to start with all that, so I push it to the side and open the first day folder instead.

I pull my phone from my pocket and catch myself trying to sneak a glance at the first day texts I've gotten from my friends, as if I'm back in school somehow and I shouldn't have my phone out in class. I look back at Thornton.

"You okay?" he asks.

"Oh, yeah . . . I'm just checking the time," I lie. I exit out of my texts and return to the home screen where the time stares back at me. So much for my alibi.

"What room are you guys in for onboarding?" Thornton asks. Hani takes off her headphones and is now following along. I check my schedule.

"Snoopy?"

"Okay, so first you look for the little red dog house," Hani says. An expectant smile spreads across her face. She waits. Thornton and I laugh. She joins in, her laughter louder than both of ours put together. "JK, JK. It's down the stairs, all the way across the main floor and then you'll see another staircase? Snoopy is at the tippy top."

"I'll walk you over," Thornton says, standing.

"Thank you," I say.

"I couldn't find it for months, TBH," Hani says, putting on her headphones.

"Bring your laptop and that folder," Thornton says, pointing to both. I grab both, making a mental note to Google "TBH" later on today.

As Thornton and I walk through the main area, I see Chris and Asher step out of the Scooby Doo conference room along with a host of important-looking adults. Without Thornton and Hani there to edit his long-winded pontificating, I can only imagine what Asher subjected them to. Thornton gestures to the staircase leading up to Snoopy. We climb the stairs in silence. I'm just about to go in when he raises his hand again. An arched eyebrow. He flicks his head toward his hand.

"I believe in you," he says. His eyes flick to his own elbow. I focus on his elbow and the plumes of feathers and black and white swirls tattooed down his inner forearm. I slap his hand. The crack of it reverberates throughout the main area.

"Feels good to have a win," I say. Thornton smiles, looks down the stairs, then back at me. "You'd better get in there, but—" He steps closer. Conspiratorially. The closeness. The heat of him. He finally whispers, "Two hats." A wry smile and he's off, bounding back down the stairs.

I wander into the conference room, thinking Thornton has given me some kind of code word maybe? Nothing would surprise me at this point, and if this onboarding is actually some kind of summer camp scavenger hunt and that was the first clue—par for the course.

There are seven seats around one long conference table. A pale, swanlike man with dyed gray hair, his tight oxford-cloth shirt buttoned all the way up to his neck, sits at the far end of the table. He looks up, notes my presence in the room, has no reaction one way or the other, and sighs as he looks back down at his phone. An Asian woman who's doodling in the bright blue journal that came in our swag bag sits closest to the door. She's wearing chunky black glasses, and her black hair is cut in a blunt bob with short bangs. Her curvy body is hugged by a tea-length cotton dress that's covered in bespectacled dinosaurs along with a fuchsia sweater that's being held together by an enamel cardigan clasp that looks like stacks of books.

As I sit down across from her, she greets me with a warm smile. I return her smile much too quickly and spend the next few quiet moments wondering if, maybe just one time today, I could be not quite so desperate.

Trying to think about anything else, I pull out my phone and Google "TBH" and learn that TBH means "to be honest." TBH, it's probably easier to just say "to be honest."

I scroll through my group text. Congratulatory emojis and wishes of good luck. I text back that I am, at this very moment, sitting in a conference room named after Snoopy and sharing the table with someone who has dyed their perfectly good brown hair gray.

"It's all the rage," Hugo texts back, along with three old lady emojis.

"I don't get it," Lynn texts.

"Such a young person's thing to do," Reuben adds.

Just then, a blond guy with a mustache, a paisley waistcoat, thick gold hoop earrings, and two baseball caps (one forward, one backward) strides into the conference room. Without a word, the young man sets his laptop down and starts fidgeting with the remotes and the cords. My phone goes limp in my hand as I . . . just stare. A wide smile breaks across my face as I remember Thornton's cryptic words: two hats.

"A word?" Two Hats turns toward the entrance. It's Ria. He hurries over to her as she scans the table, sees me. I smile. She gives me a very efficient, unsmiling nod. She and Two Hats speak quietly at the door.

I want to text Thornton, but I don't have his phone number or remotely the relationship that would warrant such a familiar communication. Instead, I look over at the other woman sitting across from me at the conference room table. Please see what I see. Dear god, it's two hats.

The girl looks up from her doodle. She sees the blond guy, looks him up and down. Her brow furrows. She leans in, bends her body a little, and then . . . her eyebrows shoot up. She saw it. It's not just me. I thought this was something kids today were doing, but from the look on this woman's face, that is most definitely not the case. She looks over at me and stifles a laugh. I shake my head and smile over at her. Two Hats finishes with Ria and walks back into the room.

"Okay, let's get this party started," Two Hats says. With a flicker, his computer connects to the flat-screen TV on the far wall. "My name's Kyle, but everyone here just calls me Fox."

The girl whips her eyes over at me. Her face is a contortion of WHAT THE FUCK IS HAPPENING. I have to look away. I'm getting those "I'm not supposed to be laughing here" giggles. It feels wonderful.

"So, I should have Joan Dixon, our new junior copywriter." I raise my hand. "Dylan Davies, starting over in Graphics and Animation." Gray Hair flicks his head. "And Elise Nakamura is in Hardware Operations." Unable to keep from laughing, the girl turns the uninvited eruption into a bursting hello. "Well, all right, that's the kind of enthusiasm I like to see on a first day!" After a few pressed buttons, Fox begins his presentation.

I look up at the TV. The slide Fox is opening his first day orientation presentation with is a GIF of the Muppet Elmo, in front of a raging fire, his hands raised high in panic. Fox turns around, the look on his face downright smug. We all smile and nod.

When Fox turns back toward the TV to talk about how first days are hard and that there's nothing to panic about, Elise continues to shake in hysterics. I am coming dangerously close to losing it myself. The combination of first day jitters, so many emotions tamped down, Fox Two Hats, and now—finally—the prospect of someone to share it all with. Unable to hold it down any longer, I bark out a laugh. Fox whips around.

"I just got it," I say, pointing to the flaming Elmo GIF. "I just got it."

"Oh. Oh, good," Fox says. Elise's entire body is convulsing as she covers her wide smile with her hand. "Man, this is a great group today." Fox Two Hats looks over at Gray-Haired Dylan with disdain: these two get it, what's your deal?

Elise and I manage to hold it together for the remaining hour as Fox walks us through our first day packets. We log into our computers, get email addresses and calendars, save passwords, sign into our 401(k)s, get links and information about our medical insurance and a schedule for our paychecks, find out where to park, go through commuter benefits, and review a list of classes Bloom offers its workforce that range from understanding your stock options all the way to how to communicate better via email.

I find myself waiting for the cult-like initiation portion of the programming. Like, maybe Fox Two Hats will cheerily tell us how the higher-ups monitor our joy through some chip we've already ingested or that HR would really appreciate if we sign this binding agreement to eat organic and if we'd follow him, they'll be giving us Bloom tattoos just down the hall along with our company skateboard.

But it never happens.

At the end of the class, Fox Two Hats walks us down to a long hallway next to the canteen, stands us up against a bright blue wall, and takes the photos for our employee badges. Elise goes first, so our goodbyes aren't as binding as I'd like. A shy wave and a knowing smile will have to do for now. Gray-Haired Dylan goes second. He makes a peace sign in his picture. Fox Two Hats is displeased. Makes him do it again. No hand gestures. Fox Two Hats takes the picture as Dylan mopes. Dylan objects, but Fox Two Hats shrugs.

Do I love Fox Two Hats?

Fox Two Hats hands me a lanyard with my bright blue employee

badge dangling at the end. I don't dare look at it. Having an appall-
ingly shitty employee photo that I am forced to wear around my neck
daily would really be quite the punctuation . . . quite the punctuation to . . . to what? I run back over what I've "endured" so far today. I
stood in a lobby. I made coffee. I got a desk and a comfortable chair.
I met my decent, kind manager and my open and friendly team
member. I had the single best HR experience of my life. And I maybe
made a new work friend.

What a trial.

"Thanks," I say to Fox, lacing the lanyard around my neck.

"You're welcome." Fox stacks his stuff up and tucks it under his
arm. "And if you need anything or want to sign up for classes, let me
know." Fox situates his waistcoat. "Just stop by my desk anytime." He
means it. He earnestly means it.

"I will," I say.

"Have a good first day," he says, hurrying to places unknown. I
take a second to scan the main area to see if I can spot where Elise is
sitting. There at the front desk, waving and waving, is Caspian. I shoot
my arm into the air and without thinking begin waving back. He gives
an exuberant thumbs up before helping someone sign in. I scan the
rest of the barn-like space, but can't find Elise, so I continue back up
to the loft.

As my smile fades, my shoulder muscles still warm from waving,
I am forced to see how not bad this day has been. Of course, I know
why I'm having a difficult time admitting it. There's a particular kind
of guilt that happens when you have a good job, but also have dreams
of something beyond. Shame, ingratitude, and selfishness start to
crawl around inside you like an insidious snail's trail. I don't have the
right to dream. I should be thankful for this opportunity. A lot of
people would kill for this job. Do I think I'm better than the other
people who work here?

Who do I think I am?

The delusional dreams of Pulitzers and smart indie movies sting my eyes as I bite back feelings of ingratitude. I look down at my badge, take a deep breath, and finally look at my employee photo.

The picture is fine. Not good or bad. I'm kind of smiling in it. The bright blue of the background is cheerful. I let the badge drop and walk (carefully) back up the stairs to the loft.

When I get back, there is a tiny Batmobile toy car sitting on my desk. Hani starts giggling. I turn around and look over at Thornton. He looks up and, without missing a beat, winks at me.

7

Box Fries

"Joan?" A shake. "Joan?" I jerk awake.

The bus driver is standing over me, bending down, his hand resting gently on my shoulder. I take a quick inventory of my surroundings. I'm on a bus. Yes, that's drool on my chin. He takes his hand off my shoulder. I wipe the drool off as quickly as I can. "You fell asleep."

"Oh, god. I'm so sorry." My voice is desperate and gravelly. But then . . . "How'd you know my name?" The bus driver points to the employee badge still hanging around my neck. I nod and then see his badge. "Why, thank you, Tom." A look of confusion . . . then he looks down at his own name badge and smiles.

"You got me there," he says, walking up the center aisle of the bus.

"Where am I?" I ask, straightening up.

"My final stop. Altadena, right at the top of Lincoln Boulevard," he says, picking up a stray sweater. I look around, and pick up the goddamn *Golden Notebook*.

"Thanks . . . thank you for waking me up," I say, pulling myself up to standing.

"Happens all the time," he says, now walking down the aisle with a trash bag. He bends down to pick up an empty water bottle. I thank him again, stepping down out of the bus. He smiles as he pulls the door closed and I attempt a weary wave.

I stand on the sidewalk and pull my phone out my pocket. It's 8:13 P.M. I walk over to the curb and sit down. Workbag, giant book, pigeon-toed feet and knees pulled up to my chest. Not half a mile from my old high school. And just like back then, I call Billy to come pick me up. And just like back then, Billy pulls up in the old nursery pickup truck, blasting some awful yacht rock music, making some joke about not picking up hitchhikers, but maybe just this once. I tug the passenger side door open and crawl inside the cab.

"So, fell asleep on a bus," Billy says. His voice is playful, yet poking in that sibling kind of way where you know for sure you're walking into a trap, but maybe not this once?

"Yeah," I say.

"Exhausting work at the internet, is it?" I look over at Billy. His T-shirt is filthy with dirt and sweat. His work gloves are tucked into his jean belt loop. His hands are calloused. Billy has clearly been working the land all day. And yet he's managed to not fall asleep on any forms of public transport.

"I know, I don't understand it either," I say. Billy just looks over. An arched eyebrow.

"The internet or why it seems to be so exhausting?"

"Both." Billy laughs. "I had it in my head that I'd be so pathetic that you'd offer to drive through In-N-Out Burger. You know, as a treat."

"As a treat." He looks over at me. I hold my ground. In-N-Out's on the line. "Well, we already had dinner . . . nice roast chicken." Billy pauses. "But, if you're starving." I sit up tall in my seat and clap my hands together. Billy continues, "Maybe I could. For you."

"Thank you, thank you, thank you," I say.

Billy and I drive down to In-N-Out and wait in the always in-sanely long line. I tell him about my day. Thornton and Hani. The Holicray email. Onboarding. Getting started on the tasks Thornton laid out. Plus, I was even looped into an email thread with Chris and Asher about the advisability of using the word "granular" in a bit of advertising. I argued that the word was too "inside baseball" and would come off as aloof, at best, and condescending, at worst. Instead, I suggested the word "personal," because it conveyed a more human focus, rather than an antiseptic one. Everyone agreed and it even gar-nered a flurry of celebratory GIFs from all on the thread, culminat-ing in Chris's own GIF addition of the Tenth Doctor standing nobly in the pouring rain. It felt good to be acknowledged for a job well done.

"Sounds like a really good day," Billy says, almost surprised.

"It does, doesn't it?" I look out the truck's window. The cool night air feels so good on my face. We are quiet, studying a menu we've both had memorized for decades.

"You getting your usual?" Billy asks. I nod. The yacht rock blasts, Billy's hand lazily rests on the gear shift. He jostles it back and forth every time he thinks the line might move. I'm tired and raw in a com-pletely new way. I begin talking before I even know what words will spill out.

"It's not like any office I've ever been in before." Billy turns down the music. "None of the usual sounds. None of the burning coffee smell and getting mad at the last person who drained the coffee pot but didn't start a new one. No one has an actual office, so it's this constant buzzing hive." Thornton's words bubble up, finally making sense. "And maybe they think that creates a collaborative environment, but without actual walls people have to make sure their body language tells passersby that they're not to be disturbed. So, it's a bunch of huddled-over, non-smiling people with giant headphones on just trying to get their work done. And, in a newsroom, that's fine. No one's trying to act like it's anything else. But at this place? They're trying to sell it as some big love-in. And—" All of it pours out. Every observation, every thought I've had. "And how would these kids even know what a love-in was? That's another thing. I have none of the same pop culture markers to make any referential jokes and I certainly don't get any of theirs. And? I don't have anywhere near enough GIFs to accurately react to anything, apparently. I'm so completely out of the loop, I can't even see the loop. And I feel dumb. So dumb. Even when journalism was . . . is . . . whatever—I never felt dumb." Billy waits. I catch my breath and look over at him. "So, yeah. It was a good day, but none of it is the same. Not even the same as when I was temping at that law office however long ago that was."

"You were still pitching stories when you were at that law office, though." I ignore Billy and press on.

"There aren't even phones on desks anymore. I finally realized that was why it felt so eerily quiet. No phones ringing. No copy machines. No clients. No outsiders even. Which is weird, now that I say it out loud."

"Maybe it's a tech thing," Billy says, fast-forwarding the cassette tape in his truck. "Have you figured out what the company actually does?"

"It's like a computer file cabinet, essentially . . . I think. I don't actually know for sure."

Billy rolls his eyes, just before he leans out of the car window to give the girl his order. He chooses his usual Double Double Animal

Style, fries, and a LemonUp. I lean over Billy and tell the girl I'd like a grilled cheese, tomato and ketchup only (Billy groans), fries, and a root beer. The girl gives us a total and walks toward the next car in line. Billy's old pickup rattles and idles, the smell of exhaust and manure now wafting all around us.

"How do you work somewhere and not know what the company does for sure?" The truck lurches forward like a bucking horse.

"I guess people are excited about it."

"Excited about what?"

"Whatever it is they're excited about. It's tech, right? The entire culture is shrouded in secrecy. No one's exactly sure how any of it works, but . . . I don't . . . Look, all I need to do for my job is to write some Instagram captions and make sure no one sends out an email with a lengthy explanation about that one time they totally raged in Ibiza." Billy laughs. It's not a good laugh.

"What? What's that laugh for?" He shrugs and laughs again. "What?"

"I never thought I'd see the day where you didn't—" Billy stops. He looks over at me. I brace myself. He looks me dead in the eye. "I never thought I'd see the day when you wouldn't try to figure it out." Another shoulder shrug. He clunks the old trunk into gear and pulls forward.

"Yeah, well." Billy doesn't know about The Dry Cleaning Story or lunch drinks with Tavia or, as it turns out, that I was probably a pretty shitty reporter anyway. "How was your day?" My voice is sharp and confrontational. Billy gives me a long look and I can actually see him decide to let me off the hook. A long sigh. When he speaks his voice is joking and light.

"Well, first off—I know what my job is. Put things into the ground. Water and tend those things. Harvest those things."

"And what things did you tend today?"

"The roses are coming in beautifully," he says.

"Out by the weed?"

"Weeds?"

"No—weed. Marijuana? Dad's growing it in the greenhouse," I say confidently. Billy and I pull up to the window, pay our money, and get our food. The smell of wafting deliciousness instantly takes over the entire cab. I pull a fry from the bottom of the box and pop it into my mouth.

"We haven't discussed who gets the Box Fries yet," Billy says. His voice dead serious.

"It's one fry," I say.

"Oh, is it?" Billy reaches into the box with his giant mitt of a hand, careful to only grab fries from the bottom of the box and not from our individual fry boats.

"Wait, no—those . . . those are the Box Fries. Fine. Fine. I won't. I won't," I say, pushing the box of food closer to him. We are silent for a while. Billy shakes his head.

"It's never just one fry," he says. "And you *god*damn know it."

We both throw our heads back and laugh. When we were little, Mom and Dad never let us swear, so when we were by ourselves we would, naturally, curse up a storm. One Saturday morning we decided that "And you *god*damn know it" was hilarious. "Those Legos are mine . . . and you *god*damn know it." "You took the last piece of strawberry rhubarb pie . . . and you *god*damn know it." "I called shotgun . . . and you *god*damn know it." From then on, it worked its way into our vocabulary pantheon—although we still have yet to say it in front of our parents.

"And nice subject change from Dad growing weed," I say, taking a long sip of my root beer.

"You do this all the time," Billy says, plucking a fry from his own fry boat.

"Do what all the time?" I pull a felted giraffe from between the seats.

"Pajama Man was really a Russian spy?"

"We still don't know that that's not true."

"He was a postman. He was *our* postman."

"Perfect cover."

"What about your ongoing theory that Mom and Dad's lifelong friend—"

"I stand by this one."

"That Sylvia, my godmother, has been secretly in love with Dad for decades."

"Tragic, right? So sad."

"It's not . . . she's been married for twenty-two years."

"Poor Greg. He has no idea."

"And what was that pyramid scheme?"

"What isn't a pyramid scheme?"

"You're not . . . you're really not doing yourself any favors here," he says, pulling into our driveway. He shuts off the old truck, grabs the box of In-N-Out, and looks over. "You can put your Tin Foil Reporter Hat away, Bumble, there's no great conspiracy here."

"Hey, that Tin Foil Reporter Hat has been right more times than not. Besides, aren't you the one who was just saying how concerned you were that I wasn't figuring things out anymore?"

"Fuzzpicking doesn't count." My family has its own dictionary of invented words. The term "fuzzpicking" originated when Mom told the story of how when she was a little kid, she picked the fuzz off blankets and sweaters when she got anxious. In the decades since, fuzzpicking has come to mean obsessing, monologuing, and fixating _____ s fluff in an attempt to avoid facing the real issues at _____ ing the term, Billy has thrown down the gauntlet. _____ izzpicking," I say.

"Of course you're not." Billy hops out of the truck. Before he shuts the door: "But, maybe ask yourself why you're talking about this nonexistent weed, instead of what happened on your first day of a job that didn't involve journalism." I'm just about to bark back what I'm certain would have been an erudite version of "NO, YOU SHUT UP" when he reaches his arm inside the cab and points. "Bring the giraffe, Poppy's been looking for that everywhere."

I follow Billy into the house and both Mom and Dad immediately want to know why in the world we stopped for food when there was perfectly good food in the house. I momentarily miss the days of eating late-night ill-advised takeout and surviving solely on the cheese popcorn I shoved into my mouth. Anne is pacing around the kitchen with a sleepy Poppy slumped over her shoulder and rubbing her eyes.

"She's not down yet?" Billy asks, setting his food on the table and reaching for the baby, but Poppy reaches for me (or the giraffe, as the case may be). Anne gratefully passes her over.

"Hello, you sleepy girl," I say, eyeing Billy as he steals a Box Fry. Poppy pulls the felted giraffe into the crook of her neck and the smell of baby soap surrounds me. I smell her head.

"Head smeller," Billy says.

"We're all head smellers here," Mom says, folding up her reading glasses.

"You smell like sunshine," I whisper to Poppy. She lifts her head up, her eyes blinking closed longer and longer. A weary smile and she's back slumped over my shoulder.

"She was down and then we had a bit of an accident," Anne says, motioning all up her back. "It was everywhere."

"The crib, the walls, I've never seen anything like it," Dad adds. Mom gives him a look.

Anne cracks open a beer. The look on her face is one of hollowed-out terror. The things she's seen.

"She's asleep now," Dad says, motioning to Poppy. I tilt my head back, although I don't really have to. Poppy's snores ring in my ears like church bells.

"Do you want—" Billy reaches for Poppy, his mouth full of Double Double.

"I'll put her down," I say. I begin to walk down the hallway, but then turn around. "Don't even think about eating any of my fries." Billy puts his hands up in surrender. I look to Anne. She nods. She's got this.

I continue down the hallway, careful not to wake the baby. I step inside her darkened room, the little turtle I gave her for Christmas lighting up the ceiling with stars. As I'm about to put her down, Poppy fusses, so, rather than wake her back up, I sit down in the rocking chair to give her a few more minutes to fall asleep. I might also be doing this because sitting in a starry bedroom that smells like sunshine while holding a snoozing Poppy, finally free of coffee machines I can't work and redacted emotional pleas in an In-N-Out line, feels so good my heart is about to burst. My breathing steadies. My shoulders come down. I feel my entire body unclench and I'm no longer bracing for the next new thing I can't understand.

I think about what Billy said. He thought he'd never see the day when I didn't try to figure something out. All that did was remind me that I'm no longer who I once was. No longer where I once was. And why some temporary job at a temporary place with temporary people has me falling asleep on buses, I honestly don't know. And, quite frankly, I'm weary of my weariness. I'll start feeling normal again soon. It's just the end of a long nine months. That's all. Being unemployed is hard. Worrying about money is hard. People seeing me like this—is hard. Seeing myself like this—is hard.

I rock back and forth. My hand moves over Poppy's back in little soothing circles. The occasional sucking of a now long gone pacifier breaks up her quiet snores. I sneak another inhalation of Poppy's baby wisps of hair and feel the soft weight of her body on mine. In the peaceful darkness of Poppy's sanctuary, I look up at her ceiling and let the lit-up stars soothe me.

When I was younger we used to have this dog. Dad always thought the nursery could use a pet, and one day he found this scruffy-looking terrier mix by the freeway and brought him home. He named the dog Alan. Dad said the dog "just looked like an Alan."

After a few weeks, it became clear that Alan had anxiety issues, maybe because he'd been on his own for however long. So Dad went to the pet store and came home with a tiny backpack for Alan. He'd read an article about how sometimes a backpack calmed down anxious dogs. The psychology being that a backpack meant the dog had a job. A purpose. People were counting on him.

And that was that. Once Alan had his little backpack he was fine—better than fine. He thrived. He trotted happily around that nursery like he owned the place, slept in the sun, and let anyone and everyone pet him. He had his backpack. He was useful and part of something bigger than himself. Alan lived a full life, finally passing away peacefully under Dad's workbench . . . with his backpack on.

I too need a backpack. I too need to feel like I'm part of something bigger than myself. I too need to feel useful. What would it take—or who would I have to be—to belong somewhere? Actually belong, not just trying to fit in. How many backpacks would I need to feel that ease of acceptance? To look around and think, these are my people, I can be who I am. Yes, you can rub my belly. I trust you.

Even with my friends, I feel like I need a layer of protection. Even with my family. There is a stillness they luxuriate in with one another that I find myself stopping just short of. Except with Poppy, of course. She has a way of bringing out the best in everyone. I k___ ___ her head.

that's why I hold on to journalism so fiercely. Because each ... it a darker layer of myself, it embraced me. No layer of pro... needed.

But I was wrong.

That warm embrace I felt with journalism wasn't a backpack like Alan's. It didn't lessen my anxiety, loneliness, or fear. It simply became my whole world, shutting out everything and everyone. Too busy to examine anything other than Stories! Looking under rocks! Pulling on threads!

What if that ease and belonging came from inside me? Rooted and anchored in something that couldn't be taken away. Not a desk, or a job, or a relationship, or even a fantasy of what success looks like. To feel certain I'm good enough despite an ever-changing landscape that keeps telling me quite the opposite. To be my own true north.

To have an internal backpack.

I lay Poppy down in her crib, putting the felted giraffe next to her. My hand lingers on her back just long enough for her to settle.

"Nunight," I whisper, bending over Poppy's crib. "Thank you for choosing me." In response, Poppy sticks her butt up in the air and shoots her arm out with a yawn. I watch her sleep for a little while longer and then finally tiptoe my way back out into the hallway, latching the door closed as quietly as I can.

I pad back into the kitchen just as Mom and Dad are saying their good-nights. Hugs and kisses all around. It takes fewer than ten minutes to inhale my dinner, and soon enough I gather up my stuff and say my own good-nights.

I throw away my trash and do up the dishes left over from dinner. I start to walk down the hall toward my bedroom.

"Did you get a chance to start the book?" Anne asks, motioning to *The Golden Notebook*.

"Oh—" I turn around. I lift the book up and glare at it. I can't hide the utter disdain from my voice. "No."

"Tomorrow then?" Anne asks, her face open and kind. "I'm dying for someone to read it so I'll have someone to talk to about it."

Fuck.

Billy and Anne got married around two years ago. It was one of those outdoor weddings with Mason jars and sunflowers right here at the nursery. Maybe twenty people were invited. It was small and intimate. Everyone cried. It was perfect.

And I missed it.

I was following a lead for some story I don't even remember. When Poppy was born, I was in Sacramento chasing down a lobbyist I thought could crack a story I was working on wide open. I was wrong. All he wanted was to spread rumors about a bill he was working on. He wanted to see if I would be open to planting some of them in my story. I was not. He was pissed. The meeting ended quickly.

What seemed to soothe me, in those moments when I disappointed everyone in my life, was that I was killing it and I knew journalism wasn't something I could take time off from, I had to be relentless. I was trying to make my mark. I was trying to be somebody.

"I will crack it open tomorrow," I say to Anne. I hoist the book high like some kind of call to battle. She gives me a big thumbs-up and says I'm really going to like it. I say my good-nights once again, hoping that my utter despair at carrying around that book for one more day will be hidden in the darkness of the hallway.

I walk into my bedroom and close the door behind me. I take off my clothes, put on my pajamas, and crawl into bed. I plug my phone into the charger, answer texts from my friends. Yes, I'm so excited about my new job. Yes, it's a great opportunity at a super-hot company. Yes, I'm lucky to have it. Yes, I'm so happy to be back to work.

Yes, all of the millennials are ridiculous. Yes, the workplace is absurd. Yes, this does sound like a fun adventure. I don't tell them about how dumb or how out of my depth I felt today. I don't tell them I just want to feel like myself again and have my old life back, but I'm afraid there's no future for me but one of middling okayness. They're all so relieved. So happy for me. I make a joke about falling asleep on the bus, but I don't elaborate on the emotional bloodletting it seems to have triggered. I don't have the right. I was unemployed and now I'm lucky to have a job. I don't get to have any other feelings about all this except gratitude. Unable to keep my eyes open, I sign off for the night.

Journalism made me feel like a titan. Big, powerful, and someone to be reckoned with. So, however wonderful Bloom seems to be— even temporarily—I still feel small there.

Lately, I feel small everywhere.

8

I Can Do This

A fresh whipped coffee sits atop *The Golden Notebook,* now boasting an energy bar wrapper as a bookmark. Unfortunately, the energy bar wrapper is thicker than the pages I've read.

A reminder email comes through at the end of the day. Something called Field is happening in ten minutes in the main area. Apparently, there will be beer and pizza. I take out my ear buds and spin around and all I see are empty desks. Thornton and Hani are gone and the people in the graphics department aren't at their desks either. Immediately, I envision the entire Bloom workforce sitting together and listening attentively as Chris and Asher outline the importance of professionalism and being on time. Now in full panic, I throw my ear buds on my desk and quietly pick my way down the stairs.

As I get to the bottom and step into the main area, I'm relieved to see that the rest of the Bloom workforce is milling around and casually sitting at desks, obviously in no hurry to get anywhere any time soon. The coffee machine bumps and whirrs on in the background— the main area's own white noise machine. I walk on in the direction of where the meeting will be taking place.

I see that a few employees are just finishing up setting up the rows and rows of chairs, the buckets of ice filled to overflowing with bottles of beer, and the card tables stacked high with greasy pizza boxes.

From what I can gather, Field is a quarterly meeting where all of Bloom's employees come together to hear announcements. And to ensure that their twentysomething workforce attends said important monthly meeting, Bloom's set up the event like a house party, complete with plenty of beer and pizza, along with Caspian spinning loud club music.

Now, *this* is the wacky start-up experience I was looking for on my first day.

Two tall director's chairs have been set up in the front of Bloom's main area, with microphones set on each.

I walk into the canteen, open one of the three glass-fronted refrigerators, and pull out a can of fancy club soda. I crack it open and head over to the back row and find a seat on the aisle.

Without emails to edit, ad copy to write, or basic calendaring to master, I start grappling with whether or not I should tell Billy about The Dry Cleaning Story and what Tavia had to say about it. I know exactly what he'll say, though. He'd probably just think I'm making excuses and feeling sorry for myself. I take a sip of my fancy club soda and get mad all over again about everything that Tavia said.

But how can I be mad at Tavia for saying the same shit I say to myself every day?

I may not have realized how bad things had gotten, but I certainly knew they weren't good. I became obsessed with the notion that my work ethic and sheer passion for writing would make up for the skill and talent I feared I lacked. In other words, they owed me.

So why did Matt get lunch while I only got lunch drinks?

Matt got the lunch because Tavia values him and his talent. And Tavia values Matt and his talent, because he values himself and his talent.

I cannot value something I don't believe I have.

I cannot expect others to put a high price on something I believe is worthless.

I cannot blame Tavia for believing me when I yell from the roof-tops that I am insignificant.

I've spent my time doing more than anyone else so no one would notice they've hired a fraud. That's where the flood of gratitude comes from. I'll make it worth their while, so they won't be sorry they took a chance on me.

Jolted, I realize all I got was lunch drinks, because that's all I ever asked for.

"You have your fun fact all ready?" Thornton steps over my legs and sits down next to me.

"What?" I ask, shaken out of my chilling realization that the "in-spirational" pep talk ending in my vow to prove Tavia wrong was nothing but the deluded ramblings of a talentless failure.

"Fun fact? Do you have it all ready?" He hands me a bottle of beer.

"Thank you," I say, taking it. I set the empty club soda can on the floor and immediately kick it over. I stand up, bend over, and reach under the chair as the can anemically rolls around.

"You got it?" Thornton asks. I swat at it, finally grabbing it.

"Yep." I fold back up, turn around, and hold the now crumpled soda can along with the bottle of beer Thornton just handed me. "What do you mean by fun fact?"

"You're definitely going to hate it," Thornton says, taking a swig of his beer.

"Hate what?" Hani asks, holding her reusable water bottle. Thornton looks over at me.

"When you wear a romper and then have to use the bathroom, so you're just sitting on the toilet completely naked," I say.

"Oh my god, I was just saying that!" As Hani launches into what sounds like a pretty well-rehearsed lecture, I see Elise threading her way through the crowd. The look on her face is a blend of bewilderment and annoyed amusement. I've never felt more connected to another person in my whole life.

I try to catch her eye, but she's too far away and too lost in the crowd of the Bloom workers who are sifting through the buckets of beer searching for that perfect IPA no one's ever heard of. I shift in my chair. I raise my hand. High. High. Higher. I wave it a little. I bring my hand back down. Thornton and Hani look over, confused.

"I know her. We were in onboarding together," I say. They nod and I immediately hope I haven't jinxed the fragile formation of our group in some way by being too greedy at the prospect of adding one more. She looks over and before I can think better of it, I shoot my hand up again.

"Elise!" The people in front of me jerk around at my loud yelp, but she smiles and waves back. I let out a huge sigh of relief as she picks her way through the crowd and heads toward our little trio in the back.

"Hey!" I say, smiling from ear to ear.

"Hey," she says, settling in next to Hani.

"Hani Khadra," Hani says, introducing herself to Elise.

"Oh, so sorry. Elise Nakamura, this is Hani." Elise smiles at Hani.

"Hani Khadra," Hani repeats. Elise and I both smile and nod.

Hani has her hand up and looks like she's about to say something else. We wait. Hani's hand freezes mid-wave.

"Okay." I turn Elise's attention over to Thornton. "And this is Thornton Yu. My manager." Thornton smiles.

"So great to meet you," Hani blurts. "Elise Nakamura." All three of us turn back to Hani. Nod. Smile. She takes a long pull from her water and sits back in her chair.

"Have you heard about this fun fact business and how can we get out of it?" Elise asks.

"I love fun facts," Hani says.

"What was yours?" I ask.

"That I named every family dog I ever had the same name because I was too sad to ever admit that any of them had"—Hani's voice drops to a whisper—"passed away." There is a lull. "Mrs. Pennybaker."

"How many are we talking?" Elise asks.

"Including the one right now?" We all nod. "Five." Hani pulls out her phone from her pocket and shows us the photo she has saved as her wallpaper. It's a close-up shot of a very happy mutt charging at whoever is taking the photo.

Fox Two Hats and Ria immediately appear over our shoulders like Fun Fact Vultures. Fox's outfit today is a pair of tie-dyed hemp overalls and an old Grateful Dead T-shirt. He's paired this look with a pumpkin-colored wool beanie that sits perched on the back of his head. Another classic.

"It's fun fact time," Fox Two Hats says, gesturing to the growing crowd of new employees forming around Chris and Asher in the front of the main area. Elise and I both stand and begin speaking in quick hushed tones.

"We'll save your seats," Hani says, putting her cell phone on my seat and a crumpled bag of Cheez-Its down on Elise's.

"It'll be over before you know it," Thornton adds, taking my half-full bottle of beer.

"You'll have to tell me later what your fun fact was," I say.

"Oh, I didn't do it." My mouth drops open. "But, good for you." I am actually speechless. "You'd better get going." Thornton gestures to the rest of my group. I hurry to catch up with Elise. We settle in with the other new employees. Gray-Haired Dylan from onboarding is chatting with a couple of the other new hires.

I am struggling. Nothing brings home the point that I don't know who I am anymore better than being asked to present a simple fun fact about myself to a room full of strangers. Any fun facts I may have had about myself are being debunked at such a rate I can hardly keep track. Chris gives Caspian a nod and the music fades. I struggle to drag one true thing about myself up from the still choppy depths. The room quiets as everyone finds their seats and focuses in on Chris and Asher.

"Thanks for gathering, everyone, I know how busy we all are," Chris says.

"But, there's beer, so—" Asher adds, lifting his own bottle in toast. "We figured you guys would show up anyway." The crowd laughs and cheers.

"We have a bunch of announcements, but first I wanted to turn the mic over to Fox and Ria so they could introduce you to our newest Bloom employees," Chris says.

"Hey, everyone, thanks for giving us your attention and energy. I'm so grateful to be a part of your day and life," Fox says. So earnest. So disarmingly earnest.

"We've had eleven new hires this past month, so please make them feel welcome as they share a fun fact about themselves with you," Ria says. She looks over at the pack of us just as Elise suddenly leaps forward. Ria hands her the microphone and I can see Elise's knuckles whiten as she tightens her grip.

"My name is Elise Nakamura." Elise's voice is loud and she's way too close to the microphone. The feedback is immediate. She quickly moves the microphone away from her face and says, "My name is Elise Nakamura and my fun fact is that I hate fun facts." The crowd erupts in whistles and applause. A huge smile breaks across Elise's face as she hands Fox back the microphone.

As an outdoorsy blond girl walks up and shares that she has one tiny dreadlock at the nape of her neck so that she can "always have a hair tie," Elise bolts past me with a huge grin and a thumbs-up. She settles back next to Hani.

One after another, all the new employees share something, from hiking Machu Picchu to winning third prize in a Tennessee turkey-calling contest. When the crowd dares the turkey-calling girl to re-create the bronze medal–winning holler, she obliges with an ear-piercing rendition to everyone's cheers. At the end, just Gray-Haired Dylan and I are left. No way am I going to go last.

When I get up to the front of the room, Fox hands me the microphone. It's slick with sweat, and something about this heartens me. Everyone who's been up here was nervous.

"Hi, my name is Joan and—" I scan the crowd as everyone leans in. My name is Joan and I'm an old maid of thirty-six who still lives at home with my parents! My name is Joan and I'm maybe your mom's age and I struggle to value myself!

My name is Joan and I'm scared.

My name is Joan and I'm lost.

"My name is Joan and—" I lift my hand in the air and bend my pointer finger back with my middle finger, making it look almost like a little finger archery bow. "And I can do this."

There's this lull. In those quiet milliseconds, I look at my bent-back fingers in all their weirdo glory. My stomach drops. It's not that the bent-back pointer finger looks dislocated, but it looks just dislodged enough to be a bit of a parlor trick. A parlor trick I've been doing for pretty much my entire life to no one's amusement but my own.

I force myself to look from my bent-back finger out into the audience and realize the lull is because everyone's trying to do the finger thing I just did. I hand the microphone back to Fox and he gives me a warm smile.

"You did great," Hani says as I sit back down. She looks from me to Elise. Hani opens her mouth to say something to Elise. Deflates slightly, but then blurts, "You were wonderful." Hani pulls out the word "wonderful," every syllable melty and lush.

"Oh. Thank you," Elise says. Hani nods, sits back in her chair, and smiles. As Fox and Ria finish up their presentation and say their thank-yous, Elise sneaks a quick glance at Hani.

I look from Elise to Hani, then back over to Thornton.

My name is Joan Dixon and I am no longer sitting alone.

9

Piggybacking

It's twenty minutes into Field and Chris and Asher have taken a very important question from the audience. They are cautious as they answer. Long pauses, searching glances at each other, and tense scrapes through boyishly tousled hair. Chris's light blue Pumas twitch in syncopation with his thoughts. Asher flips his cell phone on his knee as he formulates his justifications. They make a good team.

I look around at the Bloom workforce. Heads are shaking and people are muttering under their breath as Chris and Asher answer the clearly controversial question. The crowd is not happy.

The question? Why did Chris and Asher decide to discontinue the Maruchan Instant Lunch ramen noodles in the canteen?

"I wonder what'd happen if someone actually asked a real question?" I whisper to Elise.

"I think they think this is a real question," Elise says.

How can anyone think that was a real question?

I sit back in my chair. Then lean forward. Cross one leg, then the other. I bite my nails for a bit.

Someone from the audience "piggybacks" off the ramen question asking what happened to the Rice Krispies treats that have very quietly gone AWOL. The office manager chimes in that the vendor they deal with stopped carrying them. But, before he elaborates further, the wet-headed blond girl from the coffee line interrupts. She'd like to "circle back" to a question she'd asked at the last Field about whether Chris and Asher would be offering a bigger variety of healthy snacks. Chris and Asher explain that they're actually in early talks with a produce company that specializes in imperfect fruit and vegetables. The wet-headed girl sits back and snaps her fingers. Confused, Elise and I look around as several other Bloom workers join her finger snapping.

"It's good. That means they like it," Hani whispers. Elise and I nod.

I look over at Thornton, who has one long leg crossed over the other at the ankle. I look back over at Elise and Hani. Hani is scrolling through Mrs. Pennybaker's personal Instagram feed as Elise smiles and leans in. Here's Mrs. Pennybaker hiking Runyon Canyon and here's Mrs. Pennybaker playing peekaboo under the covers and here's Mrs. Pennybaker writing her first novel on a tiny dog-sized laptop.

How wonderful it is to be sitting with new work friends as we breezily look through fun photos of one another's pets and talk about pleasurable hikes. What a relaxing and community-building experience I'm having in this permanent job of mine.

. . .

. . .

"I think they think this is a real question."

. . .

. . .

"I never thought I'd see the day
when you wouldn't try to figure it out."

. . .

. . .

"Doesn't this bother you?" I whisper to Thornton.

"Which part?" Thornton asks. He pushes his foot down and tilts his chair back, teetering dangerously on the back legs of his chair. He rocks back and forth with annoying, youthful ease.

I blink and fidget as a feather-haired man in the front row has a "comment more than a question" regarding the benefits of natural light and whether Chris and Asher have thought about going "bulbless."

"What part? This." I motion to everything and everyone around me. "All of it." Thornton clunks his chair back down onto all four legs. He leans forward and lets his elbows rest on his knees, his beer lazily dangling in his long fingers. I feel like I should say something to break what is fast becoming an awkward (for me), intense (for him) silence. "Doesn't it bother you?"

My voice is quiet . . . and real. It's *my* voice. No weaponized niceness. No forced carefreeness. I don't think I noticed its absence. Thornton is thinking. He looks over at me, tucking a chunk of hair behind his ear.

"Sure it does. But—" He leans in closer, his voice now a low gravelly whisper. I can smell the beer on his breath. "It feels like—you know that wooden block game where you pull pieces out and if it goes off balance—"

"Jenga."

"If I recognize I'm bothered at having to sit here as grown adults ask their bosses to provide snacks for them like they're their parents, then—" Thornton pulls out an imaginary Jenga piece, throws up his hands and we both watch as the whole tower comes tumbling down.

"Yeah," I say, staring at the invisible wreckage.

"So, I'm appreciative of their beer and for the money to pay down my student loans while I figure out what I want—"

I interrupt, "What you want to be when you grow up."

"No, while I figure out what I want." His eyes lock on mine. "Period." Thornton sits back in his chair. He looks over at me and I nod.

"Yeah," I say again.

"It's not going great," Thornton says with a frustrated sigh. I sit back in my chair, crossing my arms over my chest.

What do I want?

I let one of my hands loose. *What do I want?* Place it over my mouth. *What do I want?* Rake it through my hair. *What do I want?*

Then shoot my hand up into the air.

Asher makes eye contact with me, sees my raised hand, and his gaze slips away.

"Joan, right?" Chris asks, pointing at me.

"Yeah, yes," I say.

"You have a question?" Chris asks.

"Hi, it's my second day here, so forgive me if this is a little basic . . ." A wave of giggles and snorts ripples through the audience. I look over at Thornton.

"Remind me later to tell you what 'basic' means," Thornton whispers. TBH, I'd rather you just didn't. I take a deep breath and continue.

"Does Bloom have a mission statement?" The giggles die down as the audience looks from me to Chris and Asher.

"Mission statement?" Asher asks.

"It's a formal statement that outlines the values of—"

"I know what a mission statement is, Ms.—"

"Joan Dixon. So, what's Bloom's? I've looked all over the website, as well as all the supplementary content, and couldn't find one." I lean forward in my chair and hold Asher's gaze. It's not a kind gaze to hold. His dark brown eyes are not a place you linger, every moment feeling a deeper sense of connection and understanding. No, Asher Lyndon's gaze is both violent and irritated.

"Bloom doesn't have an official mission statement. Chris and I talked at length about how we wanted the concept of innovation to be our mission statement. I know that's not customarily what companies label as a mission statement, but . . ." Asher trails off, allowing time for the audience's self-satisfied "hmphs" and "tsks" to die down. Yeah, what a bunch of mission statement–wanting squares! Asher inhales and the room falls silent once again. "But, for me . . ." He looks up to the raftered ceiling. Thinking. The main area is quiet as a tomb; even the coffee machine has been muzzled. Asher makes eye contact with me. His scrutiny hits me like a punch. "The secret to success in this internet age—at least, from what I can see—isn't trying to be everything to everyone, but exactly the opposite. To support the daily lives of people in a granular way." Asher smiles. "Or, in your own words, Joan—a more personal way." I nod. "One to one." Asher puts his hand on his chest. "For all that technology has changed people's lives, we essentially remain the same." The audience erupts in finger-snapping fireworks.

I search Asher's answer for something to hang a follow-up question on, but I come up empty. I can't help but smile. Here he is, this alpha tech-bro earnestly speaking from his heart . . . and as far as I can tell, he—quite purposefully—said absolutely nothing of substance. Seeing my smile, his face relaxes.

This is a classic technique of well-trained public figures. Pad your answers with inspirational clichés and heartfelt generalizations, so people don't realize you've completely dodged the original question.

Like magpies, we'll focus only on the shiny bits: Supporting people in a more personal way is a good thing! Technology has changed people's lives, but he's so right—we are still the same! I love working for a company that values one-to-one service!

Asher Lyndon is good.

"Does that answer your question?" Asher asks.

"Actually, no," I say. Asher's smile fades. People in the audience shift and turn around in their chairs to get a good look at me.

"What are you not getting?" Asher asks.

"Without a mission statement, how do your employees know how they fit into not only the day-to-day business at hand, but the future of this company in any kind of meaningful way?" I ask. Murmurs spread throughout the audience. Asher looks from me to Chris. Chris sits back in his chair. Asher looks out at me.

"This feels like a bigger conversation, so . . ." Asher trails off, scanning the audience. A black-haired man in the front row lazily raises a single finger. Asher calls on him.

"Piggybacking off that, will you and Chris be amending your policy on bringing dogs into this new building? And if we're not allowed to bring our dogs into work, will Bloom provide a stipend so we can take them to doggie day care? A lot of us adopted dogs because we were allowed to bring them to the last workspace, so . . . something to morally contemplate." The congratulatory finger-snapping sounds like rain falling, drowning out any heated moment I thought I had going with the whole mission statement thing.

As Asher details the ins and outs of their new building's draconian no-dogs-allowed lease, Chris cuts in with their planned future partnership with several local doggie day cares and then mentions the possibility that the Bloom workforce will be eligible for discounts as well as charitable and volunteer opportunities.

I am stuck. Motionless at the edge of my seat. My chest is still puffed out, shoulders tight, hand still held slightly aloft like I'm back in a reporters' scrum waiting for the next opportunity to be the loudest, my succinct, blistering question at the ready.

"You tried," Thornton says, jerking me out of my momentary paralysis. I whip my head around and turn my body all the way toward him. My voice comes out as a violent, offended whisper.

"On top of no one knowing what 'piggybacking' means, how was I just eclipsed by ugly fruit and dogs?" Thornton laughs. It's the first time I've seen him smile, let alone laugh, and . . . it's wonderful. I don't bother to scan the audience to see if anyone is insulted by Thornton's laughter, because why would I? They'd probably finger-snap him for being impulsively joyous.

"No one cares," Thornton says, shaking his head.

"How can no one care what this company stands for, let alone what it actually does or how it's done?"

"Ah, there's your problem: no one here cares what Bloom does or how they do it." Thornton motions to the rapt workforce as they listen to Asher explain how fostering a senior dog will earn you paid time off. "All they care about is snack-sized hummus and bringing their dogs to work."

"That can't be all they care about," I say.

"It's all they care about right now."

"How is that possible?"

"Because this is their first real job. All they want is to—" Thornton seems to catch himself. A quick, almost disgusted shake of his head and then: "—be appreciative of their beer and have money to pay down their student loans."

"You forgot the part where you said you were using this time to figure out what you wanted."

"I didn't forget it."

"You just left it off."

"I edited me."

"Yeah, but you cut the part that made you"—I shoot my hand forward, and lock eyes with Thornton—"have a plan."

"No, I cut the part of what I said that proved my point." He pauses. "And yours."

"But I don't think you're easily manipulated." I pause while my eyes scan the other employees at Bloom. "I think *they're* easily manipulated." Thornton laughs.

"No, you're right. What a great business plan. Develop a billion-dollar algorithm, build a start-up, and then hire a bunch of kids just out of college to ferry your vision to greatness," Thornton says.

"No, that's—" I cut myself off with a quick intake of breath.

Wait. Holy shit.

So, Bloom isn't like those other stuffy companies with mission statements, business plans, and an impenetrable hierarchy that only cares about the bottom line. No, Chris and Asher will serve you beer and pizza and let anyone—yes, anyone—ask them anything—yes, anything. Details about office leases, specifics about upcoming contracts, and utter transparency about everything that matters to their carefully chosen workforce.

Bloom's very specific workforce is mostly comprised of people right out of college, who've probably never had a real, "corporate" job. Their bank accounts are either connected to their parents' or are being actively pillaged by student loan officers, exorbitant Los Angeles rent that's split seven ways, or cheap fast food.

"What? What are you thinking?" Thornton asks.

"Nothing," I say, breathless.

"You're never thinking about nothing," Thornton says.

"And you've known me how long?" I ask, pushing away his uncomfortably accurate character assessment.

"Long enough." He uncrosses his legs and leans in. "What were you thinking?"

I look at him. Really look at him. I don't know Thornton Yu at all. But that emboldens me to actually tell the truth. He leans closer. And waits.

"Why would Bloom handpick a workforce that would never ask what your company does or how they do it?"

Thornton stares at me.

"I don't know."

"What are they trying to hide?"

"Could be nothing," Thornton says.

"But it could be something," I say. I sit back in my chair. Thornton sits back in his. I look over at him. He's smiling.

"What?"

"I knew you were going to say that." He takes a long drink of his beer. Chris and Asher talk. We listen.

What are they trying to hide?

If Asher and Chris don't want their workforce to know how the sausage is made, then there could be something wrong with the sausage. And if there's something wrong with the sausage, then that means the sausage isn't made up of the things Asher and Chris say it is. So the first question becomes: what's really in the sausage?

My hands start twitching.

I need to write all this stuff down. When I get home tonight, I'll dig an old, unused notebook out of the moving boxes in my room. I can get my old whiteboard out of Dad's potting shed and, once I get paid, buy some index cards—or maybe there are some unused ones in the moving boxes.

My phone buzzes in my pocket. I pull it out to see a Bloom email from someone named Mackenzie. I click on it, look down at her embedded signature, and see that Mackenzie is apparently Chris and Asher's assistant. She's inviting me to a meeting with them tomorrow morning. Mackenzie has called this meeting "Chat with Chris and Asher." I zoom in on the little avatar next to Mackenzie's name to see that Mackenzie is none other than the wet-headed blond girl.

I click Accept, close out of my email, and flip over to my calendar for tomorrow. Tomorrow: my third day on the job. My schedule is absolutely empty, except for the chunk of time Thornton set aside to start on the press release for the official Bloom launch, a newly added lunchtime meditation, and now a half-hour meeting with the two founders of a soon-to-be billion-dollar company. I take this opportunity to decline the invitation to meditation and remove it from my calendar.

Once Field ends, I say quick goodbyes to everyone, gather my stuff, and can't get out of Bloom fast enough. My mind races as I wait for the bus. Should I record tomorrow's meeting? I have so much research to do between now and then. Once I get that whiteboard out of the shed and . . . wait, I was supposed to watch Poppy tonight. Should I tell Billy and Anne I can't? Mom and Dad can do it, they won't mind. Plus, this is kind of Billy's fault anyway because of his whole "why don't you figure things out anymore" speech. If this meeting is tomorrow morning, I'm going to need all the time I can to—shit. I'm doing it again.

My name is Joan and I am desperate to believe I've learned something important so I can have my goddamned life back.

10

Just Don't Say Tit

I don't sleep that night. I try, but then I just end up sitting in the kitchen at Mom and Dad's ancient computer doing as much research as I can on Chris and Asher. I already know most of the stuff. Caltech roommates. CAM. Bloom. I make a note to dig deeper into the time between Caltech and the launch of Bloom. Everywhere I look, that time period seems to be consistently hazy.

I look up old classmates, find them on social media, and stalk all of their old photos from Caltech, hoping to find either Chris or Asher in the background. The closest I get is a series of photos from their Caltech Ditch Day—an annual tradition there, in which seniors ditch their classes, but just to make sure their now unprotected dorm rooms are safe from marauding underclassmen, the seniors set up a series of "stacks"—booby traps, puzzles, and challenges—to keep their dorm rooms secured until their return.

Chris and Asher were part of a group that set up a series of stacks that ensnared a pack of underclassmen who were trying to break into their dorm room. As they entered the dorm room, the underclassmen were hit with a cringe-worthy film festival of all of the porn each of the underclassmen had downloaded just that week. But, that wasn't the worst of it. In a little video posted by one of the team members, Chris talks about how it's not about the content, it's about the user. So, as the grainy porn played on one screen, the other screen live-streamed the underclassmen watching this porn.

I can't imagine the social scars that Chris and Asher's little prank left on those underclassmen. But it wasn't nearly as bad as another stack that ended with the now breached dorm room being filled to capacity with a giant, inflatable USS *Enterprise*.

As the sun comes up, I take a quick shower and then send a flurry of texts to my friends filling them in on the last couple of days in a feeble attempt to keep them in the loop. I'm trying to avoid getting another stern talking-to in a taco line on Sunset Boulevard. It's early yet, so the only response I get is from Hugo.

"As an accountant, I can verify that people their age aren't thinking about this stuff yet." I wait as another text bubble zooms in. "And, may I remind you, neither did we at that age."

I text back, "You're right, of course."

To which Hugo sends back a series of baby head emojis and then an entire line of old man emojis.

I send back the requisite "hahahahahaha" and head out to a now full kitchen in an outfit I hope is cool enough for my meeting with Chris and Asher. A pair of caramel-colored corduroy pants, a shirt with dogs on it, and an oversized gray cardigan. My hair is still wet, but the three bus rides and almost half-mile-long walk to work will take care of that.

As I fill my travel mug with not enough coffee in the world, I watch as Mom and Dad seamlessly thread into each other's morning routine—here's your coffee, here are your vitamins, did you make that appointment, I added something to the grocery list, where are my glasses, right where you left them—and the ballet ends with a handing over of those lost glasses with an affectionate peck on the cheek.

The other side of the kitchen is not quite so lyrical. Billy is trying to put on Poppy's tiny shoe as she kicks and squirms, giggling and reaching for another apple slice while Anne tries to hide the healthier vegetables deep in the blender of Poppy's breakfast. Baby food is everywhere, tiny socks are everywhere, the shoe is not going on, and Billy wasn't fast enough with the bib, so the shirt he just finagled onto her tiny body is already stained.

I venture over to the refrigerator and pour a glug of creamer into my coffee.

"What's with all the notes?" Billy asks, scanning the pad of paper next to Mom and Dad's computer.

"I'm not going to tell you," I say.

"What? Why not?"

"Because you're going to either make fun of me or do some weird I-told-you-so thing about something you don't know anything about," I say, taking a sip and immediately burning my entire mouth. Billy shoves Poppy's shoe on, tightens the Velcro, and stands in a victorious swoop. He wipes the sweat off his brow and turns to face me.

"Seeing as how you write in—" Billy picks up the pad of paper, tries to decipher my coded shorthand.

"It's so people can't read what I write," I say, feeling pretty good about myself.

"Oh, leave her alone. You're just early morning fuzzpicking," Anne says to Billy. She sits down in front of Poppy with a bowl full of baby food that definitely doesn't contain vegetables.

"Well, well, well . . . look who's fuzzpicking now," I say.

"I was gently floating some questions is all," Billy says, picking up his coffee mug and taking a long swig.

"Okay, then. Let me ask you a question," I say, turning to Billy.

"Yes, you look like a retired wizard," Billy says.

"Oh, shit—" I realize I still have to get sorted into my Hogwarts house. Everyone looks from me to Poppy. It's then that I realize I've said a bad word. Which, of course, makes me want to say five more bad words.

"You gotta say words that rhyme with it so she doesn't think that bad word is special in any way," Billy says.

"Bit, wit—"

"Just don't say tit," Billy whispers, laughing.

"Bit, wit, lit, mitt," I say.

"That was a close one," Mom says, with a sigh.

"God forbid a two-year-old hears a word she has no idea is a bad word," Dad says, flipping open his newspaper.

"What was the question, sweetheart?" Mom asks, setting down a fresh-baked loaf of bread. Just next to the bread, she sets down a little stack of printed papers. Mom pats my arm. "For when you're ready." I scan the papers and see that Mom has printed out the entire 'About' section for a local school that accepts "life experience" toward a college degree. Mom's circled the phone number of the school with hot-pink highlighter. I neatly restack the papers and smile at her as warmly as I can. Dad reaches past the little stack of papers to cut himself a slice of bread and starts slathering on butter.

"What do you think could be the reason why someone won't give you a straight answer?" I ask.

"Like hypothetically?" Billy asks.

"Are you . . . are you doing it now or—"

"Oh, no!" Billy laughs. "But, I mean yeah!"

"I don't give someone a straight answer when I think it will hurt their feelings in some way," Anne says, looping a scoop of baby food into Poppy's mouth.

"I would be more general if it's not my information to tell or it's above your pay grade," Dad adds from behind his newspaper.

"Maybe I don't know the answer and I'm trying to hide it," Billy says.

"I'm lying," Mom says, spreading butter on a steaming slice of bread.

"Who's not giving you a straight answer?" Billy asks.

"Anyone at Bloom. Everything they say is shrouded in all this feel-good doublespeak and, I don't know, how they infantilize their workforce . . . it just feels like they're hiding something," I say, sitting down at the table.

"What do you think they're hiding?" Anne asks.

"What if it doesn't work?"

"What doesn't work? The whole company?" Dad asks.

"The whole company only does one thing. It's an actual one-trick pony. It stores your computer stuff." I stand up, go get my pad of paper, and read from my notes. "Bloom runs on this CAM algorithm. CAM scrunches down all the stuff you save on your computer and is able to store it without a server farm. Server farms aren't as secure, cost money to run, and you have to rent or buy the land. CAM will essentially bring about the extinction of server farms."

"No one here knows what a server farm is, right? Not just me?" Billy asks. Everyone nods in agreement. "Thank god. I thought it was some kind of new farm that would put us out of business."

"It's like a data center." I walk over to Mom and Dad's computer and point to their dusty external hard drive. Even Poppy turns around. "Imagine whole city blocks filled up with these. But way bigger. Like as big as Billy." Everyone looks from the tiny, dusty hard drive to my bear of a brother. Blank faces. "But see? This is my point. Tech stuff?

Is boring. It's tedious and no one cares. It's the perfect question not to give a straight answer to, because no one actually wants a straight answer. In fact, if someone did give me a straight answer, I'd think they were being a tedious windbag and super condescending." I flip the pad of paper over to the next sheet of notes. "It's the timing. Rumors about them going public, maybe getting acquired . . . Billions of dollars in play if Bloom just does what it says it does and holds on long enough." I look up from my fugue state to see my entire family just staring at me. I clear my throat, flip the pages back, smooth out the crinkles in the paper, and set it down on the table. "I haven't slept."

"No shit." Billy says. Everyone looks at him. "Bit, lit, zit, fit."

"If CAM doesn't work . . ." Anne says, trailing off.

"They're trucked," Billy says.

11

I Got It

Without *The Golden Notebook* to distract me on my morning commute, I am forced to sit with my thoughts as the bus labors on toward work. The talking points I've prepared for my meeting with Chris and Asher recede as I board the second bus. I've done the research. I know what I'm going to say. Or not say.

I find a seat in the back of the second bus. My travel mug full of scalding coffee is still too hot to drink. I take a deep breath that doesn't quite catch at the top. I take another long inhalation, the breath finally expanding in my lungs. I open the lid of the travel mug and let myself smell the wafting, calming aromas of the coffee.

As my stop nears, I stand and wobble up the aisle. The bus jerks to a stop and we all climb off. I find an unpopulated corner of the bus stop and wait for my third and final bus. I wonder if I'm going to just forget—happily forget, once again—all I've been confronted with over the last couple of days.

But all of this brainwork makes me feel like some whiny fainting couch flopper who can't just walk this off. Back toward all of the same goals I had before the slump.

The third bus smokes and coughs to a stop in front of the bus stop and we all climb in. This bus is usually the most crowded, so I find a little pocket of humanity to stand in, easing my hand around the steadying bar just overhead.

I realize I need to find my own internal backpack. But does that mean I have to keep dismantling myself and challenging every aspect of why I think certain things? How do I know when it's over? I've dissected the slump, had a good cry, and talked to people about it—so there's got to be an end to all this introspection. Otherwise what's it all for?

I'm finally able to take a blessed sip of my coffee. We get to my final stop and I shuffle to the exit along with everyone else, lost in our morning thoughts. Once on the sidewalk, I hitch my workbag higher up my shoulder and walk the half a mile or so to Bloom.

I'm walking along when I realize that a car has slowed down next to me. I flick my eyes over. It's an old 1980s rumbling, diesel-exhaling orange Volvo station wagon. I pick up my pace, but quickly come to grips with the fact that me fast-walking anywhere just isn't in the cards. Just as I'm about to step down from the curb and cross the street, the ancient Volvo pulls in front of me.

"Hey," Thornton says, stretching across the passenger's side to roll down the window.

"Hey," I say.

"You want a ride?" He pulls on the door latch and pushes the door open.

"Sure," I say, unable to come up with a reason why not. I get in the rickety car that was definitely Thornton's parents' old car. It's immaculate. The old leather seats creak under me as I pull the seat belt taut across my body, my workbag still tight around my neck.

"Why don't you put your bag down before you put your seat belt on?" Thornton asks, putting the car into gear.

"Oh, I don't know. Never thought about it, I guess." Thornton's left arm hangs on the steering wheel as he lazily shifts the car into second gear. He has that clean early morning smell. I look over at his hand as it rests on the gearshift and see that he still has a crease on his arm from where his bed sheet left an imprint last night.

"So, where'd you go after Field last night?" Thornton rumbles the old Volvo to a stop at a red light. He turns to look at me. His slightly damp black hair is tied back at the nape of his neck, the wetness leaving little droplet stains on his plain white T-shirt.

"I just went home," I say.

"I thought about what we talked about a lot last night," he says, inching forward in traffic.

"And?" Thornton speeds into third gear as he zooms through a yellow light. I keep sneaking looks over at him. He turns onto Melrose and we roll to a stop behind a wall of traffic.

"I was one of the first people hired. Chris brought me on because we both worked for this video game company back in the day. I interviewed for one of the software engineering jobs."

"Why—"

"Exactly. When he offered me the head copywriter position, he told me it was because he needed someone with my background to make sure anyone could understand what it was that Bloom was trying to do. He said I was 'the Nerd Translator.' But then I started seeing other software engineers around Bloom, and none of them were hired on as software engineers."

"I know Elise is in hardware, but—"

"See, that's the thing. Elise is a little older." I happen to know Elise is, in fact, younger than me. "She just moved into town. I think she's from Boston. I know this sounds like a bit of a jump—" Thornton looks over at me.

"I like jumping."

Thornton pulls into the parking lot just across from Bloom. He shuts the car off. I curl my fingers around the door handle, but Thornton doesn't move. I sit back in my seat.

"Most of Bloom thinks that this job is just another opportunity to socialize, right?" I nod. "Everyone talks about everything here. Their jobs, their daily tasks, the problems with their bosses or whatever. So why would you consistently hire employees that no one wanted to hang out with?"

I wince. "Because you don't want anyone talking to them."

"Or you don't want them talking to anyone else."

"Right."

"Bloom is a popularity contest. No one knows that better than Chris and Asher. So the best way to make it so your secret can hide in plain sight?"

"Tell it to the unpopular kids."

"Exactly."

Thornton and I sit in silence for a few moments.

"I don't think CAM works," I say.

"What?"

"Yeah. I think that's the secret."

"Can you prove it?"

"Not yet. But I will." I reach for the door handle and climb out of Thornton's car. He does the same. I slam the door shut, just as he's pulling his workbag out of the back seat. I watch as he loops it over his head and situates the strap on his shoulder. "Do you want to help?" My voice is loud and robotic.

"With my bag?" He walks to the back of the car and we start walking through the parking lot.

"No . . . do you want to help me?"

"I thought that's what I was already doing?" Thornton pushes open the security gate and motions for me to walk through. I thank him a thousand times, catching myself on a thousand and one. We step out into the daylight and hurry across the street to Bloom. Well, I hurry, Thornton just walks normally.

"Why are you helping me?" I ask. Thornton stops and pulls me off to the side of Bloom's front entrance. He starts and stops several sentences and thoughts.

"They think they're smarter than everyone else." He pauses. "And—" He is fighting his own words. "I don't like when people think they're smarter than me and I'm sure it's an ego thing, but there it is." Thornton makes eye contact with me. "Why are you doing it?"

His simple question paralyzes me. My mouth hangs open, waiting for some neuron to fire with the right words that will somehow encapsulate the maelstrom of reasons and circumstances and humiliations that have led me to this moment. Finally—

"I don't know." That's as good as it's going to get. In a panic, I add, "There's something not right here. Also, it would make a good story."

"Are you thinking about turning this into a story?"

"I mean, yeah—if it all checks out." Thornton looks down at the ground. "I'm a journalist, after all."

"No, I know. It's . . . and I know this is a very luxurious point of view to have, but—"

"But what?"

"Doing something because it's the right thing to do feels different than doing something because you're going to get something out of it." His words knock the wind out of me. I question every impulse that allowed me to be so unguarded with this man.

"You're right." Thornton looks up. "That is a luxurious point of view." Pissed and closed off, I start walking to the door.

"No, wait. Joan—" Thornton calls out after me and I turn around, my whole body stiff and cold.

"Something can have impact and still sully its hands in commerce," I say. My words hit Thornton like a bolt to the chest. "Why does me amplifying how fucked up this is—or could be, shit, this could be nothing, for all I know, even though I seriously doubt it is . . . If I'm right about what they're doing, I want them to eat shit in the most public way possible. And I want them to know it was me who did it. Should I feel badly about that?"

"No." Thornton's face is calm now and . . . almost amused.

"What?" I ask, feeling totally exposed that I lost it on him. I wait for him to announce that I'm like a dog with a bone, and shit, Joan, why do you have to ruin everything?

"I was wrong."

"What?"

"I was wrong."

I . . . have no response to that. We just stand there in awkward silence.

"Thank you for saying that," I finally say. "I got it," I say, reaching for the door.

"I got it," Thornton says, one millisecond after me.

I wait. He waits.

"I'm not good at trust," I blurt as we stand outside the front door to Bloom.

"Well, let's hope I can earn it then," Thornton says, reaching for the front door. I let him open it and finally walk into Bloom. He follows close behind. I stop and turn around.

"Why?" I ask as Thornton walks right into me.

"Why, what?" he asks, taking hold of both my arms as he steadies himself. A line of Bloom employees stream in just behind us. I don't know where the guts to ask this question are coming from. I do know, however, that it feels right. I don't feel sick to my stomach, not at all. Quite the opposite. I feel relieved that the words are out in the world and no longer clanging around inside my head like some maniacal echo.

Maybe this is the first step on the way to asking for lunch.

"Why do you want to earn my trust?" I shuffle a bit to one side of the entrance. Thornton runs his hands down my arms. He takes my hand in his. It's a small gesture. It lasts maybe half of a second, but the feeling of his fingers curling around mine sends a jolt through my entire body. He lets me go.

"I don't know," he says. He looks down for a moment and then back up at me. I hold his gaze and don't feel the need to say or do anything. I like that he doesn't know. Maybe we have more in common than I thought.

"You're Joan, right?" Mackenzie curls in between Thornton and me. In her hand is a bruised apple. Looks like that imperfect produce arrived pretty quickly. As I'm about to answer her, she turns from me to Thornton. "Oh, hey, Thornton. We missed you at karaoke last night. Everyone was there."

"Was there something you needed me for?" I ask, wanting to extricate myself from whatever conversation is about to happen.

"Chris and Asher are ready for you. They've actually already been waiting for like five minutes," Mackenzie says.

"That meeting isn't until 9:30?" I ask. I look around the Bloom offices. I don't even know where their offices are.

"Mackenzie?" Thornton tries to get her attention.

"Hm?" She sighs, taking a long sip of her matcha tea.

"Is Joan's meeting in Chris's office or Asher's?" Thornton asks.

"Chris's," Mackenzie answers him. She takes a giant bite out of the grainy apple and is about to launch into some more talk about how fun karaoke was last night when Thornton cuts her off and turns to me.

"Remember Snoopy?" I nod. "Go up those stairs, past Snoopy. You'll pass the Fortress of Solitude. Chris's office is just across from it," Thornton says, pointing me in the right direction.

"Fortress of Solitude," I repeat.

"Good luck," Thornton says, getting sucked back into a riveting karaoke conversation with Mackenzie.

I hurry through the main area of Bloom, my workbag bouncing on my hip as I run. My travel mug is hot in my hand and as useless as I feared it would be. I climb the stairs past Snoopy, and find another tiny conference room with just enough room for two chairs.

"Fortress of Solitude," I mutter to myself. I turn around and see an open door. I walk down the long hallway and see **chris lawrence** in bold black lowercase letters on the door. As I get closer, I hear him and Asher talking. Nothing juicy. I step around the corner of the doorjamb and offer a weak knock on the door.

"Joan, hey," Chris says, sitting perched on the edge of a desk that I notice can, at the turn of a handle, be made into a standing desk.

"You're late," Asher says, not bothering to turn around in his chair.

"So sorry," I say, resisting the urge to launch into a tirade about their completely incompetent assistant. I walk the rest of the way into Chris's office. The art on the walls is expensive. The furnishings are modern and sterile. No photos of family or friends. No bits and bobs on his desk. There are two straight-backed chairs in front of Chris's desk. Asher is sitting in one of them.

Then I notice a nearly waist-high rafter beam, running the length of Chris's office. The giant beam divides the office and separates anyone entering from Chris's desk and chairs. I look from the beam to Chris and Asher, then back at the beam.

"Most people just hop over it," Chris says.

I take a step forward, pushing my workbag back. I set my travel mug on top of the beam. Chris has supplied what looks like a little crate to step on. I guess I'm supposed to spin around and leap to the other side, straddle it, or pole vault over it. I don't see how anyone could hop over it.

"You could just crawl under it," Asher says without looking up from his phone. What I want to say is what the fuck kind of mind games are you playing? Do you need people to actually crawl or hop or be humiliated before they get to have a conversation with you? What adult professional would choose to put their office in the one place where people had to demean themselves in order to enter?

I'm sure Asher's office doesn't have a beam running through it. These two chose this office, the office with the beam, for our meeting this morning and then proceeded to start ten minutes before it was scheduled. Noted.

Fine. Fuck it. Fuck it.

As Chris and Asher watch, I back up from the beam and get down on my knees. I shove my workbag further onto my back, push the crate out of the way, duck my head, and crawl under the beam. Once clear, I haul myself up, red-faced and winded from holding my breath in rage. I turn around to grab my travel mug off the beam, using this opportunity to collect myself. It doesn't work, of course, because it can't, in fact, erase that—as an adult person—I had to crawl into a meeting with the two founders of Bloom before, I might add, I've had hardly any coffee.

I take a seat in the other chair, my workbag still slung around my body.

"Please. Make yourself comfortable," Chris says, crossing behind his desk and finally settling in at his aerodynamic, back-friendly chair. I control my temper as I loop my workbag off and lean it against the leg of my chair. I hold my travel mug of coffee, not wanting to set it on what looks to be a very expensive side table.

"Thank you for taking the time to meet with me," I say.

"We like to be accessible to all employees at Bloom," Chris says. Asher lets out a long, annoyed sigh.

"So, the mission statement thing," Asher says. Chris looks over at him.

"Yes?" One of my favorite journalism tricks is letting people talk. Holding the silence. Not finishing sentences or letting them off the hook of ideas they don't really want to say aloud. And after that little beam stunt, I'm not going to say a damn thing. Asher shifts in his chair. He waits. I smile as harmlessly as I can. Chris is silent. His face is as unreadable as mine.

"What's that about?" Asher finally says.

"What's a mission statement about?" I ask, my voice light and airy.

"No—" Asher looks over at Chris. "You know what I mean. Can you jump in here?" I look from Asher to Chris. Chris doesn't answer. Instead—

"Where do you see Bloom going in the coming years?" I ask, hoping to catch them a bit off guard.

"We want to revolutionize cloud storage. Get rid of server farms altogether," Asher says.

"Is that what you set out to do all those years ago at Caltech?" I ask.

"We asked one simple question," Chris says.

"And what question was that?" I ask.

"How can we get a passing grade in this class," Chris says, laughing. Asher smiles. I read that exact quote in no less than four interviews Chris and Asher have given. It was even in their TED talk.

"No, but really," I say as the "laughter" dies down.

"It was something about an artichoke, wasn't it?" Asher asks Chris.

"An artichoke?" I ask.

"I don't—" Chris starts.

Asher cuts him off. "Yeah, we were super high and you said that you wanted to build a digital artichoke so we could eat all the butter we wanted." Asher shakes his head. "I never understood half the shit you said."

"Can you tell me more about the culture here at Bloom?" I say, trying to lighten the mood and distract Chris from the digital artichoke idea Asher blurted out. I've never heard or read that anywhere else. That's a breadcrumb.

Chris launches into a long, practiced speech about what being an employee at Bloom means. On top of all the social aspects, they also offer classes in retirement funds, stock options, and even trust documents. Chris jokes that he knows his workforce can be a bit young, but that just means it's their moral obligation to ferry these kids into adulthood with some life skills.

I nod and smile along, happy that Chris seems to have picked right back up on his much-practiced keynote speech. To his credit, it's actually word for word the talk he gave at a local high school that was uploaded to YouTube. Sentences here and there are verbatim from an interview he and Asher did for *Wired*.

As our meeting begins to wind down I steer the conversation back to Caltech. How did they like it there, what do they think of their alumnae program, and would they consider starting an internship just for Caltech students? Chris and Asher debate that last point a bit, before Chris taps something into his laptop.

"I really like the idea of an internship program," Chris says, pressing Enter with enthusiasm.

"Your guys' class has gone on to do some pretty impressive things," I say. Chris and Asher absently nod. "Jason Chu's company just got bought." I made myself memorize the names of the people who appeared the most in the pictures I pulled off social media where Chris and Asher were tagged. "You mentioned him in the *Wired* article."

"Yeah, he was a great dude. Heard he bought a resort in the Caymans." Asher says, swiping open his phone. Chris nods.

"And Jon Tyner—he was one of the first people who tested CAM, right?"

"Yeah," Chris says, pushing back from his desk and standing.

"He's got that start-up about . . ."

"It's like Tinder, but for animal rescue," Asher says, swiping through his phone.

"Right," I say.

"It's where we get all our kittens," Asher adds. I nod.

"Once again, we really are thrilled to have you join the Bloom team. Thanks so much for taking time out of your schedule to meet with us today," Chris says. Getting the hint, I stand, gather my workbag, loop it over my head, and mean-mug the beam. I pick up my travel mug full of the most-awaited coffee in the history of the world. "You remember that first day when I told you that you would hopefully add some much-needed age and wisdom to our team?"

"With perfect clarity," I say.

"Well, I was right. You have already begun a dialogue about what is at the root of this company and how we can better connect our workforce to that vision," Chris says, coming out from behind his desk. Asher is tapping away on his phone, answering an email.

"You guys still in contact with Meera Rao?" Asher stops typing for just the tiniest sliver of a moment. A quick twitch of the neck and he picks right back up.

"You know, we lost touch with Meera. She was brilliant," Chris says, his face completely unperturbed. Mackenzie appears at the door with two Starbucks cups and holds them out for Asher and Chris.

"The car is here, the packets for the board have been shipped, and your flight is on time, last I checked," she says. Asher pockets his phone, stands, walks up to the beam, sits atop it briefly, and then effortlessly spins to the other side, as he hops down with a sigh. He takes one of the drinks from Mackenzie and continues down the long hallway.

"Thank you again," I say to Chris.

"My door is always open," Chris says. He looks past me to Mackenzie. "I'll meet you in the lobby in five." Mackenzie spins on her heel and clumps down the long hallway toward the Fortress of Solitude.

I turn back around to Chris and notice that he has moved closer. My instinct is to take a step back, but the fucking beam won't let me move an inch.

"I read some of your work," Chris says. I can feel the wooden beam knock my workbag as I reflexively pendulum away from him. "When Ria told me that an ex-journalist had applied for such a junior position, I must admit, I was suspicious."

"Suspicious of me?" I lock eyes with him. His ice-blue eyes are unblinking and hard.

"We get a lot of people who think they're going to catch us in some kind of . . . well, I don't know what they're expecting, to be quite honest." I loop my hand around my workbag strap.

"You get a lot of people? I don't . . . like, other journalists?"

"Thing is, for you to be a real threat in any way you probably should have worked as a reporter in the last—what's it been . . . over a year?"

I am quiet.

"So, I guess I just wanted to let you know that I am absolutely positive you are not, in fact, here on some undercover reporting gig, but that you do indeed need that entry-level position at my company after all."

"Well, that's comforting," I say.

"It is."

Chris and I stand in silence for what feels like an eternity, until he gives me a final nod and an attempt at a smile. I respond with what I hope is a breezy smile and turn around. I set my travel mug on top of the beam, shove my workbag back behind me, fall to my knees, and once again crawl under the beam as Chris looks on.

"Do you need some help?" Chris asks from behind me.

"Nope, I got it." I hoist myself up as effortlessly as I can.

"Most people just hop over it," he adds.

I walk down the hallway. The rage inside me is building. I need to scream. I need to punch something. I need to scream and punch something. I look into the Fortress of Solitude. It's empty. I check the tablet and see that the next meeting doesn't take place until 10 A.M. I look back at Chris's office and see that he's back behind his desk, bending down to gather his things for whatever flight he's supposed to be catching. I slip inside the Fortress of Solitude and close the door behind me.

I ball up my fists, tighten my entire body, open my mouth, and let out an explosive silent scream that lasts until I am gasping. I bend over and put my hands on my knees, close my eyes, and focus on catching my breath. Minutes pass and finally I'm able to stand, my breathing normalized. I straighten my workbag, tighten my grip around my travel mug, and reach for the door. Before I turn the latch, I whisper to myself, "I'm going to bring that motherfucker down."

I pull open the door, walk past Snoopy, down the stairs, through the main area, up the stairs, and plop down at my desk, my workbag still slung across my chest and my travel mug still clutched in my barely caffeinated fingers. Thornton and Hani both look up. I set down my coffee, pull out the pad of paper from my workbag, tamp down my swirling emotions, flip the pages until I find the list of names. I cross out Jason Chu and Jon Tyner. I focus on the name Meera Rao.

"Who is Meera Rao?" I mutter to myself.

Thornton stands up and walks over.

"Is this the next step?" he asks, holding out his hand for my pad of paper. But once he takes a look at the coded writing he pulls his hand back.

"Wait, is this what you guys were talking about yesterday at Field?" Hani asks. I look at Thornton. Trusting one person is hard enough, but I don't know if Hani can stand to keep anything to herself if her life depended on it. I also know that Hani has a degree in computer science from UCLA. She would know how to decipher any code or whatever it is that I'd need if I wanted to understand anything about the computer part of this very tech-heavy path I'm headed down.

"How good are you at keeping secrets?" I ask.

"Oh, I'm terrible at it. Phew, I've just been on the other end of it too many times, you know? People keeping secrets from me and then when I finally get a line on a live one, I just . . . I just feel bad for the person who doesn't know, you know?" Thornton and I are quiet. "Was that the wrong answer?"

"Do you remember Elise? From yesterday?" I ask.

"You mean the most beautiful woman in the world?" Hani asks. Thornton and I both can't help but smile. "I'm sorry, but she is. She just is! She lights up a room. Sunshine. Pure sunshine. I don't know if she . . . you know, likes girls? But, I mean we could be just friends, too, it would . . . I mean, maybe it would be enough? I just want to be around her, you know? Getting ahead of yourself, Hani! First off, we've got to see if Mrs. Pennybaker likes her. Then we'll cross all those other bridges."

"Do you know where she sits?" I ask.

"I can find anyone. You want me to see if she's free?"

"That would be awesome," I say. Hani leaps up and is immediately jerked back by her headphones. Laughs hysterically, takes the headphones off, sets them next to her computer, and hurries toward the stairs. She stops and turns around.

"And then bring her back here?" Hani asks. Thornton lets his head fall into his hands.

"Yes, please," I say. Hani gives me a huge thumbs-up and bounds down the stairs.

"She means well," Thornton says, rolling Hani's chair over and sitting down.

"I know, but I am definitely wary of letting her in on all this," I say, twisting open the lid on my travel mug and finally, *finally* taking a long sip. It is delicious.

"So, who's Meera Rao?" Thornton asks in a whisper. The graphics department is huddled around in their daily morning check-in. From the balloons and the cupcakes, it looks like today is one of their birthdays. The raucous noise is actually perfect to obscure our conversation.

"She was in Chris and Asher's Caltech class. They were on the same team for their Senior Ditch Day. Their team was Chris, Asher, Jason Chu, Jon Tyner, and this Meera Rao. Jason and Jon are pretty well documented. Entrepreneurs, start-ups, supermodel girlfriends, thoughtful interviews talking about how down-to-earth they are . . . the whole nine. When I mentioned them in my little 9:30 meeting, they didn't flinch." My voice is as quiet as his. We continue to speak in barely audible hushed tones. I don't tell Thornton about what Chris said to me when it was just the two of us. I haven't figured out if I'm not sharing what he said because it's not pertinent, or because I'm ashamed of how much it got to me.

"But she was different?" he asks.

"She's got no social media presence. She's mentioned in one article in *The California Tech*, which is Caltech's little newspaper. And it's just that she, Asher, and Chris built the best go-kart and won this goofy race. But the picture . . . they looked like friends." The realization takes my breath away. "Oh my god." I open up my computer.

"What?" I sign in and retrace my research steps from last night. But then . . . I stop. I pull my hands back from the keyboard.

"This is a Bloom computer."

"Yeah."

"They've gotta track where you visit," I say.

"Oh, definitely," Thornton says.

"Shit," I say, quickly closing all of my windows.

"What's going on?"

"It was there the whole time. Right in front of us," I say, pulling out my phone from my pocket. I remember the research breadcrumbs from last night, finally sniffing my way back to the *California Tech* article with Asher, Chris, and Meera smiling wide in front of their ramshackle homemade go-kart. I show the photo to Thornton. He reads the caption.

"Holy shit," he says.

"Chris. Asher. Meera," I whisper, my finger pointing to each initial.

"C. A. M." His voice is barely audible.

"CAM."

12

Blood Oath?

"You guys will never guess it, not in a million years," Hani says, breathless from her run up the stairs. I instinctively flip my phone over on my desk. "I said, you guys will never guess it, not in a million years." Elise walks up the stairs behind Hani, a tad out of breath. A look over to me. These kids and their boundless energy, the look says. Oh, I know. I know.

"Can you give us a hint?" Elise says, plopping down in Hani's chair. I see Hani notice that Elise is sitting in her chair and her face flushes. When she speaks, her voice cracks.

"Yes! Okay! Now, that's the kind of audience interaction I'm looking for," Hani says, slightly losing her train of thought. We wait as she gazes at Elise. I clear my throat. "Right! It's something at work!" Hani lunges down into a "ta-da" position, throwing her hands up into the air.

I want to yell out, "Is it that this whole company is built on a lie?"

"Is this about the ball pit?" Thornton asks.

That's perfect.

"Yes!" Hani says, jumping up into the air. "Isn't it wonderful!? Caspian is taking photos and there's even a slushy machine!" Hani ambles around the loft. "This is the best day of my life." Thornton, Elise, and I all react in similarly lukewarm ways. "What? What . . . could possibly be more important than a ball pit?" Thornton looks over at me.

"So, I need your help," I say.

"Wait. *Wait.* Is this a secret, you know I'm bad with secrets. Please don't entrust them to me. I wasn't supposed to even tell anyone about the ball pit, but I told Caspian I'd keep it a secret and I literally ran up here and couldn't tell you fast enough. I played the guessing game, but we all know I was going to maybe go another . . . what? Two rounds and then just blurt it out. Couldn't wait. Thornton already knew, but he always knows stuff. All of your reactions were a bit disappointing, TBH, but . . ."

As Hani paces and monologues about the unrivaled majesty of a ball pit, I ask myself why I'm even talking about this with them at all. The overconfident voice inside me yells out something about thinking these three people are super temporary and insignificant, so might as well use them for what I can. Another, far more guarded, cautious voice, warns me off them completely. You can go it alone, Joan. Don't risk it. You'll be fine. You always have been. You'll figure it out. They'll screw it up. A third tells me that I shouldn't drag them into this mess. They could be fired, they could be blackballed, they could be hurt. They're at the beginning of their careers, do I really want to give them a black mark on their work history so early?

But, bursting up through the cracks brought on by lovely self-reflection that I'm, you know, I guess, thankful for, there's a new voice in the arena now. One that I envision standing in between all the other voices with its arms outstretched, keeping them from kill-ing one another. This new voice speaks of a gray area and leaving my comfort zone and maybe not playing everything safe. Maybe try to trust Thornton, Elise, and Hani, as long as they earn it. To give my-self the chance to be thoughtful and discerning and not be the overly grateful workhorse who does whatever it is you ask her as quickly as possible. To take my time and understand that I'm capable enough and confident enough to weather any growing pains, all while recog-nizing the benefits of having a team of people with different skills. That the unease I'm experiencing isn't about Thornton, Elise, and Hani. It's that sneaking feeling that keeping this story to myself, in the end, will only shine a light on my limitations.

Elise is a computer genius, Hani can find anyone anywhere, and Thornton has been at Bloom since the beginning. This means he knows the ins and outs of the company, and would be able to finesse any networking with other employees we might need. Meaning, Mackenzie won't give me access to Chris's or Asher's offices or cal-endars, but she would definitely let Thornton do whatever he wanted.

Looking at it on a logistical level, the story will be far better re-searched and more thorough with their involvement. They can give me expert advice on the ground so I can navigate the momentum of the story as it's happening. I'll ask smarter questions and get more in-depth answers. Not only will they know what a server farm is, they'll know what to do besides stand outside one and say, "Yep, that's a server farm."

I've researched everything from the Russian mob's tattoos to the ins and outs of local zone permitting, plus the secret methods used to bribe a small-town councilwoman. But this story is something else entirely. Chris and Asher have hidden the perfect crime at Bloom in-side an inexperienced workforce hopped up on ball pits and expensive beer. What actual tech there is at the core of the company is known by only a handful of overworked and siloed thirtysomething social outcasts who've been put in positions where they don't interact. Not even with the other thirtysomething social outcasts. No one sees the whole thing. No one knows where all the bodies are buried. That's how this ongoing scam has been hidden (almost) in plain sight.

Plus, I like hanging around Thornton, Hani, and Elise. Isn't there a place for community in all this? Or should I—with this fun, new-found, crippling introspection—look at why I'm on the cusp of be-friending the Millennial 2.0 version of my actual, age-appropriate friends when I've just been not-so-gently reminded that I need to work on my communication and intimacy skills?

Jesus, maybe the question I should be asking is why they should trust me.

In the past, this is right where I would drop off the grid for as long as it took until the story was finished. I'd roll out my old whiteboard, turn my whole house into one of those murder walls—index cards, crime scene photos—and survive off of Cheerios and tea, shambling around my house in stained shirts and yoga pants that hadn't seen an actual yoga class in months* (*years). The people in my life would govern themselves accordingly, they'd check in now and again with a text that they'd see me when I "came out of the cave."

But what I never allowed myself to see was that this arrangement wasn't working for the people in my life. For me. For anyone.

How have I existed on so little for so long? But I guess that's what all of this is about. How I do one thing is how I do everything. I only asked for the lunch drinks of friendships. I only asked for the lunch drinks of family bonding. I only asked for the lunch drinks of stories. I only asked for the lunch drinks of my own talent and skill. I only asked for the lunch drinks of dreams and goals. And I only asked for the lunch drinks of myself.

"It's not a secret. It's more of a puzzle," I say.

"A puzzle?" Elise asks.

"A secret puzzle?" Hani adds.

"Nope, just a puzzle puzzle," I say. Thornton closely watches the back and forth.

The thing is, Hani could yell from the rooftops that "that lady who can't work the coffee machine" thinks CAM doesn't work and literally not one person would believe her or care. While I may adore Hani, I've noticed that she's not the most popular of kids here at Bloom. Her open-hearted exuberance is often met with disdain in this social gladiator's arena where the top champion is the one who acts like they care the least.

The thing that we all have in common is that our unpopularity (minus Thornton, of course) gives us the ability to work utterly in secret simply because no one gives a shit about us or what we do or say.

If you want to keep a secret, tell it to the unpopular kids.

"I like puzzle puzzles," Hani says, almost to herself.

"Haven't you ever wanted to be a part of a crime-solving band of misfits?" I ask.

"What did you just say?" Hani asks.

"Haven't you ever wanted to be a part of a crime-solving band of misfits?" I repeat.

"I swear to god if you are joking me right now—"

"I am not joking you right now." Thornton puts his hand over his mouth, hiding what is most certainly a growing smile. He stands, walks back over to his computer, and clicks and taps as we talk.

"Crime-solving?" Elise asks. "Please expand."

"I've checked out the Fortress of Solitude conference room. Shall we continue the discussion over there?" Thornton asks, gesturing toward the stairs. Hani runs down the stairs, taking them two at a time. Thornton, Elise, and I are careful and quiet as we follow her.

Just as I previously noted, the Fortress of Solitude conference room is only big enough for two chairs. When the rest of us arrive, Hani is standing in the corner.

"I want to be the one who cracks all the jokes." We all look over at her. "There's always a wisenheimer in a crime-solving band of misfits. I'm just saying, I would like that to be me."

"I think we can arrange that," I say. Hani pumps her fist. Thornton closes the door behind us and leans against it. Elise and I sit in the two seats.

"This is the only conference room with no shared walls, no cameras, and no teleconference hookups. It's as close as we're going to get to the most secure option," Thornton says, turning the lock on the door.

"This is so cool," Hani mutters to herself. Elise crosses her arms across her chest. She's waiting for me to explain what the hell is going on here.

"Back in the day I worked as a journalist. I'm telling you this so you know not only what I bring to the table, but also that I intend to write a story about all this—if it does turn out to be true."

"If what turns out to be true?" Elise asks.

"I am not good at trust." I sneak a quick look at Thornton. A smile. "So, before I tell, may I ask that, if you don't want to be involved in this, you simply opt out and keep what we've talked about here confidential." Elise nods that she agrees to those terms.

"Blood oath?" Hani asks, pulling a small, pink Swiss Army knife from her pocket.

"No, I think a simple nod or yes will suffice," I say. Hani nods. "Thank you."

"You're making me nervous," Elise says. Hani thinks Elise's words are about her and quickly pockets the Swiss Army knife.

"I know. I have that effect on people," I say. They laugh. The room gets quiet. "I believe that the CAM algorithm doesn't work." Elise uncrosses her arms. Hani is quiet. Too quiet.

"Joan has a couple of leads, one of which is a woman named Meera Rao. She believes that Meera is the M in CAM," Thornton says.

"I've never heard of her," Elise says.

"But CAM stands for 'Contains All Materials,'" Hani says.

"What if it doesn't?" I ask.

"What if it does?" Hani asks.

"Okay, we can . . . I think they made that up after Meera distanced herself from the company. Probably because she realized that the algorithm didn't work and wasn't super cool with being part of a company that was built on a lie."

"Why do you think CAM doesn't work?" Elise asks, keeping us focused.

"All of the breadcrumbs I have right now don't really add up to much. I just want to find Meera. Ask her some questions. If it's a dead end, then this is over. If it's something? Then . . ."

"What if we get caught?" Hani asks. Her voice is quiet and serious. Thornton and Elise look from Hani to me.

I want to blurt out a thousand reassurances about how nothing we're doing is technically worthy of firing. We're just asking some questions. But I realize now that I'm splitting hairs and making excuses. Hani has worked her whole life to do well in school and get a job exactly like the one she has now. And I'm asking her to put all of that in jeopardy because I have a "hunch." She deserves an answer worthy of all that she's risking. As I'm about to speak, Thornton beats me to it.

"On our side of things, we need to make sure we don't leave any kind of trail they can follow," Thornton says specifically to Hani and

Elise about the tech end of this investigation. "Secure everything. Even everyday shit like . . . we can no longer connect our text threads to our computers, no emails or communications through any server that Bloom has access to or can subpoena through discovery. If you go digging somewhere you're not supposed to be, make sure you're the only one who knows you were there." Hani's face twists from the worry that comes from asking a seemingly simple question and getting back an answer that is way more complicated and troubling than you were expecting. I know the feeling.

"If you talk to someone or ask questions, make sure it doesn't send up any suspicious flares. Easy breezy," I say.

"Easy breezy," Hani repeats, her voice compressed in horror.

"I'm a little rusty at this myself." Rusty? What an adorable word I picked to describe the complete and utter wreckage my life has become.

"You are?" Hani's voice is a nervous yelp.

"Yeah. You really don't have to be a part of this. I can't guarantee that you won't be fired. Shit, I can't even guarantee that I'm right or that there's even a story here. Honestly—" I look down at my hands. My bloodied and bitten-down fingernails, and the word "charger" written on the back of my hand so I'd remember to bring my phone charger into work* (*I still haven't). "This could all be a wild goose chase."

"Can't get fired for a wild goose chase," Hani says. I look up. Hani is smiling.

"No, you can't," Thornton says.

"I mean, you actually can, but—" I say and am cut off by Hani laughing.

"I'm in. Count me in. I'll make team shirts," Hani says.

"Thank you." I turn to Elise, who is less enthusiastic. "This is just about finding the next thread to pull. That's it," I say.

"Just one thread," Elise says.

"That's it." I look over at Thornton. He is watching intently. Elise looks over at Hani. Hani is utterly caught off guard at Elise checking in with her. She freezes. Elise smiles and looks back over at me. Hani lets out a long breath.

"And if that one thread unravels the whole sweater?" Elise asks.

"Then it wasn't much of a sweater," I say. Elise nods. We sit across from each other at the smallest table in the world, in the smallest conference room in the world. Thornton and Hani stand noiselessly on the fringes, watching us as if we're in the final match at the World Chess Championship.

"Here's my concern." Elise pushes up her chunky black glasses and swipes her bangs to one side. We all wait as she thinks. "So, if you're wrong, then it was just a wild goose chase." I nod. "But what happens if you're right?" I am quiet as a stream of fantasies where I get my old life back flood my brain. "Let's say we uncover that CAM doesn't work, and Bloom, inevitably, closes down. We're looking at a hundred people, including all of us, who are now suddenly unemployed with no severance." I'm about to jump in when Elise continues. "The only one who has gained anything from this"—Elise makes eye contact with me—"is you." Hani and Thornton look from Elise to me. The room is breathtakingly quiet.

"I don't . . . I don't—" I stop. Think. "They're doing something shitty and they think they can get away with it. I want to tell people about it. I want to tell a lot of people about it. I don't think . . . that's not me benefiting, that's me putting a spotlight on the fact that these arrogant douchebags decided to tangle up all of these people and families and livelihoods into their bullshit scheme. If what I think is happening is true—" I stop. All of the emotion of the last few months is dangerously close to the surface now. The passion in my voice is on the brink of becoming just outright sobbing. "Don't you want to be a part of the team that brings them down?" I make eye contact with each person in the tiniest room in the world. Except Elise. She won't look at me. I'm holding my breath as I see her inhale and begin to speak.

"Yeah." Elise's voice is a whisper. She turns her gaze to me and nods. "Yes." Her voice is loud and clear and strong. I can't help but smile and find myself almost reaching across the table to grasp Elise's hand in mine. I pull my gaze from Elise over to Thornton and the relief on his face is plain.

"That was—" Hani rests her hand on the wall and leans into it. "Good night, I did *not* know which way she was going to go."

"So we find Meera Rao," Elise says.

"That's it," I repeat.

"I'm in," she says.

13

That Enamel Pin Life

I spend my nights researching the story, my days trying to keep up on work, and my lunches trying to maniacally learn a New Edition dance routine for a birthday party I completely forgot about.

I've used the Fortress of Solitude conference room during the week, to practice the dance on Skype with Lynn and Hugo. I'm Ronnie, of course. Whichever boy band member is the tallest, that's the one I'll be stuck with. I'm almost more terrified of someone recording those lunchtime dance-offs than any talk of Meera Rao or whether or not CAM works.

Even though we said it would only be one thread, we decide instead to pull four threads:

1. Who and where is Meera Rao?
2. Is there a Bloom server farm?

3. Who are Chris and Asher meeting with and why?
4. What are the inner workings of Bloom and how and where would one hide within it?

We've taken all communication offline. Instead we now have a group text thread dedicated to all things CAM. The fact that I now have Thornton's phone number and he has mine is not lost on me. Of course, I'd never think to text him about anything that wasn't related to the story.

Since Hani can find anyone, she's put in charge of trying to find Meera Rao. It's a common enough name, so she's had to follow more than a few leads—which have unfortunately all led to dead ends. Whenever we meet up for coffee, Hani marvels at someone just disappearing. In this day and age, she says, mustering the same level of wonder every single day. As the week progresses, Hani becomes a bit obsessed, culminating in a particularly heated argument when she mistakenly calls Thornton Meera.

Because of her background, Elise has focused on the notion that Chris and Asher would need a server farm if CAM doesn't work. She thought she found something, but it turned out to be just a clerical error on the lease to the first building where Bloom was housed. She said she thought Chris and Asher were covertly holding on to the old space for the server farm. But it was just a tanning salon that'd picked up the lease and that's why the electrical bills were so high. She really thought she had something.

Thornton accepted a lunch invitation from Mackenzie and a smattering of the other popular kids to see if he could find an inroad to Chris's and Asher's calendars. By the time the vegan nachos hit the table, he'd gained access, but all he found was countless meetings with VCs and donors and moneymen. They're filling the coffers, seating a board, and shoring up the bottom line. Thornton's next task is to see if he can gain access to their finances. He thinks this might be a little more difficult than the whole calendar thing.

I've decided to try to get a bird's-eye view of the inner workings of Bloom itself. Who is hired for what, what do they do, where did they come from, and how are they being utilized here at Bloom. What I've found is that the majority of people working for Bloom are in sales, marketing, and public relations. Social media, post-production, and something called "Web Scouts" are now hiring at a faster rate than they can find desks for.

They're shooting feel-good videos right here on campus, where they're cut and adapted to fit to each social media platform. Brainstorms about hashtags and Bloom swag are treated with the same gravity one would find in discussions at the Pentagon. There's also a team simply known as Brouhaha, a group of people hired to make sure the employees at Bloom are having a fun time (see: the Ball Pit).

I've also learned that no one knows what anyone else does, or who's being hired and how they fit into the landscape that already exists. And despite our job titles and descriptions, there is no hierarchy, no leveling, and no power structure.

For a tech company, there are only a handful of software engineers, and fewer than that working with Elise in hardware. As Thornton pointed out, the people hired in those positions tend to be ancient Gen X fringe dwellers with families and mortgages. There's even one poor guy who bought a Ducati motorcycle and dyed his hair green in an attempt to fit in. He was ostracized for being desperate. He was thirty-eight and a Stanford graduate with two kids.

What's genius about all of these tactics is that every human being understands the currency of popularity. If you're not successful because you're not popular enough to network with the right people, then that's your fault. Predictably, these employees will then internalize the blame instead of looking to Chris and Asher to take responsibility for building a company with such an adolescent mentality.

It has become patently clear that there are no adults at Bloom. On purpose. We are all working in a very plush version of *Lord of the Flies*.

And I blame my mission to figure out what people actually do here at Bloom for the fact that I now find myself crashing a brainstorm in the Freddie conference room entitled "Memes, Unlikely Animal Friends, and Celebs Behaving Badly: Unlocking Instagram."

I am the first to arrive, so I set my laptop down in the middle of the table. With glass walls and glass doors, each of the conference rooms at Bloom is designed so everyone can see inside. The meeting subjects are displayed on tablets just outside the conference rooms and anything written on the whiteboard is on display for anyone who happens to walk by and look in. Utter transparency in every possible way. I scan the room and notice that someone has written the words "your mom!" on our whiteboard.

Perfect.

The door to Freddie is pushed open.

"Hi." Her dyed pink hair is in a loose crown braid. She's wearing a peasant-style dress with no bra and has finished off the outfit with worn-in Birkenstocks. She is carrying a tray of tiny Mason jars that are filled with a watery caramel-colored liquid.

"Hi." I sit up straight and fumble with my laptop, waiting for the rest of the group to arrive.

"Ivy," she says.

"Joan."

"You're new, right?" She sets the Mason jars out on the table.

"Yeah, yes. I'm—"

"Do you want to try something new?"

"Oh, um . . . I'm just here for the Instagram meeting?"

"You're going to love it." Sigh.

"Sure." She hands me a small glass jar.

"Drink," she says, her brown saucer eyes now fixed intently on me. I take the glass jar.

Is this millennial drugs?

"Oh, I—" I try to hand the glass jar back to her; she pushes it back toward me.

"Just give it a try!" I look inside. Looks like rusty water.

I did this story once on a guy who wandered off at Burning Man after drinking what he believed to be liquefied peyote. Before he went missing, he told those around him that he believed himself to be some kind of shaman. He's still missing. Of course, Burning Man lore is that he turned into an eagle. My theory—and the theory of the police and emergency services—is that it was more likely that he died of thirst and exposure.

I smell the glass jar. A tart, vinegary odor pierces my nostrils. I wince. Ivy is rapt. I swirl the liquid around as I look beyond the glass walls of my conference room.

Help.

Help.

"Your discovery process is invigorating to observe." I lift the Mason jar in a toast and drink Ivy's brew in one shot. The seltzer-y bubbles tingle as the sour tang warms my throat.

"It's kombucha," I say, relieved. Ish. It may not be millennial drugs, but it *is* still kombucha. So, really, best-case scenario of all of the worst-case scenarios. Ivy takes my now emptied jar from my hand. "Thank you."

"Do you want a baby?" Ivy asks.

"I'm sorry?"

"A baby," she says. She turns around and picks up a Mason jar that's got a brown liquid in the bottom of it. On top of the brown liquid is what looks like a circle of . . . welp, it looks like a disc of human skin.

"Are you . . . are you growing a real baby in that jar?" I can't believe the words even as they pour out of my mouth.

"This is a good one, too. Here!" Ivy pushes the Mason jar into my hands. My fingers curl around the cold glass and I bring the Mason jar up to my face for closer inspection. "I'll email you the details of how to start your own brew later!"

"My own brew?"

"Yeah, it's a SCOBY. It's where kombucha comes from. I give you a baby from my mother and then you can start making your own." I just look at her. "It's like sourdough bread?"

Three people stream into the conference room already in deep conversation. They settle in around the table, opening up laptops, setting down cans of fancy club soda, and oohing and aahing over Ivy's home brew.

"Oh . . . *oh*." Billy's teasing about my Tin Foil Reporter hat screams through my head and my face flushes hot.

"—were talking about finding a back door into her feed and I thought he was talking about something else—" The woman sets her laptop down at the head of the table and curls her legs underneath her, digging her dirt-encrusted shoes into one of Bloom's eight-hundred-dollar office chairs. "We cleared it up, but I just wanted them to know that I was open—no judgment, you know—to whichever way they decided to go."

What the fuck kind of meeting is this?

"Everyone, this is Joan. She's a junior copywriter and I'm so glad she decided to join us. I can't wait to see what you bring to the discussion," Ivy says, pulling her knees up to her chest.

"Thank you," I say, genuinely touched by her openness to my presence at a brainstorm I was definitely not invited to.

"I don't think we've met," I say, looking at the other three coworkers.

"Oh, so sorry. Joan, this is my team. Jessica, Malaya and Mike J." Each member of Ivy's team looks as if they're part of a new line of fashion dolls that have been styled in outfits that resemble the others just enough so you know that you must collect all four.

"What team are you guys on?" I ask, as breezily as I can muster.

"We're on Jiffy," Mike J. says.

"Jiffy?"

"Everything we make has to be under ten seconds," Malaya adds, opening a laptop that's covered in unicorn stickers.

"We maximize content that thrives on the more minimal platforms," Ivy says, typing away on her computer.

We maximize.

Content.

That thrives.

On the more.

Minimal platforms.

"So, you make ads," I say, finally putting it together.

"We like to think of what we do as more of an invitation for people to join the Bloom family," Jessica says.

Ads.

Ivy launches into a series of prompts, using viral content as inspiration for future "invitations for people to join the Bloom family." She hooks her computer up to the television in the conference room and screens the most popular short-form content of the past year. Mike J. then follows up each ad with a rundown of how it performed, where it performed the best, and which demographics clicked the most.

Malaya then dives into the different iterations of the original ad—and how that particular ad became a phenomenon, and what each platform and region did with that original nugget of an idea. Ivy then throws the meeting over to Jessica, who talks hard and fast numbers. How many of those clicks turned into subscribers and how much revenue those subscribers added to the company's bottom line.

I sit in stunned silence.

These Bloom kids—however much they need to get their shoes off the furniture and be a little less outraged about the lack of free ramen in the canteen—know their shit. In all the years I've spent in newsrooms, the conversation between the members of the Jiffy team in the Freddie glass conference room with "your mom!" written on the whiteboard behind us is right up there with that of any group of experts that's ever broken down advertising.

Ivy turns to me for help on how to word a sequence of ads and I'm, quite frankly, relieved I can help in any way. By the time the meeting ends, and we're closing our laptops and streaming out of the conference room, I am officially hoisted on my own petard.

Once again, I came in here looking to make fun of a generation of people because they appear to be doing work that is thought of as silly or unimportant. The truth is, they're doing the same work people have done throughout the ages with the same level of thoughtfulness. But this time it's identified by cutesy names and takes place in glass conference rooms with whiteboards that are never without a scrawled bit of graffiti. Unlike us, however, they have an eye and a respect for innovation and looking to the future instead of proclaiming that "this is how we've always done things."

This is an odd realization, knowing of their blind reverence for the founders of Bloom and their failure to question the very DNA of the company to which they're devoting so much of their hearts and souls. Case in point, the Jiffy team spent more time breaking down why a five-second video of a stalker swan creeping on a duck went viral than they've ever spent on whether or not the ads they're creating are for a company that actually does what it says it does.

Walking back to my desk, SCOBY in hand, I think about how much these kids have to learn. Their bravado and certainty is like a flare sent up in the dark of the night as proof of their youthful swagger. But then I think about my slump and the denial of how small my life had gotten and realize that maybe the kids at Bloom are not alone in how much they have to learn.

All of this introspection evaporates later that afternoon while I'm trying to set up a meeting with Thornton and Hani to send Jiffy's ads through final review. I notice a new addition to Thornton's schedule. Mackenzie has set up a calendar invite for her birthday party the same Friday night as Reuben's birthday party. There's a party bus and something about a climbing wall, which feels a bit cavalier, but . . . eff those spinal injuries, hey, Mackenzie?

But this means that all us fringe dwellers have to look at Mackenzie's birthday invite—and know that we weren't invited—every time we want to schedule a meeting with someone who was.

Elise tries to ease my annoyance by saying that it was probably done like that because Mackenzie didn't have anyone's outside contact information, meaning that they're actually not that close of friends. This was cold comfort, on top of the sharp pangs of feeling silly that it bumped me at all. Why do I care if I'm not invited to Mackenzie's dumb party?

This inherent talent Bloom has for pushing every pubescent button is awe-inspiring. I'm hunting down a story that'll bring back my career and here I am sending angry texts to my friends and monologuing at my family later that night about not getting invited to Mackenzie's birthday party and what does she know, if she doesn't see how great I am, then she's not any kind of friend that I want. Mom tells me not to play with Mackenzie anymore and maybe I should get some sleep and eat an apple. I stomp to my room, flounce down on my bed, and find myself, once again, proclaiming that I'm gonna show 'em. I'm gonna show 'em all.

In the days before Reuben's party, it's as if time has lost all meaning. I get my coffee, I write new content for the website, I get some more coffee, I ride the bus, I dance to New Edition, I make myself nod breezy greetings to a busy and dismissive Chris Lawrence, I sleep, I "b-storm" with Jiffy, I almost tell Thornton what Chris said to me that day in his office about how he'd read up on me and was positive I wasn't a threat, and I check my emails. The highlight of the three weeks is getting my first paycheck and being able to pay a few bills, give my parents money for food and rent, and actually go see a movie for the first time in months. I get popcorn and everything.

At work, I study the seating chart I've made of everyone at Bloom and try to find some method to the madness. Why are they sitting next to them and why are they sequestered all the way over there? And why is Bloom hiring sales and marketing people at such a rate that they've had to make onboarding an everyday thing to accommodate it?

On the Friday of Reuben's party, Elise and I grab lunch at a sandwich place around the corner from Bloom. We asked Thornton if he wanted to come, but he was doing his own thing. Which was super great to hear. Hani asked us to bring back a market salad, with light lettuce.

As we walk over, our conversation is strained and exhausted. It's been three weeks of dead ends. Some crime-solving band of misfits we turned out to be. I wish the heat of intrigue fueled us and we were staking out some server farm in the arctic waiting for Chris and Asher to snowmobile up wearing parkas made of baby seal fur. But we're not. Instead, we're asking some poor teenager what kinds of chips come with the sandwich special as a line of people shift and look at their phones behind us.

I have feelers out to a few connections I've worked with in the past. A retired cop who works security at a local bank, a bankruptcy attorney with a Lexis password who charges me $25 to see if anyone's been sued, a woman who works at the DMV, and a real estate agent with whom I trade See's Candies for property information.

I've heard back from the lawyer. Chris and Asher have not been sued, Bloom has not been sued, but he'll do some more digging. The real estate agent is honeymooning on the Big Island and says she'll get back to me first thing. For payment, she'd like a box of milk chocolate Bordeaux as well as whatever their seasonal candy is for spring. I haven't been able to get in touch with the cop, but decide that I can stop by his bank if something urgent arises that he can help with. The woman at the DMV is a tricky one. She gives me the best information, but the last time I asked for something she made me go to a bunny museum with her—which turned out to be more of a person's house who collected bunnies than an actual museum.

In a fit of desperation late one night, I almost texted Matt to see if he had any way of tracking down Meera Rao. I pulled up his phone number and was about to text, right up until I saw the last exchange we had. And when I say "exchange," I mean my own series of unanswered texts that serves as a perfect epitaph for our relationship.

"saw a guy dressed as waldo crossing the street. We can all stop looking."

"running late. be there in 5"

"left your key in the mailbox"

I exit out of our text thread with a sigh.

As Friday finally comes to an end, we all pack up our computers and head down into the main area where Elise is waiting for us to walk out. I hate seeing Hani so deflated and try to tell her that we are just laying the groundwork right now and that I swear it will pick up. She nods bravely as we thread through the hustle and bustle of a Friday night at Bloom.

"I want to get an orange soda for the drive home," Hani says, pointing to the canteen. We all nod and settle in next to the front wall to wait. I watch as Mackenzie flits from desk to desk, asking if they're super excited about her party. The people who weren't invited act like they don't hear, but one by one I see them turn up their music or pack up their stuff quickly and leave. We all thought we'd outgrown this kind of playground behavior. Mackenzie sees Thornton and immediately makes a beeline over to us. I sneak a glance over at him as she approaches and he's unreadable. Always unreadable.

"Hey, you," she says to him, completely ignoring Elise and me.

"Hey," Thornton says. He turns to Elise and me. "You remember Joan and Elise?" Nuthin'.

"You never RSVPed to my party," she says.

"Hey, Mackenzie. Happy birthday!" Hani says, leaping over to us with one orange soda in her hand and one in each of her jean pockets. "Cute shirt. And jacket. Wow, is that one of those enamel pins, is that a . . . who is that? Oh, it's a sushi. Thought it was one of the Spice Girls. You know, I wish I lived an enamel pin life, but I just don't have the right jean jacket for it maybe—"

"If you could just . . . I'm only over here to see if Thornton is coming on the party bus or if he is going to meet us at the rock climbing place," Mackenzie says, raising her voice.

"Is this for a birthday party? You're having a birthday party? Oh, I . . ." Hani stumbles and stutters as it dawns on her that she wasn't invited. "I've never been on a party bus."

I will kill you, Mackenzie.

"We're going to an '80s-themed birthday blowout over in Burbank," I blurt. "Go-go boys, DJs, New Edition dance-offs . . . food. We
rented out a whole place. Elks Lodge or something. It's going to be
huge." Everyone looks over at me. "I was reminding Hani that we
already had plans, so . . . sorry we can't make it to your exercise party."
Hani's eyes well up in tears. Elise puts her arm around Hani and pulls
her in.

"I've always wanted to go to an '80s-themed party," Hani whispers.

"Uh . . . I didn't invite you—"

"Good. Because we can *not* go," I say, blowing out a long breath.

"Okay, good. Thornton, are you coming on the bus or meeting
us there?"

"I'm going to the '80s party, so I won't be able to do either," he
says, stepping closer to Hani. "I should have RSVPed no earlier."

"Maybe we'll see you later then at the after party," Mackenzie says.

"How many parties are you having?" Elise asks.

"I'm RSVPing no to all the parties, but thank you for inviting
me," Thornton says.

"You're welcome." Mackenzie is about to say something else.

"Yes, thank you for inviting us," I say.

"Okay, well—" Mackenzie says, finally walking away. "I didn't
invite you!"

"Bye!" Elise yells.

"You guys are the best," Hani says, tears streaming down her face,
a little orange soda smile curling at the edges of her mouth.

"She's the worst," I say.

"Is there really an '80s-themed party?" Hani asks. Elise and
Thornton look to me with expressions that suggest that I better have
an '80s-themed birthday party or what kind of monster am I?

"Yes!" I say. Hani beams. Elise and Thornton exhale. "Do you
want to come?" I ask.

"Do I get to wear a costume?" Hani asks.

"Hell, yeah," I say.

"Then I'm in," Hani says and then starts laughing. "I'm just kidding, I was going to be in whether I got to wear a costume or not, sheesh!" She takes a long drink of her orange soda. "You'll text me the deets? I gotta get to finding this costume. This is the best—you know, I thought knowing that there were party buses out in the world was going to be the best part of my day, but then—boom, '80s-themed party. Man. What a rollercoaster. Okay, see you guys there!" Hani skips out of the main area and right out the front door.

"You guys don't have to come, but I couldn't let Mackenzie . . . I just couldn't—"

"What kind of person is mean to Hani? She's literally the nicest, sweetest joy . . ." Elise trails off. Thornton and I give each other a knowing, slightly hopeful look. "Just tell me when and where and I'll be there. Until then, I'd better scrounge up a costume." Elise waves her goodbyes.

"You don't have to come," I repeat to Thornton.

"You kidding? A party with food? Where am I going to find something as rare and precious as that?" I smile. He gestures toward the front door and we walk in silence. He opens the door and waits for me to walk out first. I thank him and lunge toward the outside as quickly and conveniently as I can. We stand in front of Bloom in an expanding awkward silence.

"So, I'll see you there," I say.

"You need a ride or anything?"

"Oh, I'm all the way in Altadena."

"I'm just in Echo Park, so it's not that out of the way."

"It's totally out of the way."

"Okay, fine. It's out of the way. And yet I am still offering."

"I hadn't even thought about taking a bus in my whole costume and everything." I look up. Thornton waits. "I would love a ride."

"Good, I'll pick you up at . . ."

"Eight thirty?" Thornton nods. "See you then, then." There is a beat. Where both of us try to decipher if "See you then, then" is a real sentence. At about the same time, we both come to the same conclusion: it is not. "Let's just not speak of it." Thornton nods. I say my goodbyes and start walking to the bus stop. From behind me I hear Thornton yell.

"See you then, then."

14

The Pumpkin Drop

"Wait, who's coming to get you?" Billy yells down the hallway toward my room. I can hear him talking to someone in the kitchen and all I want is to get this costume on and go wait by the curb. Oh, no. What if Thornton gets here early and knocks on the door?

And has to sit with my family.

I text Lynn, Hugo, and Reuben to let them know that the three Bloom kids will be joining us tonight. Hugo and Reuben reply with a tidal wave of questions: Are they attending ironically? Will they be on their phones the whole time? Will they be in costume? Were they even born in the '80s? Will they make me feel old? And then just a string of old man emojis.

Lynn replies with a simple and unpunctuated, "can't wait to meet them." Then I proceed to spend the remainder of the time I'm getting ready spinning Lynn's one text into an entire indictment of my

life choices. She probably thinks I'm inviting these three twentysome-
things because my fragile ego needs a malleable set of child-friends
to revere me as a wise sage. All Lynn asked was that I have the cour-
age to connect and love my peers in an authentic way and in response
I dove into the shallow, millennial-infested end of the pool. She probably doesn't have the heart to tell me that I'm a silly coward who re-
fuses to dig deeper into my own consciousness and will continue to
remove myself from any and all adult relationships that challenge me.

Now in a full panic, I pull on my black Converse, grab my black
scarf and gray sling bag, and run out into the kitchen.

"Who are you supposed to be?" Billy asks, holding up Poppy while
Dad wipes whatever blended food was not to her liking off her entire body. "Don't tell Mom or Anne anything you're seeing, by the
way."

"I'm Allison Reynolds from *The Breakfast Club*." They both look
confused. I turn to Billy and speak sibling. I act out everything I'm
saying. "The basketcase? From that '80s John Hughes movie with the
dancing and the pot and the running through the empty school?" I
bend over, let my head fall, and tousle and shake my hair. It dawns
on me that all of the basket case's clothes were essentially already
in my closet. The old black cardigan, the skirt, and the black Converse. This isn't so much a costume as just another comfy work outfit
for me.

"Ohhhhhh. That's a bit on the nose, isn't it?" Billy asks, pepper-
ing Poppy's belly with raspberries. Poppy lunges over to Dad and he
scoops her up and flies her around the kitchen.

"Where are Mom and Anne?" I ask.

"Seeing a movie with Sylvia," Billy says.

"Oh, you'll never believe it. Apparently, Sylvia and Greg are getting a divorce," Dad says. I immediately look over at Billy. He just rolls
his eyes.

"Did they give a reason?" I ask, tying the black scarf loose around my neck.

"I'm sure your mom'll get it out of her tonight," Dad says, giving Poppy a raspberry on her belly.

"I'll be curious to hear," I say, eyeing Billy. "Verrrrrrry curious."

"So, who's picking you up?" Billy asks, changing the subject.

"It's someone from work and I'm going to wait by the curb so you don't embarrass me," I say.

"Is it a boy?" Billy asks, drawing out the word "booooooooyyyyyy yyyy." Dad tickles Poppy, but I can see that he's listening. "A gentleman caller, mayhap?"

"Oh my god," I say, transferring the contents from my workbag over to the gray sling bag—also from my closet.

"Does this work colleague have a name?" Dad asks.

"Thornton Yu."

"And is Thornton Yu your new boooooooooooyyyyyyyyfriend?" Billy asks.

"No, but you're going to be my new"—my mind rifles through a quick succession of options, finally blurting out—"deadfriend."

"That's just embarrassing," Billy says, pulling a couple of beers out of the refrigerator. He cracks them both open, sets one on the table for Dad, takes a long swig of his beer, and stifles a giant burp.

"Here's what's going to happen. You're going to shut up about Thornton Yu or else I'm gonna—" A knock on the door. A giant smile breaks across Billy's face. He slowly sets his beer on the table. We lock eyes. And then all hell breaks loose as we fight and claw and shove at each other trying to get to the door first. Billy dives into the door and pulls it open. I am panting and sweaty. And there's Thornton. Standing at my front door. Dressed as Maverick from *Top Gun*.

"Hey, Mav," Billy says, opening the door wide. Thornton's aviator sunglasses are tucked into the collar of his flight suit. His black hair is slicked back. "Please! Come on in!" Thornton looks from Billy to me, smiles, and steps inside my house. I keep the door open. We won't be staying long. Billy reaches around, shoulders past me, and closes the door.

"Thornton, this is my brother, Billy," I say, trying to get in front of this. They shake hands. So far so good.

"Nice to meet you," Thornton says.

"Nice to meet you, too," Billy says, clapping Thornton on the back and downright pushing him into the kitchen. "Come on in."

"We're actually in a hurry, so . . ." I rush past Billy and Thornton and grab my gray sling bag off the kitchen table. "Welp, it was nice—"

"Thornton Yu," Thornton says, extending his hand to my dad. Poppy leans down and rests the side of her face on Thornton's forearm.

"William Dixon, and this is Poppy," Dad says. Poppy puts her arms out toward Thornton. We are all ready to jump in, but Thornton doesn't hesitate. He loops his hands under Poppy's arms and brings her in close.

"I have nieces," he says as we all stand watching Poppy place a dimpled hand on the side of his face. She "casually" flicks her eyes down to Thornton's collar and acts like "Oh, I hadn't seen these supercool sunglasses hanging there. What a surprise!" Thornton is quick, though. He distracts her for mere milliseconds with a noisy kiss on the top of her head, and deftly loops the sunglasses off his collar, slipping them into the flight suit's pocket. By the time Poppy looks back over at Thornton's collar, they're gone. She looks back up at him, her eyes slow-blinking in wonder.

Thornton paces around the kitchen, rocking a sleepier and sleepier Poppy. He talks to her in a low lullaby of a voice. As Billy, Dad, and I look on, Thornton asks Poppy how her day was, what she thinks she'll do tomorrow, and, eyeing Mom's kitchen herb garden on the windowsill, lists each herb and which dishes he thinks they'd be delicious in.

"I know what those herbs are too," Billy says. "Just sayin'." He sniffs, picks up his beer, and won't look at me.

"Looks like someone has a new best friend," Dad says, settling back in at the kitchen table. Billy grunts out an assent through gritted teeth.

"I'm so glad you invited Thornton in," I say to Billy. He takes a long drink of his beer. Yes, I'm gloating. By the time Thornton circles back to us, Poppy is draped over his shoulder, fast asleep. Billy stands up and Thornton hands over the little ragdoll of a girl. Billy offers Thornton a respectful nod while Thornton disentangles himself.

"Say goodnight, sweetie girl." Billy brings Poppy over to me. He knows I can't be mad at him when he comes armed with a cute baby. Poppy rubs and swipes at her eyes, but attempts to give me a kiss goodnight. A little reaching hand to Thornton and they're down the hall in search of bedtimes.

"We should get going," I say. Thornton gives me a nod. Dad stands.

"Nice meeting you," Dad says to Thornton.

"You, too," Thornton says. Once outside I feel the need to explain everything.

"I didn't know how to tell you I lived at home and I know I should have, but . . . it's temporary. It's been a weird year," I say. Thornton walks up to the passenger's side door and creaks it open.

"I know." He waits. "You've got it." I can feel my face flushing. His chivalry makes me queasy. "But maybe every once in a while, you can let me get it." He motions to the passenger's seat.

"You were this close to saying 'let me get it,' weren't you?"

"How dare you," he says. I laugh and grunt a thanks as I sit down in the passenger's seat, my gray sling bag still tight around my body. Thornton extends a hand. The sling bag. I dip my head forward and untangle myself from the bag. He takes it and shuts the passenger's side door.

He crosses in front of the car in all his *Top Gun* glory. I don't know in what world this exact moment is allowed to happen. I find myself holding my breath, careful not to spook these suspended seconds where I let myself get swept away in the idea that Thornton would want to be an us.

Do I want Thornton and me to be an us?

Thornton opens his door, slides into the driver's seat, and pulls the door closed behind him. All of the sudden I am very aware that Thornton and I are alone together on a Friday night outside of work. Something about this knowledge paralyzes me in my seat.

"I can put the address to the place into my phone," I say, realizing my phone is in my sling bag. I look into the back seat. Reach an arm, then pull it back. "This is why I do the bag thing." Thornton hands me his phone. I push the Home button. Locked screen. I hold it up for him and he inputs a series of numbers that I try to act like I'm not memorizing: 8793. As I input the address to the totally hip and cool Elks Lodge somewhere in the belly of Burbank, I talk myself off the ledge that 8793 is probably Thornton's birthday. August 7, 1993. That would make Thornton Yu twenty-four years old, almost twenty-five, but right now? This is a twenty-four-year-old man sitting next to me in this car . . . being thoughtful and kind and chivalrous and like I said, he's way out of my league and oh looka there, that fleeting moment of being swept away with the idea of An Us has evaporated.

"Your family seems nice," Thornton says, backing out of our driveway.

"They're pretty great," I say, honestly. The phone tells us to turn left at the stop sign. "You're just going right down here to the free-way." Thornton nods and flips on his blinker. "So, did you grow up here, or . . ." Oh, god. It's so painful. Usually Thornton and I have a work-related topic to discuss.

"I actually grew up just outside Indianapolis, moved out here for school, and then got the gig at Bloom." He shifts into fourth gear as we speed toward the freeway.

"Which school?"

"Caltech," he says.

"You went to Caltech?"

"Yeah."

"Jesus."

Thornton laughs.

"You're just super smart is all."

"Where'd you go?"

"Nowhere." Thornton looks over at me. "Yeah, no college. I got an internship right out of high school with *The LA Times*, so I went there instead."

"That's not nowhere, though," he says.

"But it is not Caltech," I say. We are quiet. "So, you knew Chris before you worked at the video game place together?" Thornton nods. "I bet we could probably use that connection to get access to Chris and Asher's school stuff."

"I thought of that too. I sent a few scouting emails, and appar-ently we shared a professor. I sent her an email last week, so we shall see if it bears fruit." Thornton rumbles to a stop at a red light. This old car has no sound system, so just the clattering of the engine and my awkwardness fill the silence. The light turns green; Thornton puts the car in gear and glides down the street.

"What'd you say to her?" I ask, wondering why he didn't talk to the team about this connection or said that he'd emailed her or that

that's where he knew Chris from. I hear the clipped, slightly annoyed tone of my voice and immediately feel regret. I don't know how to be soft or generous with someone while working on a story that I am way too invested in. Picking up my tone, Thornton looks over at me.

"I told her I started working at Bloom and that Chris and Asher were my new bosses. I said it'd be much appreciated if she'd mind sharing any insights that could help me get ahead," he says.

"Hm," I say.

"Does that pass muster?"

"It's . . . ugh." I scratch my forehead and, sighing, look out the window.

"What?"

"Okay, here are my thoughts. Why wouldn't you tell the team about this connection? We have daily check-ins, three weeks of them. How have we never heard about this person?" Thornton is about to speak. "I'm the journalist here. I know I'm a junior copywriter at work and you're my manager. And that I told you I've been struggling a bit. But I do know how to be a good journalist or at least be *a* journalist, as opposed to you. So why wouldn't you talk to me about what to put in that email? That way you could get the most out of her, protect us, and not send up any red flags if she happens to be, I don't know, maybe working with Chris and Asher?" I cross my arms across my chest, hating every second that this night couldn't remain lovely and dreamlike. "Did you ever think of that?"

"No." We are quiet. Thornton speeds up as we get onto the freeway. He merges and threads through the traffic with ease. "I didn't want to bring her up, because I didn't want you guys to know I went to Caltech."

"What, why?"

"It's complicated," he says.

"Aren't we past complicated?"

"We've only known each other for three weeks. How could we even begin to be past complicated?"

"I meant past complicated when it comes to the story," I say, weakly.

"But, this is . . . it doesn't work like that."

"Why not?"

"What did you mean about this being a weird year?" Thornton looks over at me. A quick glance before his eyes are back on the road.

"We're going to do this now?" I ask.

"Now's as good a time as any," he says. I look down at my hands and start picking at my fingernails. I take a deep breath and look up at him.

"I got laid off and then tried to freelance, but couldn't find anything." Thornton nods. "And then I worked really hard on this story that I thought was compelling enough to restart my career. But my fancy newspaper contact read it and said it wasn't even good enough to run on someone's online blog." I put the necessary air quotes around Tavia's exact words. "I thought I'd lost everything. But a fun byproduct of all these realizations was finding out I really didn't have anything to lose, so . . ." I try to put my arm onto the edge of the window, but the window is up so I just slam my elbow into the glass and watch as it slides down the passenger's side door.

"How are you defining 'everything'?"

"That's a good question . . . Great question, Thornton. Yeah, thanks for that, um . . ." Thornton laughs. "Everything would be . . . my apartment, my car, my cable, I had some great saved BBC mysteries that are now lost, my TV, my electricity bill, gas bill, all utility bills actually." I stop. It's . . . ugh, fuck it. "My good credit, my journalism career, self-respect, pride, what other fun things have I lost, oh, the illusion that I was a good writer who gave everything I had, lost that . . . Turns out I've been in a slump for probably years and come to find out, my writing is definitely boring, soft, and shallow—because I'd become boring, soft, and shallow. Um, lost all the goals I set for myself when I was seventeen. I don't know where all this is going or what it's all for. I don't dig deeper or ask any uncomfortable questions of myself because I'm pretty sure I'm terrified about what I'll find down there. Lost the hope that something out there would make me feel complete or enough. And you can see the Catch-22 between that and the not digging deeper thing. So, it's pretty much up to me now to make that happen and whooeee is that a bucket of cold water thrown on my face, I'll tell you what." I am quiet. Thornton waits. I pull the sleeves of the droopy black cardigan down over my hands and try to swallow the sadness and loss and grief and hurt that comes crawling its way up my throat with every word I let out. Thornton is quiet for a long time. I shift in my seat, look out the window, and try to not leap out onto the freeway.

"I'm sorry," he says.

"No. I did it to myself. This is my fault and no one else's." I look over at him. "I did this." Thornton looks over. His brow furrows as he focuses back on the road. The silence expands. Finally—"What's complicated about Caltech?" Thornton slides his gaze over to me. In a mere moment, I see his face go from curious and open to flat and weary. He turns away from me and focuses back on the road. He gives an imperceptible nod, an unhurried swallow, followed by a clenched jaw before he speaks.

"After not sleeping for—I still don't know the exact number of days—a janitor found me sitting at the top of Milliken Library. It's where they do the pumpkin drops at Halloween." Thornton puts on his blinker, looks over his shoulder, and switches lanes.

"Fun."

"Yeah, super fun." Thornton turns off his blinker. "I actually don't remember getting up there. That always . . . I still think about that.

That someday this rush of memories is going to come spilling back into my head of stumbling through campus and climbing all the way up there, and I mean, this one girl said I had a two-minute conversation with her about Orion. No idea." Thornton stops. He looks over at me, then back at the road. The phone tells us our off ramp is coming up. I see Thornton scan the horizon and start getting over. "I just couldn't do it anymore. The pressure was unlike anything I'd ever experienced, and my parents . . . they'd sacrificed so much to get me there." I am quiet. I want to reach out and comfort him, but I don't think that's what he wants. I think, like me, he just wants to wrestle these words out from inside his own head. He just needs another human to help carry it. Even if it's just for a few minutes. "This poor janitor—he wasn't even supposed to be up there, but . . . he didn't know what to do. How to talk me down. Didn't want to say the wrong thing. I just felt bad for the guy. He showed me pictures of his kids. Nice family. I begged him to leave, that he didn't have to stick around. I was going to be fine. He knew I was lying, of course. He was quiet for a long time. And I thought he was going to go, you know? I thought I convinced him. But then he asked me if I had a favorite ice cream." I am quiet. He looks over. "Coffee." We get off the freeway and come to a stop at the bottom of the off ramp.

"I love coffee ice cream." Thornton smiles.

"Won't you miss coffee ice cream, he said." The light turns green, Thornton puts the car in first gear, and we float through the intersection. "I told him I would. He held out his hand and told me to just get down from there. Come back. Called me son." I wipe my cheek with my cardigan sleeve, trying to erase any evidence that I'd been crying. "I climbed down and we walked away together. I told myself I was going to go back up there, but every night after that I just didn't." He pauses. Shifts in his seat. Looks out the window. "It didn't get better for a long time." Thornton watches as the addresses speed past. He turns into the driveway for the Elks Lodge. He pulls into a parking space and shuts the car off. The car settles around us. He looks over at me and I hold his gaze. Broken sees broken.

"Thornton—"

"You're not the only one who's had a weird year."

KNOCK KNOCK KNOCK. Thornton and I both jump in our seats to see Hani, dressed up as Elliott from *E.T.*—red hooded sweatshirt, a crate tied around her neck filled with the glowing alien himself.

"Maverick! Basket Case! Like, gag me with a spoon, guys! Are we going to this party or what?" Hani situates E.T. in his little crate and waves to one of many Madonnas entering the Elks Lodge this evening. Thornton pulls the door handle and is about to push the door open.

"Thank you for telling me that," I say, reaching out to him. I was aiming for his arm, but instead find myself resting a firm hand on top of Thornton's knee. I will myself, make myself, not jerk my hand back. Just . . . leave it. It would look weird to pull it back now . . . as opposed to the spectacular escalating weirdness that's currently happening.

And then it gets weird. Because it's not like he can . . . do anything with my hand. What's he going to do, lay his hand over mine with Hani standing just outside his car? I've got to peel it off. Peel it off, Joan.

Take it off. Bring it back. My eyes are darting from my hand to him, to the outside, to the dashboard . . . I'm panicking. At some point during all this, Thornton sits back in his seat and just watches, the smile breaking across his entire face. I finally tug my hand off his knee. Sit back in my chair and sigh. Thornton grabs my sling bag from the back seat, climbs out of the driver's side, and slams the door behind him.

"Get it together, Joan. I swear to god—" I mutter to myself in the quiet of the now empty car. I take one last deep breath and start to grab for the door handle. Instead, Thornton pulls the door open and is standing there with his hand extended. I take his hand, turn my body to the side, and place both feet on the ground. He doesn't move, so when I finally stand we are inches apart.

Thornton pulls me clear of the car, hands me my sling bag, and slams the passenger's side door behind me. And, as we follow Hani into the venue, he doesn't let go of my hand.

15

Maverick, Elliot, and a Basket Case Walk into a Party

Thornton, Hani, and I walk down a long hallway lined with the portraits of the old white men who've led this fine organization over the years. The lighting is fluorescent and the laminate floors squeak underfoot. All three of us look around, wondering if we're in the right place.

I imagine Mackenzie's party bus and all of the cool kids from Bloom walking down this antiseptic hospital-like hallway and my stomach drops. Inviting anyone from that life into mine was a mistake. I love my friends dearly, but we aren't in our twenties anymore. Happily no longer in our twenties. We throw parties in Elks Lodges, not rock-climbing gyms. Reuben's party, however amazing, will end no later than midnight. I imagine that's about when Mackenzie's after party will be starting.

There'll definitely be children at Reuben's party and more than a few conversations will revolve around aging parents, moving out of LA so they can actually buy a home, and whether or not they're going to get that couch in gray or tweed. No matter how much I want to bash the millennial generation, the worst thing they ever did was make us feel old.

I'm just about to start apologizing and giving flight instructions and how maybe we can find somewhere else. And then we see the go-go boys.

There are two go-go boys dressed in tutus at the end of the long hallway. They're checking people into the party with clipboards kitted out in neon stickers and feathered roach clips. Bright pink wristbands are being wrapped around the wrists of every iteration of George Michael, Madonna, and Prince. Adam Ant looks like he's already had a few. We fall in line behind two Jazzercisers. Thornton and I finally let go of each other's hands without a word or a look. Hani never noticed.

"Okay, I'm going to need to see your and your IDs," one of the Go-Go boys says, pointing to everyone but me. Thornton and Hani fish their IDs out of flight suit and red hoodie. They present them to the go-go boy. He leans in. Takes a long look. "You look like babies." The go-go boy wraps a neon-pink wristband around Thornton's wrist, then Hani's. They step aside, situating their wristbands while they scan the growing line. "Don't they just make you feel old?" he asks me as he wraps the wristband around my ancient, arthritic bone of a wrist.

"You're not doing so bad a job of that yourself," I say with a stern look. He laughs and pats my hand.

"Sorry, girl," he says, motioning for the two big-haired, shoulder-padded Working Girls behind me to step forward. I join Thornton and Hani. We look back over at the go-go boy. "Down that hall. You can't miss it."

We hear the music first. Pushing open two large security doors, we are immediately transported to a 1980s school dance. Packed dance floor, tons of neon, sparkling disco ball, streamers, balloons, Salt-N-Pepa piercing everyone's eardrums as their music screams out of the giant speakers that line the stage. The DJ this evening is Reuben's niece. She's dressed up as Ronald Reagan.

"This. Is. Amazing," Hani says, beaming.

"Thank god," I say with a sigh.

"I'm going to text Elise, see where she is." Hani walks over to an empty table, takes off the crate with E.T. in it, and sits down in one of the folding chairs. Her face is immediately lit up from her phone.

"Let me see if I can find my friends. Introduce you guys," I say, scanning the packed dance floor.

"There must be two hundred people here," Thornton says.

"Yeah, that's Reuben," I say.

I spy Reuben and Lynn across the room. Reuben is dressed as Marty McFly, and Lynn is Madonna from *Desperately Seeking Susan*. I shoot my arm in the air and wave them over. Reuben grabs Hugo, who's dressed as someone right out of *Miami Vice*, and the three of them cross the crowded dance floor toward us. I don't know how to introduce Thornton to them. I don't even know how to introduce him to me yet. Maybe I'll take a page out of Chris and Asher's playbook and not give anyone a straight answer. Hani joins Thornton and me, situating her crate around her shoulders.

"Elise says she's just pulling up," Hani says, trying to play it cool.

Reuben, Hugo, and Lynn settle in front of Thornton, Hani, and me. I introduce everyone to everyone else. Hands are shaken, pleasantries are traded, and compliments and oohs and aahs are exchanged about everyone's fabulous costumes. Reuben motions to two flaming skid marks made out of poster board that are now leaning up against the stage. He assures us they make the costume. I watch as my worlds collide. Holding my breath.

"There's someone here who came dressed as Ice Man," Reuben says to Thornton.

"And not with his own Maverick?" Thornton asks, quite rightly.

"Yeah, just . . . of the characters I guess he related to Ice Man the most. All by himself," Reuben says.

"Even Goose would have been better," I say.

"He's one of Hugo's coworkers from the accounting firm," Reuben whispers conspiratorially.

"Oh, he's a lovely man," Hugo says, defending him. "Great at math."

Reuben gives us the lay of the land. Where the food is, points out the photo booth—which is just Reuben's mom and dad standing next to a painted hot-pink backdrop offering their services to use your own phone to take a photo. Reuben tells us it's an open bar, and which of the guests are already drunk (steer clear of the aforementioned Adam Ant; Reuben has already called his wife and she is on her way), and that there will be cake and ice cream later.

We all nod along, taking in the growing party. The crowd has ballooned just since we've been standing here. Hani excuses herself to go meet Elise. Reuben is tugged away by well-wishers. Which just leaves Lynn, Hugo, Thornton, and me. Hugo immediately launches into the Plan.

"Okay, he doesn't suspect a thing," Hugo says, huddling us up.

"Are we robbing this place?" Thornton asks.

"No, we're dancing," Hugo says.

"Perfect," Thornton says, smiling.

"Reuben's greatest wish is to be the lead singer of a boy band, so we are going to grant that wish tonight," I explain. Thornton nods.

"After we're done here, I'll go talk to the DJ," Hugo says. "She's acquired the version of the song from the music video. With the manager's pep talk at the beginning. Now, I figure we play that and then reveal the five microphones on the stage." We all look. I hadn't noticed them, but sure enough there they are—five microphones on the stage, utterly ignored. "I thought we were going to be found out when he leaned his flaming skid marks up against the stage, but the microphones didn't even register."

"So, the DJ will play the opening, and then what?" Lynn asks, looking over at the stage.

"Then my friend from work—"

"Ice Man?" Thornton asks.

"Yes, Ice Man," Hugo says. "What Reuben doesn't know is that while he may have odd taste in relatable characters, he's spent more than a few tense hours trying to figure out the lighting here."

"Now I feel bad," I say. Lynn and Thornton nod in agreement.

"Ice Man is going to focus the spotlight on the five microphones—and, you know, not that we are down one Ricky Bell. Hopefully, like a moth to a flame, this will draw Reuben to the stage. Where we will be waiting." Hugo takes the lavender pocket square out of his sea foam–green jacket pocket and dabs at his brow.

"We got this," Lynn says. We all bravely nod.

I see Hani and Elise walk into the party. Elise is dressed as a Ghostbuster, proton pack and all. They see us and make a beeline over to where we are. I introduce everyone to Elise; she is happy and downright glowing. That's when I see that she has an intensely bright blue carnation surrounded by baby's breath wrist corsage on. I bring my hand to my chest and nudge Thornton. I stare at Elise's wrist, willing him to follow my gaze. Thornton's lips purse as he looks from the corsage to Hani. He raises his eyebrows at her and she beams from ear to ear.

"Let's hit the dance floor already!" Hani announces, bounding over to the table and taking off E.T. She comes back over to our little group and stands in front of Elise, extending her hand. "M'lady." Elise laughs and takes Hani's hand. They nudge and cuddle and fix each other's costumes all the way to the dance floor.

"They're super cute together," Lynn says.

"When did that happen?" Thornton asks me.

"We literally saw them two hours ago," I say.

"This just happened?" Hugo asks.

"Apparently," I say, watching as they jump and leap around the dance floor. Hani's got some moves, to the surprise of no one. We all watch in stunned romantic silence.

"Or . . ." Thornton trails off.

"No, it can't be." Lynn and Hugo can only watch Thornton and me go back and forth.

"Hani kept a secret," he says.

"I never thought I'd see the day," I say. An awkward silence falls.

"If you'll excuse me," Thornton says. Hugo points to where the men's bathroom is. Thornton thanks him. We all nod and smile patiently, waiting for him to get out of earshot. Reuben comes running over.

"Spill it," Reuben says.

"He works at Bloom, he's my manager, actually." I take a deep breath. "He's twenty-four." I watch as the rippling sound waves of me saying "twenty-four" reverberate throughout the room. "And I thought he was too out of my league for there to be anything. I convinced myself it was because we were talking about this story at work and he's nice and thinks I'm some . . . older . . . friend he can look up to because I remember a time before cell phones, but . . ." I trail off, remembering holding his hand.

"But what?" Hugo asks.

"He held my hand walking in here tonight." Hugo and Lynn both clutch their chests, swoon, and clap. "But is holding hands the same thing with millennials? I thought first base was . . . like a threesome or something?"

"Honey, that's not . . . I don't think that's right," Lynn says. The happiness bursts through me and I notice that I'm physically holding the base of my neck in some last-ditch effort to choke it down.

"He's decent. And not afraid of me. He doesn't make me feel like I'm too much, but then I hear Matt's words over and over ringing inside my head—"

"*Shit, Joan, why can't you just leave it alone. You ruin fucking everything,*" we all say in droning unison.

"But do you remember why Matt said that to you?" Lynn asks. A montage of grainy footage from the last fight Matt and I had flickers through my brain.

"I never felt like he listened, so I would keep trying to get him to understand. Once I decided he didn't get it, I just wouldn't stop."

"I need you to know that this is for your own good that I'm walking you down this particular memory lane," Lynn says.

"Remember we love you," Hugo adds.

"Oh, god. Is this another let-you-love-me thing?"

"You'd decided he was flirting with that photojournalist," Hugo says.

"She was so cool," I say, reverently.

"And you thought you had him, because you'd found some texts," Lynn says.

"Yes! The texts."

"But later, you saw that that same coworker got engaged, and thanked Matt in her Facebook status as the one who helped her fiancé orchestrate the surprise proposal?"

"Doesn't mean they weren't sleeping together," I say.

"Joan. Just stop it," Lynn says. Her face is suddenly serious. Hugo is stone-faced, and all around us people are having the best night of the year. "We have to stop doing this, repeating this shit. Lying to ourselves." Lynn stifles a sob and now it's Hugo and my turn to share a look of concern. He wraps an arm around her and pulls her in.

"Has something happened?" Hugo asks, his voice heartbreakingly tender.

"Is it—" I look at Hugo. "Not something with a baby or . . ." There have been too many sad things with babies for Lynn. Lynn shakes her head, fighting the emotion. Finally—

"You guys were right about Josh. I . . . but I wouldn't listen. He never wanted a baby—you kept telling me he never wanted a baby—and—" Hugo gives her his lavender pocket square. Lynn dabs carefully at her overly mascaraed eyes. "I wanted to be a mom so badly I almost saddled my baby with a bad dad."

"Oh, honey," I say, taking one of her hands in mine.

"Phyllis and I are moving out. We've wanted to move closer to the store anyway." Lynn lets out a long exhalation and hands Hugo back his pocket square. "I am going to go into this next round of fertility treatments alone."

"You're not alone," Hugo and I say almost in unison.

"I know." Lynn pulls Hugo in close. "I have Phyllis." We all laugh, but then she refocuses back onto me. Which feels very on brand for her. "Best friend truth."

"Best friend truth," I repeat, bracing myself.

"You've turned Matt's quote into some kind of curse, but—"

"Don't . . . You don't have to say it," I say.

"All he wanted was to love you and—" Lynn waits until I look up. She brushes a strand of my unbrushed, basket-case hair out of my eyes and lets her hand linger on the side of my face.

"And I wouldn't let him," I finish. Lynn rises onto her tiptoes and kisses me on my forehead.

"Why don't you just see what happens with Thornton," Hugo says.

"I feel like if I think it's a thing it'll go away."

"It very well could," Hugo says.

"But won't it be wonderful until then?" Lynn adds.

"What'd I miss?" Thornton asks, settling back in next to me.

"We're just trying to figure out what that costume is," Hugo blurts, pointing to someone who is dressed in possibly the most iconic costume of the 1980s: Michael Jackson, dressed in head-to-toe red leather from his "Thriller" video.

"We are stumped!" Lynn says. The person dressed up as Michael Jackson moonwalks across the dance floor.

"Are you guys serious? Do you really not—" Just then the sound of crashing thunder bursts through the speakers, interrupting Thornton. Everyone knows that thunder. It's the beginning of the '80s classic "It's Raining Men." The entire party freezes. Oh my god. Everyone hurries to the dance floor as the opening chords ring out. As the chorus builds, Thornton and I are tugged out onto the dance floor, where Elise and Hani have already secured a nice pocket of space in the mosh pit of a crowd.

"This is the best night of my life!" Hani yells over the music. Elise leaps up and twirls as the first chorus hits the crowd like a tidal wave.

It's raining men! Hallelujah!

The momentum of the song is electric and the entire room moves as one, screaming along with the words. I look over at Thornton and am relieved to see that he can, thank god, dance. It's that cool, not a lot of movement dancing where he definitely has rhythm and you know that he's just warming up, and as the night goes on we'll see some more elaborate moves. He dips his head low as the song quiets down and the singers start building from the lowest range all the way up to the top. I catch myself getting looser and looser as I let myself have this. Let myself just see where this goes.

Just dance. Have fun. Let go.

Each song blends into the next. Sweaty and exhausted, we dance the night away. I am thankful that Reuben's niece never slowed things down, and revel in the fact that Thornton and I never had to have that weird . . . "Shall we?" moment and then three minutes of terror as I scream "Wait, where do my arms go?" inside my own head. Instead, we jump and dance with a crowd of people, smiling and laughing as we try to yell over the songs. I lose sight of Elise and Hani after about an hour.

It's during Lynn's particularly dramatic reenactment of "Bette Davis Eyes" that Hugo shimmies over to us on the dance floor.

"It's time," he says. My stomach drops. I nod to Hugo.

"Good luck," Thornton says.

"Just remember back to when you thought I was cool," I yell over the music.

"And when would that have been?" he answers back, resting his hand on my upper arm as he talks into my ear.

"Ah, yes. Touché," I yell, nodding. I leave Thornton and I walk up to the stage. Lynn is already waiting. Hugo scans the crowd and sees Reuben over at the photo booth with his flaming skid marks. Hugo motions to a door at the side of the stage. We creak the door open and sneak backstage. My heart is racing.

The music fades out. And then New Edition's manager's pep talk comes on. It's a twenty-eight-second speech. We watch from backstage as Reuben immediately perks up, telling everyone around him that he loves this song, he knows all the dance moves.

Hugo walks out onto the stage and with the one live microphone, says, "Happy birthday, my love." And then Ice Man lights up the five microphones. "Why don't you come up here and join us."

Reuben starts crying. And then Hugo starts crying. And then everyone at the whole party starts crying.

We all join Hugo onstage, Reuben's niece quickly takes the one live microphone, and we each settle in behind our designated prop microphone. I'm right in the middle. Which I like. Reuben runs over, leaps up onto the stage, sweeps Hugo into his arms just as the manager's speech comes to an end.

"So, let's do it one more time from the top and let's get busy," New Edition's manager's voice echoes throughout the room. Reuben takes his place at the first microphone just as the long drum roll kicks in. He can barely contain himself.

The first move of the dance has us with our hands up in the air wiggling our fingers and bringing our arms down on the beat. Classic boy band choreography. Reuben and the void of Ricky Bell that we hope no one will notice are the first to spin, and then me, and then Hugo and Lynn. After eight downbeats, we are all spinning together. We are in complete precision. By the time the cymbal countdown happens, each one of us is raising a knee and then folding over in perfect time. The crowd is going wild.

We have had months to practice this dance, but Reuben knows the whole thing without one minute of rehearsal. By the time the vocals kick in about a minute into the song, Reuben grabs the prop microphone (exactly when Ralph Tresvant grabs the microphone in the video) and lip-syncs along without missing a word.

The entire thing lasts for four minutes and fifty-five seconds, but it goes by in a blur. By the time we're gearing up for the final jumping high five that ends the video, I am sweaty and smiling and my mind is only focused on how much fun I'm having. Completely unburdened by the now-lifted curse of Matt's words, I leap as high as I ever have and high-five my three dearest friends as the song finally comes to an end. We bow and bow and hug each other. We pulled it off. The applause is raucous and just as it dies down, Reuben's parents roll out a giant birthday cake full of candles. A timid, out-of-tune voice sings the opening bars of "Happy Birthday" and then the whole room joins. Reuben and Hugo jump down off the stage and stand with Reuben's parents. Lynn and I decide that we'll be taking the stairs down, thank you very much.

We creak open the door and walk out onto the dance floor to smiles and join in with everyone singing "Happy Birthday" to Reuben. I scan the crowd for Thornton and see him standing over in the corner with Elise and Hani. What kind of . . . how . . . did they even see our dance, or the cake, or the birthday singing? I should have known. Thank god Reuben, Lynn, and Hugo don't see them.

I apologize, people of the party, that the three millennial dipshits I invited are currently ruining this very fine moment because they can't be away from their phones for even four minutes and fifty-five seconds.

Reuben's niece kicks on "The Power of Love" by Huey Lewis and the News and the entire crowd migrates exuberantly to the dance floor. Except me. I set my sights on the rudest, most disappointing trio in the world and stomp up to them ready to give them the what for.

"We found her," Hani says.

"What?"

"Meera Rao. I found her," Hani says, showing me her phone. "Someone was talking about *Full House* and, you know, one thing led to another and sure enough . . . Meera didn't disappear, she just got married. Her name is Meera Blue now. That's why we couldn't find her."

"She and her husband own a winery up by Buellton," Thornton says.

"You found her," I repeat. Hani beams.

"Road trip?" Elise asks.

"Give me a second," I say, looking over to the crowded dance floor. Hugo is smooshing cake in Reuben's face and everyone is laughing as the opening chords of "Jessie's Girl" keep everyone out on the dance floor.

"We'll meet you out by the car," Elise says, whisking Hani outside. I am frozen.

"We don't have to go tonight. We can leave first thing tomorrow," Thornton says.

"I actually posed this exact scenario to myself. If I got the chance to go back to my old life, would I take any of these lessons with me or would I remain a monster and abandon my friends once more in search of filling some unfillable void with a story?" I look away. "Looks like I got my answer."

"Uh-huh." Thornton's voice is flat. I look over at him.

"What? What's with the 'uh-huh'?" I ask, bracing for impact.

"I know . . . I don't know how to say this without—" My stomach drops.

"Oh my god, just say it. I'm a monster."

"You're wrong."

"What?"

"The party is winding down." Thornton urges me to scan the slowly emptying room. Parents peeling off with sleepy kids over their shoulders, packs of Madonnas with their stilettos in one hand and a slice of cake in the other saying their goodbyes. "Whatever this abandonment of your friends and unfillable void thing is, you went to a party, killed a dance routine—"

"You saw it?"

"Of course I saw it."

"Oh."

"And now—after saying your goodbyes along with most everyone else—you're going on a clue-finding road trip up to Buellton with a trio of people you met less than a month ago."

"But—"

Thornton steps closer. "I know how it feels not to trust yourself. But maybe we start by . . ." Thornton looks away, his brow furrowed. He looks back over and locks eyes with me. "Do you trust me?"

"Yes," I say, without thinking. My answer shocks me.

"And I trust you," he says.

We are quiet. Inches from each other.

"So, I trust you and you trust me," I say, my voice a rasp.

"Maybe that's the best we can do right now."

"I can do that."

"You're not a monster," he says. I don't believe him.

"You're not a monster." And I can see he doesn't believe me, either.

16

Flight

The energy and excitement, which propelled us out of that Elks Lodge and made us decide not to stop at our houses to get clean clothes or toiletries and just take Thornton's car right from the party, is wearing off as we pass Ventura.

We're about an hour outside of Buellton.

Elise and Hani fell asleep pretty much right away. Elise's tucked into Hani and the two of them are curled around each other so sweetly you don't know where one begins and the other ends. Except that E.T. is poking his head out from his spot right between them.

Thornton and I are mostly quiet as we speed along the ocean in search of answers that only Meera Rao can give. When we do speak, it's in quiet voices so we don't wake up Elise and Hani.

We stop to get gas at a rickety gas station, load up on road food, and quietly get back in the car. I got a couple of bottles of water, some toothpaste, a bag of plain M&M's, and a package of minidonuts for the morning. We settle into the front seats and get back on the 101. I take a long swig of my water and shift in my chair, turning my knees so that I'm facing Thornton more. I've always hated being the driver on long road trips and being left to my own devices as one by one people drop off to sleep. I offer my water to Thornton. He takes it, drinks a long slug out of it, and hands it back. I offer him an M&M and accidentally pour thousands into his hand.

"You're a good navigator," he says, popping an M&M into his mouth.

"That's the highest compliment anyone has ever paid me," I say, sitting back in my chair. I swipe open my phone and start reading off cheap hotels in Buellton that we can crash in overnight. Meera's winery opens at eleven o'clock tomorrow morning. It's up the road in Los Olivos, but that's too expensive and touristy. Buellton is a better bet. Thornton nods along.

"What if we find a room with two big queen-sized beds and a couch or a cot or something?" I say, scrolling through the dwindling options. "Save some money. It's only one night."

"That sounds good. Worse comes to worst I can sleep in the back of the car," Thornton says, motioning to the way back of the Volvo. "I've done it before." I book us into a little motel in Buellton, actually calling there to confirm since it's so late. A grumpy man answers and says yes, he'll roll a couple of cots in there and how long will it be before we get there, yeah, that's fine, but checkout is still at eleven, he wants us to know. I agree to all terms and sign off.

"When did you do it before?" I ask. I drop my phone into the pocket of my cardigan. Thank god this basket case costume is essentially just glorified pajamas. I am all set for tonight.

"Do what before?" Thornton asks.

"Sleep in the back of your car."

"Oh. I drove across the country after I graduated from Caltech. Did odd jobs along the way," he says.

"Hm." Thornton looks over at me. "I'm trying to act like that's not super cool and all I can muster was a hm." Thornton waits. "You're way cooler than me is all."

"Yeah, probably." Then he laughs. Looks over at me. Laughs some more.

"That's great. Thanks for that."

"I mean, what are you gonna do?" Thornton holds out his hand and I pour more M&M's into it. "No, I . . ." He pops the M&M's into his mouth, but then holds his hand out again. "I don't want M&M's in my hand, I want your hand in my hand."

"Oh," I say, unable to keep from laughing. I tuck the bag of M&M's into the side pocket of the passenger's side door, shove my water bottle next to me in the seat, and put my hand in his. And we drive on in silence. "This is weird."

"Only because I have melted chocolate on my hand," he says, letting go of my hand and grabbing a napkin from the gas station bag. He giggles as he wipes the chocolate off his hand. Hearing Thornton giggle is . . . something even I recognize not many get to behold. It's truly wonderful. He holds his hand out again and I take it.

Wordlessly, Thornton lifts up my hand, brings it up to his lips and gently kisses it. I watch as he lets our held hands drop to his leg and somehow it doesn't feel as weird now.

In the silence that expands, I want to ask him what he thought of my friends. Does he still get sad sometimes? Does he think Mackenzie is as awful as I do? I want to ask him if he thinks Meera Rao is going to have the answers we need and if this story will give me back journalism. I want to ask him if he thinks that's going to change what we have, whatever that is. I want to ask him if I'm a good writer.

But most of all I want to ask him why me? Why does he want my hand in his? I want to ask him if he thinks I can get used to being seen like this? Being loved like this. I want to ask him why I can be myself around him. Why I still belong to me around him.

Instead, I lift his hand to my lips and gently kiss it. Our held hands fall back on his leg. I lean over in my chair and rest my head on his shoulder.

"I'm not falling asleep, I promise," I say, my voice gravelly.

"You'd better not," he says. I can hear his voice muffled inside his body. I smile and watch as the cars speed past.

We pull into the sketchy hotel about an hour later. Thornton runs in, puts it on his card—telling us all to Venmo him later—and emerges with the key to the room.

We are all quiet as we walk across the parking lot to the bank of rooms. Thornton turns the key and pushes open the door. Two queen beds and two cots make the room look like one giant mattress.

"I'll take one of the cots," Thornton says, peeling his flight suit down to his waist and revealing the plain white T-shirt just underneath. Jesus Christ. He pulls off his shoes, sets them by the side of the cot, and crawls under the covers.

"Night, guys," he says, flipping over onto his side. We all wish him a good night and I try not to stare at how the plain white T-shirt is just see-through enough so I can see the outline of his back muscles as they shift and flex while he tries to get comfortable in a bed two inches shorter than he is.

"I'm so tired I can sleep anywhere," Hani says, doing her nightly prayers and then falling down on the other cot closest to her. Hani continues talking into her pillow. "Night, guys. This was the best night ever. What a special everything."

"I appreciate that they didn't say they would take the cots because we're older," Elise says, with a yawn. I nod. I take off my sling bag, flick off my Converse, and crawl into the queen bed by the sliding glass door.

Elise crawls into the other queen-sized bed and asks if we're ready for the main light to be turned off. We grunt that we are. She turns off the main light and wishes us a good night.

At first I think I'll have trouble falling asleep, but before I know it, the morning light is breaking through the sliding glass door. I blink open my eyes and see that Hani is sitting up in her cot, red hood drawn tightly around her face.

"There's a breakfast place called Mother Hubbard's that I want to go to," she whispers. I push the hair off my face. She looks back over at me. "It's not in a cupboard, though." Hani laughs as she swipes through her phone. "That would have been wonderful." She tightens her hoodie around her face. And then, almost to herself, she whispers, "Man. Eating pancakes in a cupboard."

"So, you and Elise?" Hani's face bursts with the joyous flush of love. It's unmistakable, but then she claps her hand over her mouth and crumples in on herself.

"It's—" Hani finally squeaks out, "I didn't know you could be this happy." I nod and feel the clawing emotion prickling my skin. I swallow and tamp down as much as I can. I will not lose my shit in a cheap hotel room in Buellton dressed up as a basket case. Hani goes back to her phone with a sigh.

Over the next hour, everyone gets up and gets ready. Thornton sits up in his cot, sleepy-eyed, his clothes wrinkled. Elise tries—to no avail—to find a way to make her Ghostbuster costume not look like . . . a Ghostbuster costume. Hani hurries us along, having decided that we, as a people, deserve pancakes.

We are packed up and out the door by 9:30 A.M., having pancakes in our costumes from last night by ten, and driving up to Los Olivos by eleven in search of Meera Rao's winery.

"There," Hani says, pointing to the wooden sign that reads "Wayfarer," the name of the winery. Thornton pulls the car down the long dusty driveway and we park next to the handful of other cars already in the lot. He shuts off the car. We are quiet.

"I think we see what kind of lady she is first and then come up with a plan," I say. Everyone nods along.

"So, we order a flight. Settle in. And Joan chats her up," Elise says.

"Yeah, I think we'll get a pretty good read on her right away," I say.

"This all of the sudden feels really real," Thornton says.

"Right? I was just going to say that," Hani says.

"This was all so academic, and now there's a person in there, and—"

"I'm good at this," I say, looking Thornton in the eye.

"I know," he says. Hani and Elise share a look. We all get out of the car and walk up to the main tasting room.

Wayfarer is exactly the kind of winery anyone would hope to own one day. Olive trees dot the property; a golden retriever underneath a white bench greets you as you step up onto the wrap-around porch. Muted whites and grays and sages. The whole place smells like a wonderful, luxurious herbal bath. We open the shiny black door and step inside the tasting room.

The seating is plush yet minimal. Stylish vignettes of comfy chairs cluster and circle around wooden tables at their center. There are a few groups of people here already. They're standing at the long reclaimed wood bar, being poured wine by a lovely man in his late twenties. Dark brown hair, wire-rimmed glasses, and a light blue oxford shirt. He brings out a nice white for the group next to us and walks them through how it was made and the different notes. They nod along.

We scan the rest of the room. We all see her at the same time. She's emerging from the back holding a bottle and calling out to her husband that she found it, and that it was right where he left it. He nods and the group oohs and aahs as she presents them with the bottle of wine. She is tiny. Curly black hair, bright eyes, and wearing those linen clothes that look good on no one, except her. She sets the bottle down, sees us, and tells her husband she'll be right back. Thornton, Hani, and Elise peel off toward the other helper behind the bar. They order a flight.

"Your friends seem to have abandoned you for wine," she says. Her voice is strong and I can tell right away that this woman is not going to put up with any of my bullshit. "What are you looking for?" She starts walking toward a shelf full of salts, rubs, and olive oils. "You're clearly not a wine drinker."

"How can you tell?"

"Come on, honey."

"That black salt looks neat," I say, pointing. Meera looks from me to the black salt. She picks it up off the shelf and hands it to me. "Is it just like regular salt?"

"Well, first off . . . it's black." I can see Thornton, Hani, and Elise stealing glances.

"I'm actually here about something else," I say.

"You don't say." Meera takes the black salt away from me and replaces it on the shelf.

"Chris Lawrence and Asher Lyndon."

Meera rolls her eyes. "What about them?"

"I think they're running a company based on something that doesn't work and that you may know something about that."

"Are you talking about CAM?"

"Yes," I say, holding my breath, in disbelief that she just came right out and said it.

"All that was in the past, I've got this lovely winery far away from tech bros and hey, honey, get me some coffee, and this is my Russian supermodel girlfriend who's now going to be the CEO of our start-up, you're cool with that, right?"

"So you moved up here to get away from them?"

"I moved up here because this is where the wine grows. I walked away from CAM because it didn't work at that time."

"Can you prove it?" Meera walks toward the back room, gesturing for me to follow her. As she disappears through the swinging doors, I look back over at Thornton, Hani, and Elise. A nod. They nod back. They're nervous. I step into the back room and find Meera waiting for me, uncorking a fresh bottle of wine.

"This is our newest," she says, offering me a glass. I take a sip.

"It's good," I say.

"So, who are you really?"

"Joan Dixon. I'm a journalist." Goddamn, does it feel good to say those words.

"I thought you'd have been here earlier. Not you, in particular, but some journalist." I am quiet. Let her talk. "I had my whole speech planned. Do you want to hear it?" I nod. "I was going to tell whomever appeared at my doorstep the hypothetical story about a local vineyard that claimed to have a high-yield grape that would allow way more wine to be made off a small plot of land." Meera refills both our glasses. She motions for me to drink. I obey her. "Turns out they just bought the garbage wine excess from a larger vineyard, selling it under the table. And wouldn't you know it? No one knew until someone found out about that other vineyard."

"Did you sign an NDA?" I don't want to spook her, but making up hypothetical vineyard stories seems to speak to a legal inability to speak freely about what happened with CAM.

"We were twenty years old when we developed CAM, living in

dorm rooms and eating ramen," she says. I wait. I need her to say it. "No, I didn't sign an NDA. I did, however, sign away my shares on the back of a King Taco receipt. No way was I going down with that ship." My heart sings. "Also, fuck that and fuck them." She walks over to the shelves and grabs another bottle of wine. She uncorks it, sets down two fresh glasses. "Now, this is my personal favorite." I drink. She drinks, watching me the whole time. "Really sit in it."

"It's good," I say, not knowing the first thing to say about wine or how to "sit in it."

"So, how'd you find me?"

"Does it matter?" I realize that I'm becoming quite drunk. I think that's the point.

"I guess not," she says, taking a long drink from her glass. She pours herself another.

"Can I record this?" Not trusting my quickly drunkening self, I pull my phone from my sling bag. She watches me.

"Are you dressed like that girl from that one movie?"

"Yeah." I look down at my outfit. After sleeping in it, the basketcase costume looks more genuine than ever.

"Should I ask why?"

"Probably not." I hold out my phone and she gives me a nod. I press Record. I ask her again if I can record this conversation and Meera says yes.

"I used to believe telling someone my story would be seen as gossip. But it was my story, so how could it be—gossip is something most people believe is at best catty, and at worst a downright lie. But my story was neither of these things." Meera pours. "And then I started paying attention. Really paying attention. Let me ask you a question, Joan. If I told you that I overheard two people gossiping about someone at work. Describe those people to me."

"I don't know . . . um . . . I'd think one of the women was—"

"Why is it a woman?"

"What?"

"Why did you imagine that it was two women I overheard? I just said two people."

"Oh, shit. Yeah . . . damn." I'm stunned by own ignorance.

"I realized that people in power use that word to debase those who would pass along information they would rather was kept secret. And isn't it odd how it seems to be only women who are called out for gossiping?" Meera puts giant air quotes around the word "gossiping."

"I've never quite thought about it like that," I say.

"Women secretly confiding in other women, arming each other with hard-won information that will allow our fellow sisters to thrive, is a true rebellion." Meera raises her glass. "To gossip."

"To gossip," I say, clinking her glass. Meera takes a long, luxurious drink, carefully sets her glass down, and locks eyes with me. Her gaze is resolute and commanding.

"CAM was never going to be what Chris wanted. He was obsessed. And it broke him. One night I was joking around that we could just do it the way everyone else does and no one would know. We hide a server farm somewhere, set up some ditzy start-up that only talks in inspirational memes, throw in some talk about America and don't you yearn for a time when you didn't have to lock your doors, and people would eat it up. No one understands this tech shit anyway. We'd seen it happen a million times. And where was the harm? People's stuff is stored just as safely in a server farm."

"So they deliberately misled people?"

"That was the plan."

"To what end?"

"All anyone in tech wants—well, guys like Chris and Asher, anyway—is to develop some app or start-up that is just shiny enough that they can get bought for some ridiculous amount of money. It doesn't even have to work. Like, that's completely legal. Because the dudes buying these things are just as fucking dumb and arrogant as the dudes making them."

"Why did you leave?"

"I tapped out when they started talking about what later became Bloom. It didn't feel right. You want to make a difference, you know?" She drinks. "Or at least be able to sleep at night."

"Why are you telling me this?"

"Because they're imperious dicks who could use a bit of a takedown." I think back to that day in Chris's office when he made me crawl under that beam. How sure he was that I wasn't a threat. Meera drains her glass. "That a good enough reason?"

"Yes." Meera raises her glass, notices it's empty, shrugs, and sets it down.

"What are you going to do with this?"

"I'm going to write a story about it."

"You've got to find the server farm first," she says, walking back into the main area.

"We will," I say, just behind her. She turns around.

"I know you will," she says. She joins her husband behind the bar, lacing her arm around his waist. "So, I guess I'll see you guys later, then." Meera looks at the flight of drinks in front of Thornton, Hani, and Elise. "On the house."

"See you soon," I say. I give a nod to Thornton, Elise, and Hani and we say our thank-yous and goodbyes. Once outside, I hold my phone up. And tap Play.

"CAM *was never going to be what Chris wanted. He was obsessed.*

And it broke him. One night I was joking around that we could just do it the way everyone else does and no one would know. We hide a server farm somewhere, set up some ditzy start-up that only talks in inspirational memes, throw in some talk about America and don't you yearn for a time when you didn't have to lock your doors, and people would eat it up. No one understands this tech shit anyway. We'd seen it happen a million times." I press Stop and look up.

"Holy shit," Thornton says.

"We need to find that server farm," I say.

"I think I've got a lead on that," Elise says.

"To the Batmobile!" Hani says, running toward Thornton's car. Elise follows her, along with the sleepy golden retriever. Elise and Hani play with the dog down by the car.

"Hani's going to want to keep him," Thornton says. I take a deep breath and it doesn't catch. I look up at him. Take another deep breath and it finally fills my lungs. Thornton steps in close.

"I want to send you this file in case anything happens to my phone or me," I say.

"Nothing is going to happen to you," he says. I send him the recording and I hear his phone ding in the pocket of his flight suit. I try to catch my breath again. My shoulders rise, but my breath doesn't catch. Another breath. Another. He steps in closer. I can't look at him.

"You were right," he says. I take a giant deep, filling breath.

"I was right," I say, my voice so soft. I take another deep, body-filling breath.

"You were right."

"I was right." My voice is louder. Stronger. Clearer. I smile and breathe so deeply and deeper still. "I was right." I want to scream it from this porch and that mountaintop and all along the 101 as we drive back to Los Angeles. Then I'm going to show Chris how much of a threat I am. Once and for all.

Thornton pulls me into him, wrapping his arms around me. So tight. I don't worry about where to put my arms, I just know how to hold him. And I smile. I smile because I was right. I'm still here, deep down inside all of my brokenness.

I was right.

17

That's the Good Stuff

We found the server farm three weeks and six days later.

After we returned from Buellton, Elise dove into figuring out how many servers Bloom would need based on the clients they're serving, as well as the future projects coming down the pipeline. Acquiring this information took way longer than we expected, since everyone in her department is so intentionally siloed. Then, once she had those hard-earned figures, we factored in the buzz on when Bloom would be acquired—now knowing that Bloom going public was probably just another gambit—and approximately how long they'd need to keep up this "CAM actually works" charade.

Elise's final conclusion was that Bloom's server farm would have to take up almost a full city block. They'd need expensive cooling systems, massive energy, and a security detail, and the lease would have to run for at least another two years, give or take.

And then, using information that Thornton pulled from Chris's and Asher's calendars, plus their expense reports, we were able to use gas receipts and vague blocked-off chunks of time to start to see a pattern. We noticed the same unexplained three-hour blocked-off span of time coincided with the same 120 miles every week. But that wasn't the interesting part. Those three-hour blocked-off chunks of time and the 120 extra miles only occurred in Asher's calendar.

However this scam was being run, the division of labor had it so the boots-on-the-ground oversight of the server farm was Asher's responsibility alone. What that confirmed to us was that—as Meera had intimated—Chris was the brains of this operation and Asher was the brawn.

Then it was my turn. Armed with a one-pound box of See's Candy milk chocolate Bordeaux and a sampler plate of Peanut Butter Eggs, Chocolate Butter Eggs, and Divinity Eggs, I called on my favorite newly married and loose-lipped real estate connection.

We'd narrowed down our search for the server farm to the Inland Empire—which is an area about sixty miles outside of Los Angeles. Land is cheap there, and Chris and Asher could buy a big abandoned warehouse and no one would think to ask any questions. And according to Asher's expense reports, he frequented a Starbucks in San Bernardino where we assumed he stopped during these weekly treks.

I plied my real estate connection with See's Candy, cooing that "ohmygod, yes, I would love to see the entire photo album of your honeymoon!" And in between blurry photos of the happy couple sitting by the pool (not the ocean) I had her run every iteration of Asher Bailey Lyndon and Christopher Villiers Lawrence she could find. Plus, thanks to Hani—and her cloak-and-dagger mission to break into Mackenzie's desk where she said all she needed were "her wits and a trusty paper clip"—we now had the last four digits of Chris's and Asher's social security numbers.

And then, in the middle of a story about her swearing a turtle said "Mahalo" back to her, my real estate connection leapt out of her ergonomic work chair and said, "Now that's the good stuff." Hani and Elise were so taken with this phrase that they immortalized it on our long-awaited and much-needed team shirts. Hani designed the team shirts herself: On the front was a crude drawing of a magnifying glass with a sash of four little paper doll friends swathed across it. On the back, the words "Now that's the good stuff!" in Comic Sans. Hani insisted that her use of Comic Sans was ironic.

The "good stuff" that my real estate connection was so excited about was a one-acre parcel with a one-and-a-half-story building that had been constructed in 2016. The warehouse was owned by a shell corporation called Budz. Thornton argued that Budz was a pot reference. Hani thought Budz was a testament to Chris and Asher's friendship. Elise just shrugged and said, "I mean, it ends in a z." But I maintained that it was actually more about them trying to be clever. Everything led back to that for them.

"A bud," I said over coffee ice cream one night. Blank faces and slurps. "A bud blooms." Ice cream dripped. "Bloom. Get it?"

"I still think it's about friends," Hani said.

It didn't take much for Hani to find out that Budz was owned by none other than Asher Bailey Lyndon and Christopher Villiers Lawrence.

Once we found the warehouse and identified Budz as the corporation they were using to hide shit they didn't want people connecting to Bloom, we met with Hugo and he gave us a crash course on Corporate Accounting 101. With his help, we were able to find the security firm they'd hired, as well as the general contractor who built the server farm and even the blueprints he used to do it.

Now all we had to do was see it. And that was what we were doing today.

But neither the investigating, the dead ends, nor the endless hours looking at honeymoon photos were the hard part about the last three weeks and six days. It was when I caught Chris watching me while I stood in line for coffee. I wanted to walk right over, grab him by the hoodie, and whisper menacingly, "I'm going to take you down, motherfucker." But I couldn't. I had to smile and act like he'd domesticated me. That I was no threat. Just like he said. It killed me.

Thornton put this little field trip in our calendars as a "Team Outing." Kayla from PR found it and wanted to give Thornton $40 for each of us "to cover fun expenses." She also sent Thornton a few suggestions that had helped other pods build trust and community: a medieval times–themed restaurant, go-karts, a schedule for ferries to Catalina Island, and finally a "lodge" that offers Jacuzzi tubs that rent by the hour.

We've taken two cars, because along with our San Bernardino server farm stakeout, Hani's taking Elise home to meet her parents, who own a restaurant up in Big Bear. To compensate for the fact that we couldn't all be in the same car, Hani has supplied us with walkie-talkies, as well as hand mirrors (to "send signals") and a series of colored bandanas that we wave just in case service is spotty and we want to:

- RED: change the route;
- YELLOW: have to pee ("Get it? Hahahahahaha");
- BLUE: need gas; or
- GREEN: just sayin' hi

Hani has waved the green flag practically every five miles while crackling through the walkie-talkie with "Breaker, breaker, this is Red Otter here with Pink Sunshine, do you read me, over?" When Thornton and I failed to use our code names (Black Fox and Bloodhound

One, respectively), Hani repeated her call sign until we did. In the end, it was just easier to refer to myself as Bloodhound One than fight her overwhelming zeal.

The drive to San Bernardino took about ninety minutes, and Thornton and I passed the time easily. That's the problem with finally finding someone you can talk to about everything. Not only do you never want it to stop, you start unearthing that version of yourself you've only seen shadows of. The tiny, joyful me that's at the core of the Russian nesting doll protective layers of myself that have formed over the years.

I can't pinpoint what it is about Thornton that so readily accesses that "tells all she knows" center—a state of being I've had a hard time revealing even to my family and friends.

Maybe it's because, somewhere in all of this, I believe that Thornton—and the conversations I can't seem to stop having with him—are fleeting. That once this story gets written, once I stop working at Bloom, the spell will be broken and we will part ways, the nesting dolls clicking back into place once more. This inevitability has been my constant companion these past three weeks.

Because, while we haven't held a single hand since Buellton, we've been taking these walks and talking. It started when I wanted to ask Thornton about something having to do with the story and the Fortress of Solitude was booked. Instead, he suggested we take a walk around the block. We talked about the story for the first half of the walk, but then I finally told him about that morning in Chris's office and the fucking beam, which led me right into talking about Tavia, the whole workhorse thing, and why do I only think I deserve lunch drinks, and what did he think it'd look like to train myself to think I deserve lunch, and then he said he did it too and why is he the head copywriter at a company that doesn't even work, when he has degrees in computer science and physics from Caltech? What are we both so afraid of?

And then we started going for walks every day at 3 P.M. We talked about messy childhoods and if we thought the root of why we're struggling now is somewhere in the past where our inability to fit into our well-meaning families led us both to believe that there was something inherently wrong with us. Or if the culprit is just the wear and tear of a life lived sitting on the wall—aiming low and playing it perpetually safe.

And somewhere along the way in these past three weeks, feelings crept in that, while Thornton may think I'm smart and hold me in high regard, his attachment might have tipped over into platonic admiration and deep friendship. Which I'm not certain is a bad thing. Because whatever this is or has become with Thornton is the closest I've ever felt to being truly seen and understood. Thornton knows me, because I've let him know me. And I know him because he's let me know him. We are the innermost Russian dolls with each other.

I was so ready to look at our stalled physical progress as a sign that I didn't like Thornton that I failed to see that I might actually be falling in love with him.

And with that startling recognition, I realize that Thornton may be falling in love with me, too, and that real love, for broken people, has to be more careful because it resides in the same place as all of our hurt and pain.

So, would it be so bad if we decided that what we have is a beautiful, loving friendship? Maybe that's what both of us need most right now in a person.

I guide Thornton off the freeway. Our tone is easy as we wind our little green flag-waving caravan through the streets of San Bernardino in search of a nondescript warehouse that holds a billion-dollar secret.

When we finally pull down the least infamous-looking street in the world, I can tell we're all just a little disappointed. Bloom's server farm sits on a street that's anchored by a strip mall on one end with a coin laundry, a donut shop, a nail salon, and a liquor store called the Come and Go boasting tenancy there. A tidy-looking motel called the Alpine Inn sits just across the street from what appears to be the nation's most popular tire store.

We flip a U-turn and find parking along with a steady stream of people going about the most mundane of daily errands. Thornton turns off the car just as Hani crackles through the walkie-talkie.

"Breaker, breaker, Black Fox, this is Red Otter, do you read, over." Thornton looks over at me with a weary smile and I hand him the walkie-talkie.

"Red Otter, this is Black Fox." Thornton unlatches his seat belt and shifts in his seat.

"You have to say over, over."

"Red Otter, this is Black Fox, over." Through the walkie-talkie we can hear Hani giggling and then Elise takes over.

"Black Fox, Pink Sunshine has to pee and also Red Otter maybe wants a donut, over," Elise says. Some jostling and laughing and then Hani is back on the walkie-talkie.

"Bloodhound One, don't get mad about the donut, over." I gesture to give me the walkie-talkie. Thornton obliges.

"Red Otter, I never get mad about donuts, over." Thornton laughs.

"Bloodhound One, do you and Black Fox want a donut, over." I look over at Thornton.

"Plain glazed, please," Thornton says, after a bit.

"Really?"

"Does that surprise you?"

"No, it's . . ." I nod and smile to myself. "It's perfect. Red Otter, Black Fox would like a plain glazed and I'd like a maple bar, over." I look over at Thornton. He's making a face. "Does that surprise you?"

"No." He smiles.

"Who'd like a maple bar, over?"

"Bloodhound One would like a maple bar, over."

"Copy that. ETA on donuts is ten minutes and what's the ETA on Wolf One, over?"

"Red Otter, Wolf One will be arriving in forty-seven minutes, over." Hani finally signs off and we see her and Elise running over to the donut shop, craning their necks, and leaping behind cars so they'll be "inconspicuous."

Our plan for today is getting photographs of Asher walking into the server farm along with pictures of inside the server farm. The first one is easy, the second one is going to take some patience.

What we do know for sure is that Chris and Asher opted for security rather than security cameras. I imagine this decision had a lot to do with not wanting any photographic evidence of what's going on—or not going on—at the server farm, come what may in the future. Their security detail is run by a shady friend of Asher's from high school. Chris and Asher clearly needed people they could trust with a very expensive lie, so it's not surprising that the people they chose are just as rarified and hypocritical as they are. It'll be my special pleasure to shed light on this web of crooked business practices in my story.

Hani and Elise will get the photos of Asher with Elise's good camera. They're going to be positioned on a little cross street just near the back of the Alpine Inn, so they can get a straight shot of the server farm entrance and possibly see if they can get a couple of shots of the inside when Asher opens and closes the main front door.

There was some discussion that this stakeout did not require all four of us. However, when she was apprised of this, Hani argued that "there is no *i* in 'crime-solving gang.'" Yet when it was pointed out that there were, in fact, two *i*'s in "crime-solving gang" she crossed her arms across her chest and said, "Exactly."

So, here we are.

Once Elise and Hani get those shots, they'll head up to Big Bear. And then it's Thornton's and my turn. We found out that Asher and Chris employ a skeleton crew of seven completely off-the-books Bloom employees to run the servers. Completely off the books, except that those seven employees were given the exact same employee badges we have. So, while there is no record of their employment in any way—no retirement, no onboarding, no shipments of imperfect fruit—we should be able to just walk into the server farm, show our badges to Asher's bro-y security guy, and have free rein. For a while, at least.

We also know that the security detail goes from four dudes during the day to just one starting at 9 P.M. And, using her tracking prowess, Hani uncovered that the 9 P.M. security guy has a penchant for frequenting a strip club just a couple of blocks over from 10 P.M. to around 11:30 P.M. Meaning, once the security guy checks the badge—we don't want to scan the badge, thus leaving a digital footprint—we'll be free to roam without anyone watching.

All of us decided that Thornton would be the one to infiltrate the server farm, given his talents at both computers and people—or as they like to call him, "the Nerd Translator." He would record everything he sees and hears via a small device Elise developed using a bunch of random computer and camera parts from her workshop. Because of course she has a workshop and of course she basically invented some new spyware in the spare time of her falling hopelessly in love with Hani.

Hani and Elise hand off the donuts and settle in at the agreed-upon little cross street across from the server farm. Hani with her binoculars and Elise with her long-range zoom lens. For the next forty-seven minutes, Thornton and I eat our donuts and field questions, concerns, and knock-knock jokes from Red Otter.

Until, with a precision he exhibits in no other area in his life, Asher rolls quietly down the small San Bernardino street in his Tesla.

"Wolf One is among the sheep, over," Hani crackles through the walkie-talkie.

18

Nights in White Satin

"We see him, over," I say. I am right on the cusp of telling Hani that this is all fun and games until her exuberance blows our cover, but it's just then that the walkie-talkie falls silent for the first time in weeks.

Asher pulls into the small, empty parking lot and idles his Tesla in front of a parking space with a large orange cone in it. One of the security guys runs over and moves the cone, and Asher pulls into the space closest to the door.

I begin to receive real-time photos from Elise's camera on my phone. She and Hani rigged it so—and don't ask me how—all of the "assets" we got today (photos, video, and audio) would be automatically uploaded to a secure location (i.e., not Bloom).

"How he finds new and ridiculous ways to be entitled, I'll never know," I say to Thornton, scanning Elise's photos. They are perfect.

Asher is in fine fettle this afternoon. In his wrinkled T-shirt, newly shaved head, and low-slung Dickies, he looks like he should be walking into a custody hearing for back child support.

"I fucking hate these guys," Thornton says, shaking his head.

Asher ambles over to the entrance and regally waves his hand, and the front door is opened for him. Barely looking up from his phone, he points to a pile of cigarette butts in the empty lot and then proceeds to wait as the security guy scurries over, picks up the cigarette butts, and throws them in the proper container. As this transaction is happening, I am receiving a stream of photos Elise is getting of Asher with the inside of the server farm through the now wide-open door.

"These are perfect," I say, showing Thornton. He takes my phone and zooms in on the photo, from Asher to beyond.

"You can see everything," Thornton says, navigating around the photo to the servers in the background.

"So how do we head off the lie that this server farm isn't connected to Bloom?" I ask, taking the phone back from Thornton.

"I'm hoping that's where I finally become useful. Once I get in there, I am pretty sure I'll be able to get proof that it's Bloom stuff on those servers," Thornton says.

"How?" I ask.

"This is where that fancy degree of mine comes in," he says with a wink.

I recognize that ease and natural confidence of his in that moment. Apparently, I'm not the only one who's getting reacquainted with my true self by pursuing this quest. But of course he's feeling that, too. We're all susceptible to the siren song of purpose and the opportunity to tap into that reservoir of potential that our high school teachers used to bang on about. In such a mundane world, it's easy to forget sometimes that we have the capacity for greatness. Or maybe not so much forget as trap those soaring feelings so they don't break our hearts.

The security guy finally finishes cleaning up the cigarette butts and is just about to return to the front door when Asher disappears inside without a word of thanks.

"Holy shit that was so cool, over," Hani crackles through the walkie-talkie. "This is Red Otter, BTW. Over."

"Pink Sunshine, your photos are incredible, over," I say.

"That arrogant bastard stands there pointing to some poor security guard to pick up cigarette butts and the whole time I'm just clicking away," Elise replies. I can hear Hani in the background. "Over."

"Did you see the cone thing, over?" Hani asks.

"There are literally five empty spaces, but nooooo. He had to have the one right next to the door, over," Elise says.

"It must be so hard for him not to put his name on that space, this being a whole secret server farm and all, over," I say.

Asher only stays for fifteen minutes and Elise gets some shots of him exiting, too. He's even acquired a cup of something inside.

"Is that a plastic straw?" I ask Thornton.

"It can't be," he says in faux-disbelief.

"They outlawed plastic straws at Bloom," I say, watching Asher climb into his Tesla.

"For the turtles," Thornton finishes.

"This server farm is lawless, I tell you. Lawless," I say. Asher pulls out of the space, waiting for the security guard to replace the orange cone. Once that's done, he speeds off down the quiet San Bernardino street, probably on his way to the Starbucks. Once he's turned the corner, the security guy lights up a cigarette and leans back against the side of the building, right where the pile of incriminating butts were.

"Did you see the straw, over?" Hani says through the walkie-talkie.

"We saw it, over!"

"Man, they're not even trying over here, over," Hani says.

"This is Pink Sunshine, Red Otter and I are going up to Big Bear to meet her parents, no biggie. Rendezvous tomorrow at yours, over?"

"Sounds like a plan, Pink Sunshine. Good luck, over," I say.

"This is Red Otter, she won't need luck, they're going to *looooooove* her, over," Hani sings.

Hani waves the green flag to us as Elise drives past on the way down the small street and on to Big Bear Lake.

"And now we wait," Thornton says, reaching into the back of the car. He grabs a water bottle and a bag of chips that were clearly taken from the Bloom canteen. "I mean, we are technically still at Bloom." He jerks his head toward the server farm and pulls open the bag of chips, offering them to me. I look over at him, and dig into the bag for a chip. The crinkling is deafening and I can't quite get my fingers around any one chip, so I decimate a whole bunch of them while trying. All of that effort and I've gotten just a crumb. Bit symbolic. I drop the chiplet in my mouth, crack open the water, and drink.

My chest is tight. But, because I don't trust myself with any feeling, I can't be sure if this is a good tight or a bad tight. Am I hungry or just having an existential crisis?

What's begun to haunt me over the last three weeks is this feeling that I'm missing something. The specter of The (boring) Dry Cleaning Story looms large over everything I've done. Can I trust that I've learned some kind of paradigm-shifting lesson well enough so the Bloom story rises above a skill set that was severely lacking only a few months ago?

What don't I know I don't know?

"Thank you for the chip," I say, as the silence expands beyond excruciating.

"You're welcome," he says. We sit in chip-eating silence.

"Five hours didn't feel like a long time when we were planning this," I say, shifting in my seat.

"Yeah, we sure pulled the short straw on this one," he says.

"My mind is racing. My heart is racing," I say, unable to calm myself down.

"Mine, too." I look over at him. We lock eyes and he nods. I take a deep breath. His hand jerks up, but just as quickly, he balls his fist and lets it fall onto his leg. Watching him force himself not to reach out to me sends a flush across my face and down my neck. He's about to say something, but—

"I don't know if it's a good racing or a bad racing, but—" I stop. Look down at my lap and shake my head. Thornton is quiet. Waiting. "I guess I don't . . ." I take a deep breath. "I want this too much."

"And you think you won't get it?"

"I think I won't get a lot of stuff," I say, making an alarming level of eye contact with him. I immediately look away and roll my window down. I need fresh air. "It's the getting-your-hopes-up thing, right?"

"Yeah," he says. We fall silent, watching the smoking security guard, the steady stream of tire store patrons, and the hustle and bustle of just another Friday afternoon in San Bernardino. I take another long drink out of the water bottle as Thornton tucks the now empty chip bag into the side pocket of the door. He brushes the chip crumbs off his hands, finally allowing them to come to rest on the bottom of the steering wheel.

I go back to watching the security guard as he drops his cigarette to the ground, stomps it out, and leaves the butt exactly where the pile once was. Another security guard comes out of the front door and together they walk the perimeter of the server farm.

"I thought you wanted to just be friends," Thornton says. His voice is quiet and raspy. I look from the disappearing security guards to Thornton, who is staring right at me.

"What?"

"I know you saw me pull my hand back and it looked like it upset you, so I'm explaining why I did it," he says. We both look down at his hand as if it has somehow gotten us into this mess.

"You don't have to explain yourself, I . . ." Fuck fuck fuck. "I like being honest with you, but not when it's about my feelings for you." I laugh and so does he. "I can talk to you about my parents or my hopes and dreams or my failings, but—" I point to him and then to me. "Us? I'd rather just—" I pull up the gesture an umpire would use to call a man safe. "I don't know if I can do it."

"How do you think I feel?" he asks, joking.

"I bet you feel pretty wonderful, but . . ." And then my entire face flushes. Running my fingers through my hair, I look up just in time to see a garbage truck pull up to the strip mall, turn on its deafening alarm, reverse its direction, and then I hear the metal crunch of hoisting bin after bin of trash into the truck.

"Super romantic," Thornton says, over the sound of the engine heaving and lifting.

"Yeah, all we need is a little 'Nights in White Satin' and we're set," I say, shifting my body over more toward the passenger's side door. One more bin is hoisted and dumped.

"Nights in white satin?" The trash falls into the truck and the bin is lowered back onto the street. The garbage truck drives away. I look over at Thornton.

"It's a song, you—" My stomach drops as I realize. "That you don't know. You don't know it, because not only do you and I not share pop-culture references, but your parents and my parents don't even have the same pop-culture references."

"My parents only listened to classical music growing up, so I would only get the music references of someone born in the 1700s."

"So, just a little older than me. Fantastic," I say. Thornton doesn't take the bait.

"Let's hear it then," Thornton says.

"Absolutely not."

"What? Why not?"

"Because it's going to be like when you're all—oh, you don't know that movie from the '90s, great let's watch this trailer and oh my god the trailers back then were awful and this movie is incredibly problematic and what was I thinking and . . . you know, now I'm embarrassed that you're trying to like something you know I'm nostalgic about but, ugh, just . . . no, I don't even know if it's aged well. I haven't listened to it in years." While I've been talking, Thornton's pulled his phone from his pocket and is searching for the song online.

"Moody Blues?" he asks, his finger hovering over the Play button.

"Can I . . . is there anything I can do to—you know what? I would rather talk about my feelings. How's that? I would—" He hits Play.

"Be quiet, I'm trying to listen to this song, please." Thornton turns the volume of his phone all the way up as the opening drumbeats break through the tinny speaker. "Roll up your window." I oblige him just as the vocals come on. The outside melts away as the song builds to its "'Cause I love you! Yes, I love you. . . . Oh, how I love you" chorus. As the song dips into its second verse, I fix my eyes on my shoes, tracing and retracing the stitching around the sole.

But then I find myself giving over as the song fills the car. I sit back in my seat, put my head back, close my eyes, and sink into the music. By the time the flute solo comes in—because of course there's a flute solo—I realize my hands are curled tightly around my seat, as if I'm afraid I'll float away. All of the anxiety and nerves, all the too-high hopes I can never control, all the times I felt rejected and lonely get mixed up and blended with these scary, soaring feelings that swell and unsettle me as I sit in this quiet car with Thornton. My heart tugs with every note and I let it expand inside my chest. And feel it. As terrifying as it is, I don't pin these feelings or overthink them down into some place where they're labeled and managed. I let the music move me, affect me. And when I open my eyes and see Thornton, I finally let him move me and affect me, too.

As the last chorus starts, I take a deep breath. I uncurl my fingers from my hold on the passenger's seat and reach out toward Thornton. He leans in just as my fingers tighten around his T-shirt, pulling him into me. His hand laces around my waist. His mouth is warm and fast on mine. My fist tightens around his shirt, pulling and pulling him closer, so my other hand can finally thread through his long black hair. I hear myself gasp and I can feel him smiling just as the song comes to an end.

In those silent, empty milliseconds we break apart. Centimeters apart.

"That's some fucking song," he whispers. "Now I'm just throwing this out there—" Another kiss. "But we've got five hours and the Alpine Inn is right there." Another kiss.

"Have I ever told you about the fantasy I have about those little Podunk motels along the freeway?"

Thornton leans back and smiles.

"No," he says.

"That I always wanted to be so swept away in a frenzy, you know, maybe we were on a road trip or just driving back from Orange County, I don't know. But, regardless, we just had to pull over to . . . you know—" I say. I look down as my face flushes. "Is that weird?"

"No."

"No?"

Thornton shakes his head, and brushes my hair out of my face. I smile.

"I'll get us a room, do you want to make a stop at the liquor store and I'll meet you over there?"

"Yeah, oh . . . good idea."

I efficiently turn to pick my purse up off the passenger's side floor, relieved that I have an errand to run now. Wordlessly, Thornton and I climb out of the car, careful to avoid being seen by the security guards. He gives me one last smile and runs over to the Alpine Inn.

In a haze, I walk to the Come and Go liquor store, unsure of what I'm in here for. I wander the aisles, pick up a bag of plain M&M's and a bottle of water, peruse the tea options for a quick second, before it dawns on me why Thornton wanted me to . . . oh my god, okay. I rush over to the aisle where the condoms are, clutching my bag of M&M's and water and am immediately overwhelmed.

Bare Skin? Ultra Thin? Enz? Pleasure pack? Is there . . . is there one that Thornton prefers or—I tear open the bag of M&M's and pour a handful out, popping them into my mouth as I pace.

A couple of construction workers walk toward me and I shift over to the next item in the aisle, hoping they'll think I am now really into lubes and sanitary napkins and definitely not condoms. They pass me, en route to the beer case. I shuffle back over in front of the condoms. It's just like being back at the Bloom coffee machine again. Just grab however many and look, I doubt there's going to be one that just ruins the whole mood altogether. I grab three random kinds of condoms from the shelf and walk to the front of the liquor store and pay for said items with as much discretion as I can muster.

As I exit the liquor store, I can see Thornton standing just out front of the Alpine Inn, his hands lazing in his pockets, waiting for me. I twist the M&M bag closed, pull out the condom boxes from the bag, and replace them with the candy. I can see that Thornton's

trying to figure out what I'm carrying, furrowed brow, slightly leaning over to . . . what in the hell is that and a shake of the head as he
finally figures out what's in my hand.

"I know we've got five hours, but I think you're being a bit ambi-
tious," he says, taking the three boxes of condoms from me.

"Oh?"

Thornton balances the boxes of condoms in his hand. He pulls
me close. "We'll see." Still with my hand in his, Thornton leads me
over to room 9 on the ground floor of the Alpine Inn. He lets go of
my hand, reaches into his pocket, and fishes out the key. He opens
the door and gestures for me to go in.

"Let's see if you're right," he says, stepping inside and closing the
door behind us.

"About what?" I ask, now utterly breathless.

"Whether or not I feel pretty wonderful," he says, pulling his
T-shirt over his head.

19

One Thing

As I walk from Thornton's car to the front door, I turn around and
wave to his bright headlights, in an attempt to hide the building panic
that's fully taking hold as I reach the door. I turn back around and
notice he's yet to pull down the long driveway.

Then I get that he's waiting for me to go inside before he leaves.
But if I walk inside and he pulls away, that means this afternoon, this
moment, this . . . chance will have officially come to an end. Before
I know what I'm doing, I rush toward his headlights. He turns the
car off, pushes the door open, and steps out.

"You locked out?" he asks. His hand absently rests on my waist
in an unbearably intimate way. I wrap my arms around him and pull
him in tight. Without a word, he envelops me. In that moment, I
know he feels it too. Both of us are trying to stave off the fear that

we'll go back to being the people we really are, in the world as it really is, when we wake up tomorrow morning.

I have no idea how long we stand there, but our disentanglement comes in aching waves, as if we're unable to pull away from each other all at once.

"Today was my favorite day," I say, unable to look at him. I walk away before I have a chance to regret being so sentimental.

"Joan—" Thornton calls, just before I walk inside the house. I turn around and see him one last time. He's still standing next to his car, his silhouette dark in the beam of the headlights. "Mine, too."

Heartbroken and smiling, I turn the key, push the door open, and step inside the quiet of my parents' house.

"He seems nice," Billy whispers, sitting at the dining room table with a fussy Poppy draped over his shoulder.

"Oh my god, you scared me," I say. A jolt of fear unleashes all of the tamped-down emotions of the last couple of days. Billy misses none of this.

"And where were you?" Billy asks, smoothing Poppy's hair. She fusses, so Billy has to stand up, shift her into her favorite football hold for when her tummy is bothering her—which is getting harder as she gets bigger—and proceed to pace around the kitchen.

"We were on a stakeout," I say, getting myself a glass of water. Hoping it will cool and drown the emotion.

"Is that what the kids are calling it these days?"

"You're younger than me, doofus," I say, filling another glass with tap water. I turn around and lean against the sink, noticing that Mom has tacked yet another neatly cut out article about registering at the local community college to the fridge. This time, however, she's added a stickie with my name and an arrow next to it. I walk over to the fridge and pull both the article and the stickie off with a sigh. I fold it in half and hold it as gently as I can in my hands. When I get back to my room, I'll put it with the others.

"You need to talk to her. She's just going to keep doing it," Billy says, now on the other side of the kitchen.

"I've tried. She . . . she won't listen and I don't want to hurt her feelings. She's been so supportive. I feel like a—" A quick glance at Poppy and my mind flips past all the bad words until finally settling on: "Jerk."

"I mean, is it such a bad idea?" Billy has the good sense, at least, to be across the room when he says this. I set down my glass, pissed that I can't slam it down, because of course I don't want to wake the baby.

"No, it is not a bad idea," I say, starting out as diplomatically as I can.

"Okay, then—"

"It's just not for me," I say.

"Why not? I mean, don't you want a little—" Billy looks at Poppy. Shrugs. Then walks over to the table and writes down "fuck you space" on a pad of Dixon Gardens paper.

"What's—" I point to the words on the pad of paper.

"First off, that's not my line. You and I both know I couldn't come up with something like that. This woman said it to her friend while they were walking around the nursery the other day. But I think it's—" Billy stops, shifts Poppy to the other arm. "So you're not always begging journalism for every dime. It's the whole all-your-eggs-in-one-basket thing, right?"

"How come you get to have all your eggs in one basket?" I ask, motioning to the nursery around us.

"I like my basket. I'm going to be the boss of my basket someday," he says, his voice straining to whisper.

"Oh, yeah. The basket that's full of weed?"

"What weed?"

"Oh my god, you are such a bad liar. The weed you and Dad are growing out in the greenhouse," I say, relieved to be onto another subject.

"Wait, that wasn't a joke? You actually think that's a thing?"

"Uh, yeah. Because it *is* a thing."

Billy laughs. Shakes his head. Walks over to me.

"It's a coral plant. It just looks like weed."

"What?"

"The plants inside the greenhouse are coral plants. Coral plants. Beautiful bright flowers, grow super tall, they're hard to kill . . . oh, and by the way, they're not weed." He looks down at me. "You're wrong." He locks eyes with me. "Admit you're wrong."

"I admit nothing except that you are spinning an elaborate yarn to keep me from finding out what's really going on back there," I say.

"You can never just admit you're wrong," he says.

"I can too."

"Okay, then say it."

Billy waits as I stand against the counter, trapped. He knows he's got me and I find myself getting angrier and angrier, with him and not myself, for being so stubborn. It's his fault that he's making me say it. Why can't he just know that I was wrong and move on, what kind of asshole needs me to say the actual words? But, then . . . what kind of asshole won't admit when she's wrong? Probably the same asshole who was mortified at not knowing how to work the Bloom coffee machine on her first try.

What is it that I think will happen if I admit that I don't know something? When did learning become such a point of shame for me? I imagine that timeline parallels when this whole slump started.

"Fine. I was wrong." My voice is clipped, light, and wildly insincere.

"Wow, how heartfelt and genuine," he says in a robotic voice.

"And? I like my basket. A lot," I say, trying to change the subject back to what we were talking about before Weedgate. But I hate that I can hear the doubt in my voice. And that all Billy has to do is raise an eyebrow.

"If you love your basket a lot, then—" Billy shakes his head. "If you really do love writing, why do you need Tavia or *The LA Times* or *The New Yorker* to tell you that you're a real writer?" I just sigh and Billy shakes his head. "Humor me."

"I know I'm supposed to say that it doesn't matter, but it does. It's the whole if-a-tree-falls-in-the-forest thing," I say. My voice is fast and hard. I've had this conversation with myself, my family, my friends, and then back again. And each time it's their argument that's sound and technically right and I'm just hardheadedly moving on right toward the looming cliff. Lalalalalala, I'm not listening! This is going to work out! I'm not miserable, you are! Just waiting for that one big break, but it's not that I *neeeeeed* external validation, I'd be fine just writing my life away and dancing like no one is watching!

"But the tree does make a sound. You get that your example—" I walk over to the pad of paper and write "shut up" on it. I point to it.

"No, you—" Billy points to it.

"No, you!" I point to the pad of paper.

"This is the one thing. This story is going to bring me back," I say, pulling out a chair and plopping down. My voice is raw. My brain is on overdrive as it tries to convince every cell in my body not to get used to what happened today with Thornton and feeling like a real journalist again and getting the evidence and being right and trusting myself. And as these thoughts come back to me, my chest tightens and hardens.

In that green flag–waving caravan, in Thornton's Volvo, outside of the server farm, and inside that hotel room was the first time I felt like I truly belonged. I actually had flickers of loving myself.

How do I say that to Billy? How do I communicate that feeling to anyone when I can't make sense of it myself?

"No one story . . ." Billy stops. He raises his hand and gestures out there. "No one *thing* is going to save you." Billy tries to sit down at the table with me, but Poppy immediately fusses and he hoists himself back up. He is quiet and I can tell he's thinking. I look up at him. He brings his hand down over his heart. "*You* are your one thing."

"You overhear that in the nursery too?" My voice breaks in its forced levity. Billy smiles and stifles a bark of laughter.

"Nah, every once in a while I come up with something good," he says.

"Yeah." I lean forward and put my elbows on the table, letting my hands cover my face. "What if I don't believe you?" I look up at him. "What if the tree really doesn't make a sound if no one is around to hear it?"

"I know you're trying to be dramatic, but you can't use that example because the tree clearly makes a sound."

"But what if it doesn't?"

Billy walks over to the table, slides the pad of paper over, and writes down, "You're batshit."

"No, you are," I say. Billy laughs and we grow quiet. I fold and refold the article and the stickie that Mom left on the fridge. "I'll talk to Mom tomorrow morning before everyone gets here."

"Just tell her the truth," he says. Poppy is finally and officially asleep. He walks past me toward the hallway. "You do know what the truth is, don't you?" He bumps me as he passes. "Go to bed, Jojo." I hear the door to Poppy's room open and close. And the quiet of the old house settles in around me. I open up Mom's article.

"I'm my one thing," I repeat in a choked whisper. I fold the article back up, shake my head, follow Billy quietly down the hall, and go into my bedroom.

I change into my pajamas, noticing my skin is oddly soft—thanks to the shockingly good bar of soap provided by the Alpine Inn. I switch off the light, crawl into bed, and plug in my phone. I debate texting Lynn, Hugo, and Reuben about today, but then decide against it. I can fill them in when we move Lynn out later this week. This is more of a face-to-face kind of thing. Plus, maybe I'll know by then what today even was.

I turn over on my side and pull my hair from under my neck where it's starting to tangle. I flip over onto my back. I think about what Billy said.

You are your one thing.

If I'm my one thing, maybe today happened not because of the story or the caravan or the Volvo or the hotel room, but because, for the first time in my life, I loved myself enough to believe that I belonged there. But, if I am my one thing, I should love myself even without the story and the caravan, Thornton's Volvo, or the Alpine Inn. And maybe that's why I didn't want today to end, because, like some magical enchantment that turns a pumpkin into a carriage, I finally felt what it was like to love myself, if only for as long as I lived a life I could be proud of.

20

Midnight

After a fitful night's sleep, I shamble down the hallway to the sounds of Mom clanging around the kitchen looking for her grandmother's iron skillet to use for the day's cooking. She is always the first up and today's no different. I fold and refold the article and the stickie she left on the fridge last night and realize that I'm getting more and more nervous and guilty with every step.

"Morning, you little dear," she says, without looking to see which little dear it is. She's squatting in front of the lower corner cabinet and reaching into the way back for the skillet. It's the same skillet she uses nearly every day but inexplicably keeps just out of reach.

"Morning," I say, my voice a choked rasp. I walk over to the coffee machine and pour myself a generous helping. I open the top of the machine, dump the coffee grounds in the compost bin, and get the next batch ready for the coming onslaught.

"There are banana muffins for your friends and fresh fruit in the fridge," Mom says, finally pulling the skillet from the depths of the cabinet. She stands and sets it down on the stovetop.

"They'll love it. I doubt any of them have had a home-cooked anything in months," I say. "How can I help?"

"You can hull the strawberries," she says, pointing to the sink where a pile of fresh strawberries awaits in a colander. She looks back at me just long enough to see the folded article in my hands. I set it and my coffee down on the counter, look over at her as she starts in on the Cowboy Breakfast—a dish she usually reserves for Christmas morning.

"I saw the article and stickie you left on the fridge. Thank you," I say, hulling my first bright red strawberry.

"And?" Mom cracks and whisks the eggs.

"I know you're worried about me." Taking a quick peek over at her, I can see that her lips are pursed and her eyes focused. She swipes at her brow with her shoulder. She gives me the smallest nod in agreement. "I'm worried about me too."

"It's just a couple of classes and maybe, who knows, you might find something you want to do that makes you happy," she says. I hull strawberry after strawberry. Mom and I can't look at each other.

"Mom, you make me happy. Dad makes me happy. Billy, Anne, and Poppy make me happy." Mom bends down to check the pilot light on the stovetop. A quick shake of the old iron skillet.

"I know, honey, but I want you to make you happy, and writing—"

"Writing makes me feel real," I say. I take a deep breath. "And sometimes real makes me feel happy and sometimes real makes me miserable. And I know that lately, it's been a lot more miserable, but—"

"Honey, I don't want you to stop writing, I just want you to have something that's yours outside of writing," she says. I smile as I realize that this was Mom's way of saying that I needed what Billy called "fuck you space."

"I don't know if there is a me outside of writing, and I know that sounds dramatic, but I don't—" Mom turns away from the skillet to face me. I've never said any of this to her. To anyone. "I wish I wanted the life you wanted for me. I do. I don't know what's wrong with me that I don't."

"Oh, my sweet girl," Mom says, sweeping me into her arms. "No, that's . . . that's not what this is about." She pulls away from me and makes me look at her. "This face." Mom holds my face in her hands. "I love this face." She dips my head down and kisses my forehead.

"I know I've disappointed you and I'm trying to put it right. This story . . . I think this story will make you proud of me." Mom pulls me in for a hug. "I just want you to be proud of me."

"Oh, my little girl. You make me proud every day."

I can't help but laugh.

"You have a mighty low bar for pride, then," I say, sniffling and laughing through the streams of tears. Mom pulls away from me and once again makes me look at her.

"No more articles about community college," she says. I nod. Try to smile. "But can you do something for me?"

"Anything," I say.

"There's a wonderful life in the gray area between happiness and misery, honey. Please use some of that wonderful, relentless curiosity of yours and try to find it." She gives me a squeeze, just before she returns to her now bubbling skillet.

"To learn something new," I say.

"Yes. To learn something new."

"I could definitely benefit from a computer class or two," I say.

"You could also benefit from a class where there is no f~ at all, pumpkin, except to have a little fun."

"I'm not good at fun," I say, picking up another strawberry.

"Oh, I know," she says, giving the skillet a shake. "But you weren't always like that." Poppy squeals as she runs down the hallway completely naked. "You used to be like that." Mom looks from me to the joyous Poppy. Why can't I remember what it felt like to be so free?

An exhausted Billy follows behind her with a combination of diaper and clothes. Mom switches the skillet to the back burner, lowers the flame, and picks up her naked granddaughter. Billy walks into the kitchen just as Mom feeds Poppy a newly hulled strawberry. He eyes the folded article and my red-rimmed eyes.

"You good?" he asks.

"Yeah."

"Good," Billy says, with an efficient nod. And that's that.

He walks over to Mom and collects his daughter, who laughs and giggles with delight. "There are people coming over, Pop. I have to make you presentable." Poppy arches her body back and reaches out for me. I, of course, take her. Mom takes the Cowboy Breakfast off the stovetop and puts it into the oven.

"Is your daddy being super demanding and trying to put clothes on you?" I ask, in a gasping voice of wonder.

"Okay, well—when your little boyfriend arrives you'll thank me for not having him be greeted by a naked toddler," Billy says. I stare daggers at him.

"Boyfriend?" Mom asks. Easy. Breezy. Nothing big.

"He's not my boyfriend," I say, trying to sound as carefree as I can while figuring out if I can kill Billy with this strawberry huller before everyone else gets here.

"Silly me, I thought someone who dropped you off just after midnight could be referred to as a boyfriend." Billy pours himself a cup of coffee. "But what do I know?"

"Not a lot," I say, my voice still airy and light. He leans down to the table, slides the pad of paper over with last night's "shut up" still scrawled across it, and points. "Very nice. Very nice."

"You're on the cusp of a very—" Billy sighs, sips his coffee. "Very important morning with some people that I'll wager you wouldn't want to know certain things about your past."

"I swear if you—" Poppy looks from me to Billy. "If you aren't just the cutest little brother in the whole wide world."

"Aw, thanks so much. Yeah, I need this to be a moment of clarity for you, young Joan." Another long sip. "Be nice to me or the high school yearbooks are coming out."

"You wouldn't dare," I say.

"I wonder if handsome Thornton Yu knows that you went through an even more awkward phase than the one you're enduring now," Billy says, smiling. "Was it sophomore or junior year that you had that fun 'pixie cut' that you decided would be way better if it were dyed a bright fuchsia?"

"Senior year," I say, having flashbacks.

"Ah, that's right." Billy sets his coffee down on the counter, sweeps up Poppy in his arms, and continues back down the hallway. "Indeed, what a fun morning this portends to be."

"Billy, be nice to your sister," Dad says, passing him in the hall.

"I will be the perfect gentleman," I hear Billy yell from Poppy's bedroom. Dad shakes his head and laughs as he gives Mom a kiss and asks how he can help.

~~~~~

The high school yearbooks are strewn across the dining room table and now Billy's showing Thornton the fun candid of me that perfectly captures my oversized flannel phase. Just next to the yearbooks are Elise's laptop, Thornton's laptop, and several sheets of paper with my shorthand scrawls across them. We've compiled everything we have and I've spent the last hour organizing the sources and footnotes so I can ready the story to be properly vetted. Mom, Dad, and Anne are playing with Poppy in the nursery while we do up the dishes after an incredibly successful breakfast meeting.

"I bet I have still have that flannel," I say, eyeing it just a bit too greedily.

"It's a good flannel," Thornton says, watching as Mom's skillet dries on the stovetop. When he sees that it's dry, he takes it off the flame with a macramé potholder.

"Make yourself useful," I say to Billy, handing him a pot that goes in one of the highest cabinets. He grudgingly leaves the yearbooks and takes the pot. Billy then joins Mom and Dad outside as Poppy makes a run for the roses and her beloved pile of dirt. I take this opportunity to close the yearbooks and stack them up on a faraway shelf.

Thornton, Hani, and Elise continue to clear the dishes off the table, bringing them over to the sink stack by stack. I am positive everyone knows we slept together and I've been blushing all morning as waves of embarrassment hit me anew. I put the last of the dishes into the dish drainer and scan the kitchen for any fringe dwellers. When I spy none, I fold the towel and hang it over the rim of the sink.

"So, we have news," Elise says. She looks over to Hani and I see them share a comforting smile. Thornton unlaces the sage-green apron Mom gave him so he wouldn't ruin his shirt and walks over.

"We were in Big Bear and talking about how much fun we had at the stakeout," Hani says, holding out her hand for Elise to take. Elise immediately threads her fingers through Hani's and pulls her in close.

"We're good at it," Elise says.

"And since we're all about to be out of a job . . ." Hani says.

"And also since we found out that if those two yahoos can run a business, maybe we can, too." Elise looks over at Hani and Hani blushes.

"Cheese and rice, did those guys sure make a mess of things," Hani says. Then I notice that both Hani and Elise have brand new Spice Girls enamel pins. Hani's is on the jean jacket she'd believed not cool enough and Elise has pinned hers among her already impressive enamel pin constellation near her collar.

"So, our first order of business was making sure our company actually does what we say it will," Elise says. Hani digs into her jeans pocket and hands a business card to Thornton and me. The logo is a cartoon of a dog, Mrs. Pennybaker, I assume, and circling around the drawing are the words—

"The Good Girl Computer Gang," Thornton reads.

"We were helping Hani's mom with her computer and she was talking about how all these computer guys come around and make her feel stupid. And that's when we got the idea: we should start a computer gang of women who help other women," Elise says.

"Everyone's got a mom who needs help with her computer," Hani says.

"That's actually our tag line," Elise says, laughing.

"I already bought all the domain names," Hani interjects.

"So, we help ladies with their computers during the day—" Elise says.

"And we can still dabble in being hot lady spies at night when you need some extra help on a story," Hani sings.

"Or any new tech," Elise adds.

"I'm amazed," I say, staring at their business cards.

"You did all this in one night?" Thornton asks.

"I got excited," Hani says.

"It's—" Thornton stops. Shakes his head and smiles. "Wow."

"You guys . . . this is . . ." I lunge into them for a hug and it catches everyone off guard. "This is just great." I let them go and take a step back, beaming at them.

"We figured you'd keep breaking these stories, so . . ." Hani trails off.

"What she's saying is that we really liked fighting crimes with you and we'd like to continue to do so," Elise says. I nod, not able to break it to them that who knows what's going to happen with this story and whether or not there will even be an us if and when Tavia finds a place for it.

"Speaking of, you'd better get to writing," Hani says.

"Oh, the byline. I wanted to check with you guys before I put your names on this thing," I say. I sneak a quick glance over at Thornton and immediately look away. "First, I didn't know if you wanted to be named and then I thought how would we do it, so—" I pull a newspaper from the stack yet to be taken to the recyclers and comb through the stories until I find what I'm looking for. "It's here—" I show them the story that has one name as the byline with several other names under the "Additional Reporting By" label. "If this is okay with you, I was thinking I would list your names under the Additional Reporting By." I tossed and turned about this conversation in the early morning hours. Along with everything the fuck else I'm tossing and turning about.

"I wonder if—" Elise starts and then stops.

"No, I know," Hani finishes.

"If we're going to start a computer gang and maybe dabble in having a detective agency, do we want to be named at all?" Elise asks.

"I think we do," Hani says. Thornton is quiet.

"First and last names?" Elise asks.

"Customarily, yes."

"So everyone at Bloom will know we helped," Thornton says.

"Yeah." I finally make eye contact with him. And instantaneously it's just him and me. He tilts his head and I can't . . . I can't read him. "What are you thinking?"

"It's just sad," Thornton says.

"I know. I know. It's—" Thornton puts his hand up.

"The sooner these kids get disentangled from Bloom, the better their résumés will look without spending years at basically the tech version of Enron. A posting like that could really stain their work history. Especially so early on," Elise says.

"You're right. It's just sad that people are going to lose their jobs," Thornton says.

"Yeah," Hani says. I look over at Elise. She nods in agreement.

"I don't have to put your names down at all. I can keep you guys as anonymous as you want to be," I say.

"No, I want Chris and Asher to know it was me," Thornton says.

"Me, too," Elise says.

"Yep," Hani agrees.

"Okay, then. I'll put your full names down under Additional Reporting By," I say.

"Are we going into work Monday or . . ." Hani asks Thornton. He is technically our manager. He looks over at me.

"I'll have a draft of the story to you guys this afternoon, you can give notes, and hopefully we can get it to final by tonight," I say.

"We're getting paid on Monday, and I doubt we'll see another paycheck after that, right?" Elise asks no one in particular.

"This is so surreal," Thornton says.

"I've got all that stuff on my desk," Hani says.

"You can go in and . . . we'll get it out," Elise says, soothing her.

"This is that thing you were talking about. Why you don't put stuff on your desk," Hani says to me.

"I don't put stuff on my desk because I'm an asshole," I say. Thornton laughs.

"So we'll go into work on Monday. One last time," Hani says.

"Hon, you can't walk around and say goodbye to people like you're dying. Do you think you'll be able to act normal?" Elise asks.

"No way. Not even a little bit," Hani says.

"Okay, well, we'll brainstorm some strategies on the drive home," Elise says, pulling Hani in close.

Everyone says their goodbyes and thanks my family for the breakfast spread. There are hugs and good lucks and fingers crossed and recipes are swapped and advice is given about starting a company and yes, as a matter of fact, my mom would like to contract with the Good Girl Computer Gang as soon as they're up and running. Thornton and I walk Elise and Hani to their car and watch as they drive away, green flag waving in the distance.

Then it's just Thornton and me. And just enough fairy dust from yesterday.

"Come here," he says, pulling me into him for a long, overdue kiss. "I wonder if there's an Alpine Inn around here."

"I don't think there's an Alpine Inn, but I do have a key to the outside door to my bedroom," I say, presenting him with the now sweaty key that I've been fondling all morning and almost handed to him a thousand times. He takes it.

"Shouldn't you be writing?" he asks.

"I can write all day, and then maybe later, you know, if you happen to be free . . ." I say, trailing off.

"This is pushing some pretty big fantasy buttons in me right now," he says. "Is that weird?"

"No."

"No?" I lift up onto my tippy-toes and give him a kiss.

"No."

"See you then, then," Thornton says, looping his messenger bag over his head and walking toward that old orange Volvo.

"See you then, then," I say, watching him go.

Once he disappears down the long driveway, I turn back toward the house and actually say to myself, with a little balled-up fist and everything, "Let's do this."

I'm still haunted by the rattling chains of the Ghost of The Dry Cleaning Story, but instead of agonizing over what I'm missing or whether this story is boring, I sit down at the ancient desktop computer in the kitchen and start.

As my family moves around me, I type and type and type. I get up to pee. I get up for coffee. I flip through my notes. I get up to pee. I get up for coffee. I flip through my notes.

I. Am. So. Happy.

I made the decision to keep the story short and not dip into long form. If I've learned anything from my brief time at Bloom—and the Jiffy team—it's to make the most impact, to go the most viral—content should be relatable, tightly structured, and concise. As morning becomes afternoon and afternoon becomes night, I'm finding that keeping to those constraints has kept me incredibly honest with what I'm trying to say. All of my usual hedging language and meandering, polite words from my life before—there's just no place for them here.

These are the facts. This is what happened.

I send out my first draft at dusk. I get notes back from everyone. I make the changes and send it back out. Elise comes back with some more tweaks and I find myself going back and forth with just her about a few of the notes she had. She is precise and spot on. Hugo asks about the ramifications of using certain words legally, so Elise asks if she can run it by her mom, just to make sure about the legal side of things. It's a great idea, and Elise comes back with a few changes her mom suggested to go the extra protective mile. When the rewrite comes in with Elise's mom's sanctioned words, Hugo is relieved and finally signs off. By the time Thornton turns the key in the secret door to my bedroom, the story is all but finished.

We don't say much of anything that night. It's an odd feeling to go from wanting to tell him everything, to simply not having to. With a look or a shrug I know what he's thinking as we lie in bed in the early morning hours. But I can't sleep.

Whatever this has been over the last month, whatever train we've been on feels as though it's finally coming into the station. Our whole world was this investigation, and now that we have the finished story I fear that we'll all grab our bags from the overhead bin and go our separate ways.

I sit up in bed as quietly as I can, pull the covers off, and put my feet on the floor. And in the blue hue of the morning, I try to breathe.

"You okay?" Thornton asks, turning over.

"When we were in Buellton, I asked Hani about her and Elise. She said she didn't know you got to be this happy." Thornton sits up, sweeps my hair off my neck and over my right shoulder. He traces my back with kisses. This is not helping. "At first her face looked so open and, I mean, you know Hani, it was joyous and lovely, but then she just started crying." Thornton brushes his hand across my back. "I don't think I could . . . I don't know, let myself understand why, until now." I turn around and face him. "It's like I can hear the ticking clock and midnight is coming."

"I know. Me, too."

"Why don't we get to have this?" Thornton is quiet. I can feel the answer in his chest as I know it too. His arms are tight around me. I look up at him and his arms loosen. I wait. I want him to say it. He knows I know.

"Probably because we both think we're shit," he finally says. I nod and I breathe. I dive into him with every breath, and without saying a word we get lost in each other again and again.

21

Everywhere

I load the last of Lynn's moving dregs into Billy's truck early the next morning. It's always such a bizarre assemblage of household items that serves as the final load. I set a dusty tower fan on top of a clothes hamper and tuck in the rogue toilet plunger as securely as I can.

I turn around and step aside as Hugo and Reuben shuffle over to the truck with Lynn's massive design whiteboard. We argue and maneuver with the full to bursting truck bed, finally sliding it in between her couch and a coffee table. It's not pretty.

"So, is that it?" I ask as Lynn steps down from the curb holding a stack of framed art. Reuben takes it from her and we negotiate with the truck's contents to allow just a few more items, we promise.

"This is it," Lynn says, stepping back from the truck.

"Do you have to leave a key or something?" I ask.

"I can't believe Josh didn't even offer to help. That's—" Hugo starts.

"Did you really want him to?" Reuben asks.

"To help with that couch? Yeah," Hugo says, rubbing his sore shoulder.

"No, it's perfect that he left. It's fitting," Lynn says with a sad sigh.

"Oh, honey," I say, wrapping my arm tightly around her.

"It's fine." Lynn waves a meek hand. "It's going to be fine." As much as we want to comfort Lynn in this moment, we also know that she would hate it. So—

"You guys want to lead the way over and we'll follow you?" Reuben says, moving us along. Lynn looks relieved.

"Are we all done? All locked up?" I ask, unwrapping my arm from around Lynn and motioning in the direction of her apartment building—now ex–apartment building.

"I pulled it locked behind me. Left the key," she says. Reuben, Hugo, and I share a quick look.

"Okay, then we are off like a turd of hurdles," I say. I wind my finger around as if to say "reverse that." "Herd of turtles."

"I quite like turd of hurdles," Hugo says as he and Reuben walk to their car. Lynn climbs up into Billy's truck cab and I look back one last time to see if the load is secure. I pull the driver's side door closed behind me and the truck rumbles on.

Lynn and I are quiet on the drive to her new little house over in Studio City.

"You keep thinking, how'd I miss it? How did I not see who he really was?" Lynn looks out the window; her voice is elsewhere and she's started sounding like this conversation had been going on way longer than before she started speaking. I am quiet. "Was he like this from the beginning? It'd be so easy to say that this isn't the Josh that

I fell in love with, but . . . what if it was?" Lynn traces her finger along the dirty window. She turns and finally faces me. "How did I let this happen?"

"Because it wasn't that bad," I say, repeating Lynn's own words back to her. Lynn lets out a scoff of recognition.

"And where have I heard that before?" Lynn says, looking back out the window. "Learning to be loved—"

I shake my head and try to pull together all my thoughts like I'm desperately leaping up to catch a handful of loose balloons before they float away. "It's a process." I reach across and take her hand. Unable to look at me, she squeezes tight. "You know now that he wasn't what you need." I glance over at her, willing her to look at me. She finally does. "You should be proud of yourself." Lynn allows a tight smile as she looks down at her lap.

"Proud," she whispers. She chokes back a sob and I tighten my hand around hers. "What's that feel like?"

"I wouldn't know," I say, smiling. Her choked sobs burst out into laughter. She lets go of my hand and pulls a tissue from her purse. She dabs at her eyes, wiping the tears away. A long sigh and she rolls down the window, closing her eyes as the cool wind begins to restore her.

We pull down the tree-lined street and back Billy's truck down Lynn's adorable cottage driveway. We move Lynn into her new home in grunting bursts and too-heavy loads. We bark out orders to one another and stack boxes marked KITCHEN and BEDROOM and OFFICE in the appropriate rooms. Lynn tells us to be careful and we make snide remarks behind her back that she can totally hear.

"That's the last of it," Hugo says, bringing in Lynn's rolling dress form—outfitted with half of what will most certainly be a best-selling dress. He pushes the dress form into a corner and joins the rest of us in Lynn's small galley kitchen.

Lynn drags over her desk chair and plops down into it, cradling a flat fast-food soda she bought hours ago. I move a box aside and hop up on her butcher-block counter, letting my legs blessedly dangle. Reuben drags over an ottoman, and Hugo sinks down onto the floor. We are exhausted. I can feel the moving-day grime all over my body. The mystery bruises on my legs are just starting to form.

"My mom and sisters are on their way with Phyllis," Lynn says, checking her texts.

"The next wave of fresh recruits." Reuben sighs, letting himself sink down into the ottoman.

"You guys ordering pizza? You always order pizza on the first night in a new place," I say.

"Oh, definitely," Lynn says, texting her family.

"So where are you running off to again? A spin class?" Hugo asks, deciding to just lie down on the floor.

"That can't be right," Reuben says.

"I am sitting outside of an impossible-to-get-into exercise class where a world-class DJ"—I put giant air quotes around "world class"— "plays music for a group of women and men who are lucky enough to attend this particular spin class in Culver City. One of these lucky women and men happens to be the one and only Tavia Keppel." I snap my sock away from my shin and a puff of dirt wafts away from my body.

"You're stalking Tavia Keppel," Hugo says.

"Dressed like that," Lynn adds.

"Yes and yes," I say.

"And a meeting with her is . . ." Reuben trails off.

"We're too late for that. Tavia will read our story, she will place it with the right people, and I will take down Chris Lawrence," I say, hopping down off the counter.

"Well, okay," Lynn says. Reuben and Hugo are quiet.

"I know I sound nuts. Just in case—"

"No, we weren't going to say a thing," Hugo says, smiling.

"You look nuts, but sound—" Reuben starts.

"I'd say more determined than nuts," Hugo says. Lynn and Reuben nod in agreement.

"Sound determined and look nuts." I pull Billy's truck keys out of my pocket. "I'll take it."

Lynn, Hugo, and Reuben wish me an exhausted good luck, and within the hour I'm pulling Billy's truck into a parking structure just across from the Platform in Culver City.

It's when I step out of the truck that I realize how sore I am from the morning of moving. Muscles I hardly knew I had seize and buckle as I walk to the elevator. Fortunately, I got here in plenty of time, as it'll probably take me around forty-five minutes just to walk across the street.

The Platform is a posh outdoor shopping mall located in an incredibly un-posh section of Culver City that's just under a freeway overpass. It has outdoor seating, expensive boutiques, and restaurants that serve a menu full of different kinds of salads: the Platform is the embodiment of Los Angeles.

I stop into Blue Bottle and buy a coffee and something to nosh on as I continue to the furthest corner of the Platform. This is where the most coveted spin class in Los Angeles should be letting out in fewer than twenty minutes.

I find a seat on a slatted bench just across from the spin place and in front of a fancy home goods store where everything looks amazing and comfortably unaffordable. I sip my coffee and wait.

I don't practice my pitch. I'm not nervous. I am also covered in moving dirt from head to toe, probably (definitely) stink, and am wearing a stained gray sweatshirt emblazoned with the silhouette of a woman and the words "LOWOOD INSTITUTION LACROSSE." Billy got it for me for Christmas. Said that it combined two of my favorite things: Jane Eyre and baggy clothing.

Once I finish my pastry, I pull out my phone to check the time and see that my group text with Hani, Elise, and Thornton is blowing up.

"just a pitch, take it or leave it, but maybe we should bring back the code names for this text thread," Hani texts. She is shot down almost immediately. Her next tactic is to type a string of single letters, spelling out:

G
O
O
D
L
U
C
K

Elise reminds me of the talking points that we worked out last night. Then she, like Hani, offers good luck. In the group text Thornton simply types, "you got this."

I look at his text, switch over to his contact saved into my phone, and press Call.

"Hey," he says.

"I'm calling you so I don't get nervous."

"Good plan." I am struck silent, staring at the entrance to the spin place with the heat of a thousand suns. Thornton gets the hint. "So, Lynn is all moved in?"

"Yeah, we got the last of her stuff over there just in time."

"Did you have a chance to go home before heading over to Culver?"

"Nope."

"So you went right from moving day—"

"Yep."

"Well, it'll be a conversation starter."

"I need to say this because I have to get it up and out. What if she's not even here, what if she says no and what if all of this was for nothing?"

"All of those things aren't mutually exclusive."

"Right . . . right."

"For as much as Tavia likes to think so, she's not the only game in town."

"Totally."

"This is actually one of those instances where she needs you way more than you need her." I am quiet. "I pushed it, didn't I? You were okay with those first two, but—"

"You got a bit cocky on that last one." I notice a few people starting to stream out of the spin place.

"I stand by it."

"I'd better get going. They're starting to come out."

"Okay, good luck." I scan the sweaty, beautiful people as they exit the spin place.

"Thanks." I hang up my phone, and flip it in my hands as I wait. Another sip of coffee. I stand. Sit. Stand. Throw my pastry trash away. Sit. Stand. And then I see her.

Striding out in a matching set of white leggings, a sports bra, and a chartreuse zip-up hoodie, Tavia digs out her phone from her work-out bag and bobs and weaves through the outgoing traffic. I throw my coffee in the bin and walk toward her.

"Tavia," I say. My voice is strong. Tavia stops when she sees me.

"Joan?" She walks toward me and clutches me from the side. I feel like I'm being jostled in a crowded bar rather than being hugged. At some point, I pat her shoulder to signal I'm done being "hugged." Which is when she smells me. "Are you coming from a . . . long hike?"

"Runyon Canyon," I lie.

"Oh, fun." She pokes and swipes at her phone, continuing on toward the parking structure. "Okay, well . . . Lovely to run into you!" Tavia picks up her pace, but I keep up.

"I have a story for you," I say.

"Yes, I'm sure you do, but—"

"Are you acquainted with the tech company Bloom and its two founders, Chris Lawrence and Asher Lyndon?" Tavia flicks her gaze toward me.

"We asked them to speak at a small business round table aimed at the millennials just this past quarter." Tavia sniffs. "They declined."

"Did they?"

"It was incredibly shortsighted . . . from a business standpoint." Tavia waves at a trio of women who were, by the looks of their expensive athleisure wear and copious amounts of sweat, probably in the spin class with Tavia. She scrolls through several texts as we walk. The Platform is not a big shopping mall. One block at the most and we are nearing the end of it. My time is running out.

"I've actually written my story up." I pull the printed pages from my purse. "It'll be much better if you just read it." I hand her the pages. She looks as though I've presented her with a high-caloric meal laden with carbs. She looks from the offending pages back up to me. "My writing speaks for itself." I will my hands to stop shaking before the ruffling pages give me away. "Please."

Tavia takes the pages, crumples them in her hand, shifts her workout bag to the other shoulder, and lets out a long sigh. I take a deep breath and make myself hold the space. Tavia drops her phone into her purse and with a slight sneer and a raised overly botoxed eyebrow begins reading the pages. After only a few seconds, she leans forward only slightly toward the pages.

Tavia flips the first page back and pushes her designer glasses further up her perfect nose. Her eyes race across the second page. Eyebrows shoot up. Mouth contorts. She flips the second page back onto the first and dives into the third page. She cringes. A sharp intake of breath. A hand at her chest and she almost rips the page just to get to the fourth and final sheet. A gasp as she comes to the end. She holds the pages tightly in her hand. She looks up at me and I wait. Breathless.

"Is this true?" she asks.

"Yes."

"And can you prove it?"

"Yes."

"This is big," she says, pulling her phone from her purse. "This is big."

"Tavia, if I could—"

"It'll have to be vetted within an inch of its life, but—" She taps away on her phone.

"Now, let's talk terms." I hold out my hand for the pages. Tavia hands them back to me in a reluctant haze. I fold them up and put them back in my purse. She watches every movement.

"Terms?"

"I get final approval over which publication I'd prefer, as well as any and all edits. All four names on the byline appear everywhere the story is. And lastly, the contract will be negotiated through our attorney," I say, handing Tavia Elise's mom's business card. Tavia takes it.

"Attorney," she absently repeats.

"I know what I have, Tavia." She nods. "If the negotiations meet our approval, only then will we send over a digital copy of the story." Tavia stands there, her phone now limp in her hand. She nods her head.

"Okay," she says with an efficient nod. "I'll call—" Tavia looks at the card. "Kerri Nakamura from the car."

"She's waiting for your call," I say, noticing that we've arrived at the end of the Platform and are now approaching the intersection just across from the parking structure. I push the pedestrian walk button. Tavia and I are quiet as we watch the red numbers count down. She taps away on her phone and I replay everything I just said and wonder if I should have gotten an iced tea at Blue Bottle and told her she really must try it and then give her one to take "to go."

The light turns and Tavia and I walk across the street and into the structure where we both pay our parking fees in a truly awkward silence in which I fight every urge not to apologize for being "such a bitch." We ride the elevator in silence, and just as we're about to peel off to our respective cars—

"Where is it you see this story going?" I ask, my hand curling around the door handle of Billy's truck.

"Everywhere, Joan." She looks up from her sleek black Mercedes and makes eye contact with me. "Everywhere."

~~~~~

I swipe open my phone as I sit on the curb outside my house, waiting for Thornton to come pick me up early Monday morning. I haven't heard from Tavia, but Mrs. Nakamura says they've been going back and forth about terms since yesterday.

I felt unmoored when I woke up this morning. I've lived and

breathed this story for the last month. It's been my constant companion. And now it's out of my hands and, along with it, all of the hopes and dreams for what it could be and what I fantasized it could do. And maybe even how it could save me.

But what if it doesn't?

What if the story doesn't fail, but instead does just okay? It makes a few waves, I save the name tag I get from whatever fancy movie studio I've been allowed on for just that one hour of whatever meeting I dressed up way too much for, and Bloom continues on with a slap on the wrist like nothing ever happened.

I know this is where I'm supposed to take the high road—trot out all of my learnings and stare off into the middle distance while musing about how truly noble my quiet life of anonymous scribblings will be, but . . . fuck that.

I want this story to reverberate around the world as a warning to all the Chris Lawrences out there.

We're coming for you.

We're coming for you.

Thornton pulls up; I climb in and throw my bag in the back seat. I lean across and kiss him as if it's the most natural thing in the world.

"You ready to take down a couple of tech bros?" Thornton asks.

"Every day," I say, buckling my seat belt.

"Damn right," he says, pulling down my long driveway and on toward Bloom one last time.

Thornton and I walk into Bloom. Once again, I'm in the lobby that isn't a lobby with seating options that aren't actually seating options now leaving a job that was never really a job. I look over at reception and immediately feel guilty as Caspian waves excitedly to the both of us.

"This sucks," I whisper to Thornton.

"I know," he says, waving back to Caspian. "Okay, I'm going to hit this head on." I smile and give him a sneaky wave. "See you back up in the loft."

Thornton peels off and goes over to Caspian, who chatters about the weekend and what he had planned for the day and what does Thornton think of his new kilt. Thornton likes it, he says. Caspian twirls in celebration.

I scan the main area of Bloom and see Hani embracing Ivy as if she's going off to war. Elise is just behind her, apologizing and pulling her off. Ivy, of course, lunges into Hani for an even longer hug, sermonizing about big emotions and loving as wild as she wants to!

I walk through the main area to the loft in an almost automatic haze, climb the stairs, drop my bag on my desk, and pick up my coffee mug. I zip the little Batmobile around my desk and then catch myself. How quickly this place became routine. I look over at the graphics team, huddled up in their usual Monday morning meeting. Then I glance at Hani's desk. The whole thing is cleaned off. She must have come in early. Taking her lead, I drop the Batmobile and *The Golden Notebook* that Anne still thinks I'm reading into my bag.

No matter what, today is my last day at Bloom.

I check my phone. No news from Mrs. Nakamura or Tavia. That's fine. This is fine. Now holding on a bit too tightly to my coffee mug, I pick my way down the stairs and walk toward the canteen and the Bloom coffee machine. As I walk, I catch sight of Asher and Chris. They're walking into Scooby Doo with that same group of suit-wearing adults who I now know are Bloom's board of directors. A board with no idea what's coming. Or maybe they do know? Maybe Chris and Asher are just pawns of a greedy, faceless monolith of tech business people who want success at any cost. We'll soon find out.

I set my mug in the line and force myself to look around. It really is a shame that CAM didn't work, because what Chris and Asher tried to build here could have been wonderful if it were meant to grow something instead of hide something. These kids would have done anything for them, and instead of cultivating that, they exploited it. These hardworking kids deserved better.

"It doesn't feel real," Elise says, settling in just beside me.

"I feel so guilty," I say in a whisper.

"Don't." She waits and I turn toward her. "This is our moral obligation. These kids have to learn this lesson. It's a hard one, but if they don't learn it now then somewhere down the line they're going to blindly follow someone into much more dangerous territory than this."

"You're right," I say, really hearing her. "You're right."

"This will teach them to question authority. The power and inconvenience of dissent is always a hard lesson to learn," she says. She puts her hand on my arm. "Stay strong. This is much bigger than our discomfort."

"Well, goddamn," I say, laughing.

"You like that?" she asks, shifting our mugs forward in the line.

"Holy shit."

"That's the speech I came up with last night when I woke up in a flop sweat imagining poor, innocent Caspian packing up his little desk and wondering why people had been mean to him." We both look over at Caspian as he labors over which beret to wear today. "I don't think Hani and I are going to make it to lunch."

"I saw her desk was already cleared off," I say.

"Yeah, we packed it up before anyone was in the office," she says.

"She's pretty great," I say, and Elise flat-out blushes as a smile breaks across her face.

"She is," Elise squeaks out. We are quiet. "And don't think we don't know about you and Thornton."

"What?"

"Hani thought you guys would do it in the car, but I had money on the Alpine Inn," Elise says.

"I . . . how . . ."

"Because we're hot lady spies, that's why," Elise says, holding her hands up as if she's bringing home the chorus in a '90s R&B music video.

"I don't know whether to be embarrassed or—"

"Don't be embarrassed," she says. The girl in front of me removes her mug from the drip tray and I step forward. My fingers move across the keypad with speed and ease as Elise continues talking. The machine clunks and whirrs to life. "He really is incredibly decent." I brush off some stray crumbs from the counter as my coffee streams into my awaiting mug. I can't look at her.

"I'm not used to . . ." I look back over at my mug and see that the coffee is done. I pull my mug from the drip tray as Elise sets hers down. She waits. "Things working out."

"Seeing as how all of us are going to be unemployed by day's end, might want to rethink your definition of 'working out,'" she says, punching her own arcane code for perfect coffee. She turns toward me.

"That's definitely true," I say.

"Although I'd rather be on our side than theirs right about now," Elise says, pulling her mug from the drip tray.

"You'll let me know if you hear from your mom?" I ask.

"You'll be the first," she says. We say our goodbyes as she heads over to her dark corner of the office and I walk back toward the loft.

"Joan, right?" Chris. On his phone. Hoodie and jeans. A can of fancy club soda tucked under his arm.

"Yeah. Yes," I say. He is standing just outside Scooby Doo. I wait as he taps away on his phone. Does he know? Were we wrong about there not being any security cameras at the server farm and do they know that we know?

"So, I see that you're settling in fairly well?" he finally asks.

I'm going to take you down, motherfucker.

"I am," I say. Mackenzie walks up to Chris and hands him the ledger for what is probably the meeting he's standing just outside of.

"Getting back on your feet is hard," Chris says. Mackenzie doesn't move from Chris's side. I wait for him to dismiss her, but he doesn't.

"Yeah, well, I think I'm going to be with you guys for the long haul," I say.

"Wonderful, wonderful," he says.

"Thank you again," I say, meaning every word. I look from Chris to Mackenzie and then back to Chris. "You truly have given me the opportunity of a lifetime."

"You're welcome," he says.

"Well, I'll leave you two to it," I say with a polite smile. I look past Chris and Mackenzie to Hani and Thornton watching our conversation with horrified paralysis. I step to the side and continue toward my friends. Hani bounds up the stairs in front of us as Thornton and I follow.

"What did they say to you?" Thornton asks. Hani appears at the top of the staircase.

"No, don't tell him anything yet, I can't hear you." Thornton and I get to the top of the staircase and sit at our chairs, and we all roll into a tight circle.

"It was nothing. Chris was being a dick about this being my second wind and how it's hard to get back on your feet again," I say.

"And what did you say?" Hani asks.

"I told him that I was going to be with Bloom for the long haul."

"Which is technically true," Thornton adds.

"Exactly." My phone buzzes in my pocket. "Oh!" Thornton and Hani flinch as I reach into my pocket. "It's Elise's mom." I tug my headphones from my pocket and plug them in and answer the phone. "Hello, Mrs. Nakamura. Hold on one second while I find a private place to speak freely."

I bound down the stairs, trying to find any empty room in which to have a private conversation. In the end, I sprint all the way right outside the front doors of Bloom and out onto Melrose Avenue.

Out of breath, I listen as Mrs. Nakamura walks me through her contract negotiations with Tavia. Tavia wants to place the story with the *San Francisco Chronicle* because she feels it'll have the most impact, as it relates to Silicon Valley. I text all of this to Hani, Elise, and Thornton in real time, and get their feedback and any questions they have. Once I have their sign-off, I tell Mrs. Nakamura to send over the contracts for us to sign and we will send over a digital file of the story so Tavia and the *Chronicle* can run it through legal and dot all the *i*'s and cross all the *t*'s.

I thank her for all she's done and we sign off. I'm not halfway through the main area of Bloom when my phone dings with the email from Mrs. Nakamura. I walk up the stairs to an awaiting Hani and Thornton.

"Where's Elise?" I ask, before I say another word.

"She's in a meeting. I know . . . it's . . . it's so her," Hani says, unable to keep from smiling.

"Can you get this thing off my phone and how are we going to sign it and—" Thornton takes my phone, his hand lingering on mine just long enough to lower my heart rate by about twenty points.

"I got this," he says, walking over to his desk and tapping away at his computer. I look from him to Hani.

"I knew it," Hani whispers.

"That's what Elise—"

"I knew before Elise."

"How?"

"The Batmobile. I'd never seen him do something like that. It was the first time I saw him giggle," Hani says, smiling just thinking about it.

"The Batmobile is his?"

"Yeah."

"I thought it was yours?"

"Uh, no. I'm a Marvel girl." Hani is absolutely offended. "Thornton is DC. It's . . ." Hani waves her hand in front of her face. "It's a point of contention, so . . ."

"I didn't know," I say.

"Well, now you do." Hani exhales loudly while mumbling something about the DC universe and how could I possibly think the Batmobile was hers *of all things!*

Thornton calls us over and somehow we electronically sign a contract and wait as Elise emails her signature over to join the others.

"The Batmobile was yours?" I ask, after e-signing the contract. Thornton's face colors.

"Are you blushing?" I ask, tucking a strand of hair behind his ear. He leans into my touch.

"Yes," he says, focusing back on his computer. "We're all signed. You want me to send it back to Mrs. Nakamura?" I nod, Hani gives a big thumbs-up, and Thornton sends our signed contract along with a digital copy of the story on to Tavia, who'll then send it on to the *San Francisco Chronicle.*

It is officially out of our hands.

"You know what?" Hani asks, standing up and lunging into a superhero position.

"What?" I ask, slightly numb.

"Chicken butt," Hani says unable to help herself. "No, but really. You know what?" Thornton and I are quiet. "I'm serious this time, no funny business."

"What?" Thornton asks.

"I am going to go get my lady and make like a tree and leaf," Hani says, closing down her thoroughly scrubbed work laptop. Thornton and I look at each other. Why are we hanging around? Thornton spent all morning scrubbing our laptops of anything personal. Our desks are cleaned off, and we know for a fact that, after today's, we will not be receiving another paycheck from the "good" people at Bloom. "You guys want to make like a baby and head out?" Hani tucks her chair under her desk. Thornton stands, walks over to his desk, and shuts down his computer, then tucks his chair under his desk as well. "You guys ready to make like a bread truck and haul some buns?"

"How many of these do you have?" I ask, shutting down my computer, picking up my coffee mug, and looping my messenger bag over my head.

"Millions," she says as I tuck my chair under my desk.

We stand at the top of the stairs and look back at the loft. Thornton holds his hand up in the air. The high five. Hani thwacks his hand without a second thought and bounds down the stairs.

"Oh, god," I say.

"You know you want to," he says. I look at his elbow and hear the crack of my hand on his ripple through the loft. We smile at such a small victory, hoping many more will follow. We walk down the stairs and then across the main area of Bloom. Elise and Hani are already outside waiting for us. Talking and laughing.

"You ready?" I ask.

"Yeah," he says.

"I never got sorted," I say.

"Yeah, neither did I," he says, with a wink. Thornton takes my hand in his and we walk past the front desk, say a sincere goodbye to Caspian, and without looking back, stride out the front door, never to return.

22

Redemption

"Messrs. Lyndon and Lawrence have no comment other than to commend Ms. Dixon on her thorough reporting and to thank her for shedding a light on what she believed was corruption at the highest level. Many older Americans are just as perplexed with the fine print of technology, and while Ms. Dixon is correct that Bloom does, in fact, utilize a server farm to safeguard our clients' data, it is just that and not more. A safeguard.

In a show of good faith, Messrs. Lyndon and Lawrence have donated a share of this year's profits to several organizations whose mission it is to celebrate and protect the First Amendment.

We look forward to serving the American people in the future."

I read it again and again.

"Many older Americans," I say, finally pulling into the parking space just inside the studio lot.

"Yeah, but it's not working. People are calling bullshit left and right all over social media," Lynn says as I shut off Billy's truck's engine. "That was so smart to get screenshots of their website before the story went up."

"Yeah, I'm so glad we did that. What does it say now?" I can hear Lynn clicking around on her computer.

"CAM is nowhere to be found," Lynn says.

"They're trying to get away with it," I say, putting the phone on speaker and switching over to social media, where the hashtag #bloomgoesboom is now trending.

I click on the hashtag and along with my story, and think pieces about my story, there are uploaded vlogs from Bloom of people cleaning out their desks, raiding the canteen, and giving Chris's and Asher's office doors the middle finger. Even Mackenzie has taken a selfie in which all of the stuff from her desk, along with her Bloom swag, is packed up in a box and sitting just behind her in the back seat of her car. Her caption is simply a string of wineglass emojis.

"Yeah, but they won't," Lynn says. I click through photos of the server farm, Chris and Asher pushing their way into the Bloom offices, and stock photos of Silicon Valley and all manner of computers, most of which are so outdated that they reinforce Asher and Chris's statement that most people don't know the first thing about technology other than how to post on social media. "When does your meeting start?"

"In ten minutes," I say, pulling the keys out of the ignition. I can hear my voice as I reply to Lynn. It's hard and clipped. And as we sign off and I walk toward the entrance of the bungalow, the last thing

I want is to ask myself why that is. But, of course, I know the answer to that question; I just don't like it.

I check in with the woman at the front desk, thank her for the bottle of water, and sit among the movie posters this particular production company has made over the last year. I pocket my phone as I'm called into the small development office by a young man in an expensive suit. Once inside, two other young men join us and the meeting goes just as all the others have.

The young men brood about what complicated anti-heroes Chris Lawrence and Asher Lyndon are. They want to "drill down" on what was behind such a desperate choice and really highlight the themes of societal pressure on young men these days and what their relationships with their fathers were like and, you know, have we talked to their schoolmates about whether they were bullied or not? Then, you know, they want to really build out their past, show their home lives, and isn't Asher engaged and, you know, what does his fiancée think of him as a man? They pitch several young white male actors who'd be perfect and that, you know what, this could be an Oscar vehicle for them if we play our cards right.

And then, like clockwork, the meeting builds to a swelling battle cry that what they believe this story to be about is redemption. Who among us, the young man asks. There but for the grace of God go I, another young man sighs.

"We want this movie to—" The third young man pauses, looks out the window and out onto the sprawling movie lot. "Inspire." He laughs to himself. The other two men join in. I'm positive they have no idea what they're laughing about. "We're all flawed." The other two men nod worshipfully. "We've all got a little Chris and Asher in us, you know?" All three men turn their gazes toward me.

"Uh-huh," I say. I stand, shake their hands, they tell me how excited they are to get to work and can't wait to hear from me. I smile and say my goodbyes.

I walk back out to the banged-up truck, marveling at how my story about toppling a billion-dollar tech company just became an inspirational tale about a couple of flawed anti-heroes.

I wrench the truck's door closed, drop my purse next to me, and violently shove my keys into the ignition. I bang on the steering wheel. Again and again.

"Redemption," I repeat. I start the old truck up and reverse out of the space, shaking my head. As I drive, I get progressively madder about every meeting that was billed as everything I'd ever wanted. "Redemption, my ass."

I pull the truck over on a small side street just off Highland and shut it off. I rip the name tag I got at the studio's security gate off my sweater, fold it up, and shove it into my purse with all the others like it. I roll down the window and let the cool breeze in. It's getting hotter. Almost summer. Closing in on a year since I was laid off.

I pick up my phone. Desperate not to think, even though that's exactly why I pulled over, I scroll through some texts. Thornton wants to meet me back at my house. I give him my ETA and tell him I can't wait to see him. Which is the truth. Lynn asks how the meeting went. I leave that one unanswered, and it looks as though I missed a call from Mom. I listen to her voicemail and it's just her telling me that there's an accident on the 110 freeway, so I should probably take the 134 freeway home.

I pull up my inbox. These emails are an actual fantasy sequence of responses from every person I'd ever emailed for a job in all those months and years. Would I like to write a story on this, contribute to that, there's a book agent they'd like me to meet.

And at the very top of the inbox is an email from someone at *The*

New Yorker. They'd like to chat about a long-form piece they're working on about Silicon Valley. They liked my "outsider's take" and would
I consider joining the team. It would involve moving to Palo Alto for
at least three months, possibly as long as six, but they believe it'd be
a perfect fit for me. I drop my phone back into my purse and sit.
Officially too numb to feel.

I start the old truck up again and roar down the quiet side street
toward Cahuenga Boulevard, away from the 110 freeway and toward
the 134 freeway, just like Mom advised.

I pull down our long driveway and see Thornton's old orange
Volvo waiting. He's standing just in front of it. Hands in his pockets. Sunglasses. I smile as I rumble up to him. I shut the truck off,
grab my purse, push open the door, and hop out onto the dusty
driveway.

"So how was your big, fancy meeting?" he asks, taking off his
sunglasses. I lean into him for a kiss.

"Same," I say as we continue on inside the house. "Always the
same."

"That's actually chilling—pathological, really," he says, opening
the front door and waiting for me to go in first.

I step inside and the quiet surrounds us. Dad and Billy are working at the nursery, Anne and Poppy are at the park, and Mom is vol-
unteering at the local elementary school's community garden. I drop
my purse on the dining room table and by the time I've turned around
Thornton has his laptop set up on the dining room table just next to
my purse.

"You working on something?" I ask, walking over to the sink in
search of a glass of water. I pull a squat Mason jar from the cupboard
and fill it.

"I know you haven't asked me what I want—" My stomach drops.
"What I want to do with my life, not us. Job wise." Thornton motions

to the chair just next to him. I sit. I'm growing nervous. I think about the *New Yorker* offer and the temporary move to Palo Alto that I haven't mentioned yet.

"I knew you'd tell me when you were ready. Which, I'm assuming, is . . ."

"Yeah, now." Thornton tucks his chair in closer to the table and taps away on his laptop. "When I went into the Bloom server farm, something clicked. Every single person in there lied. To me. Someone they knew for sure was on their team and even knew a little bit— more than they thought I did, anyway—about what they were talking about. And even then, they tried it."

"I didn't know that," I say.

"Before we . . . this little presentation is kind of a good news, bad news situation, so . . ."

"Oh my god, why would you tell me that?"

"I . . . I actually don't know. I saw you getting all excited and melty about me having found something to do and just felt bad about . . . you know—"

"Felt bad about what?"

"What's going to come next." Thornton taps a few keys and screen after screen of chaos comes up one after another. "This is the data— some of it, anyway—that I pulled from the servers at the Bloom server farm. I've been going through it ever since. I don't know why. At first, it was probably just a puzzle, looking at their coding, seeing how they did it, really just trying to translate what Chris and Asher were saying Bloom did, versus what the guys in the server farm said was happening. But then it became something else—I wanted to figure out what was actually going on. The facts. I'm sure it was about ego in the beginning. But then—it wasn't right what they did."

"I know," I say.

"These tech guys are out-and-out lying to people. Taking advantage because no one understands what the fuck they're talking about half the time. But I do. I want to be these tech bros' kryptonite."

"Hani said you were DC," I say. Thornton laughs and throws up his hands.

"It's the maddest I've ever seen her. A true betrayal."

"I don't understand how—"

"Normal people need a guy who can call bullshit on this tech stuff. I can be that guy. I can be the guy you hire to go in and see if that computer company actually works and whether or not it's worthy of your money or your data or your business. I can bridge the two worlds. I can be the official Nerd Translator. That's the good news."

"You'd be perfect."

"I sent some emails and started talking with a few people I knew from school and reached out to a couple of internships I worked at over the years and I think it's about figuring out if I want to first join a consulting firm to learn the ropes and then go out on my own or if I can manage going out on my own while paying bills by tending bar at this place over in Echo Park that's looking for some part-time help." He smiles. "TBD."

"I love this so much." I pull him in close. "I just want to touch you all the time. I had to say that out loud because I was about to touch—no, I was about to caress your face and I thought that would be weird, but? I kind of always want to caress your face. Is that weird?"

"No," he says.

"No?" I say.

"No." He pulls me in for a kiss. We break apart.

"So, what's the bad news?" I finally say. Thornton gives me one last kiss. And with an arched eyebrow turns back to his computer.

"I was studying the data from the Bloom server farm like I was saying. Seeing if I could spot all the ways they'd hidden shit and whether or not I could explain it to someone—"

"Like me," I finish.

"Right." He turns the computer so I can see it better. I am worried that no amount of visibility is going to make me understand anything that I'm about to look at, but don't have the heart to tell him that. I don't think now is the time to tell him about the Computer 101 course I just signed up for at the local community college. "And that's when I found it." He points to a series of bigger and bigger spikes.

"I don't—"

"See how they gradually start to expand?" he asks, pointing at the expanding width and space between each spike.

"Yeah."

"Now see right here? How this spike just becomes the new baseline?"

"Yeah."

"When I got underneath what that was measuring, I figured out that each one of those spikes is a test. And each time"—Thornton points to each spike, except the very last one—"the test failed."

"But not that one." I point to the last spike.

"Right. Whatever it was they were testing—and I think we're looking at Chris's handiwork here. I read up on his coding and this—" Thornton shakes his head in awe. "This has got him written all over it. But right here? This is where what they were testing started to work."

"If you tell me that I am a looking at a working CAM algorithm right now—"

"You are looking at a working CAM algorithm right now."

"Holy shit." I lean back in my chair. I want to stand up and walk. Run. Get in Billy's truck and drive away. Go up the coast. Maybe take a road trip across the country and swim with the whale sharks in Georgia instead of being faced with a working CAM algorithm mere days after I wrote a scathing article about a very nonworking CAM algorithm.

"But that's not the bad news." Thornton's voice is so kind. I can't say it. I can't ask. Thornton continues, his voice heartbreakingly tender as he does so. "The bad news is that what Chris designed the CAM algorithm to do—and what he's been testing this whole time, apparently using Bloom as some elaborate smoke screen—was not to store data." He waits as I take that in. "What the CAM algorithm actually does is strip the user data from the companies and people who used Bloom for storage. Completely undetected. So while your documents and your music were safe—"

"You weren't."

"Right," Thornton says.

"And now it works. He knows it works." I look back over at Thornton's computer. All those spikes. Relentless testing. Single-minded. And then that one spike. The moment CAM started working.

"Yeah."

"And Meera signed over her shares and—"

"Asher just signed away his today," Thornton finishes.

"So Asher didn't know?"

"I don't think so."

"No surprise there."

"Nope." Thornton and I have a brief second of levity as we share the tiniest of smiles knowing that of course Asher didn't know, because he's a fucking idiot.

"The digital artichoke," I say, my entire face flushing and tingling from the epiphany.

"What?"

"When Chris was super high he told Asher he wanted to invent a digital artichoke. It was the one piece that never fit."

"What does that—"

"The artichoke is just a transportation device." Thornton doesn't get it. "Bloom was the artichoke, but the user data is the melted butter. It's all about the butter. I mean, how often does anyone eat just a plain artichoke?"

"I hate artichokes, so . . ."

"It was a trap."

"Yeah."

"And I stepped right into it," I say.

"We all did."

Thornton rests his hands on my arms and makes me look at him. He's telling me how everyone missed it, no one caught it, and how my article was just the beginning, but his words muffle and disappear, as the ghost of The Dry Cleaning Story howls and moans inside my own head. Gloating and taunting me with the facts that I missed:

- Chris, Asher, and Meera developed CAM.
- CAM couldn't store data securely, but it had the potential to be able to strip-mine user data.
- Meera and Asher had no idea CAM did this.
- Chris did.
- Chris convinced Meera and Asher that CAM didn't work.
- But they could build a company off the harmless lie anyway.
- Chris needed data to test CAM.
- Bloom was born.
- Meera signed over her shares, thinking the company was built on a lie.
- Asher went all in on the big scam.
- Asher got to work on the server farm.

- And the whole time, Chris used the data Bloom gathered to test the real CAM algorithm.
- Bloom is exposed.
- Chris and Asher have written protective clauses into their contract.
- No lawsuits, fraud allegations.
- But Asher signs away his shares anyway.
- Bloom folds.
- Chris is 100 percent owner of the CAM algorithm.
- The CAM algorithm that now works.
- Chris will use the CAM algorithm to strip user data completely undetected.
- He will sell this technology to the highest bidder.
- He was smarter than everyone else.
- Even me.

23

Fuck

I was wrong.

24

Broad Street Water Pump

I'm at the sink. Getting water. I don't know how I got here. I can't remember getting up or walking over. Thornton is watching me, witnessing this. Witnessing me. Seeing me be wrong and watching as that single realization throws me into such a frenzied tantrum that I'm like some spoiled toddler being denied a shiny balloon.

I fill up my glass with water. And drink. Fill up my glass with water. And drink. I don't know what else to do, because I'm afraid if I don't give myself a mindless job I may take this house apart with my bare hands, one piece of wood at a time. I turn around from the sink and face Thornton, the glass of water still in my hand, my shirt stained with wet droplets of rogue water spray.

"I hate that he won," I say.

"He didn't win shit," Thornton says, standing. "This is the first domino, that's all. They'll all fall, I promise you."

"That little piece of shit was smarter than me the whole time, and if you hadn't found that stuff from the server farm I would never have known." I hear myself in that moment. It's not about the story or the truth. It's about who won: Joan Dixon or Chris Lawrence. "Jesus Christ, how did I get here?" I walk over to the dining room table, pull out a chair, and sit. Because I know exactly how I got here. I fought tooth and nail to get here. I thought about one thing day in and day out and sacrificed everything and anything in order to get it. I am here because I put myself here. I am here because I keep putting myself here. I am here because I made choice after choice in order to get here. "No, that's not . . ." I close Thornton's laptop, unable to watch as CAM mocks and taunts me.

I think back to the inspirational pep talk I gave myself while interviewing for jobs. It was all there. I only tolerated rock-bottom because I was certain it'd lead to a plucky and inspirational commencement speech at an Ivy League college. I valiantly weathered this fun, disruptive detour because I fully planned on laughing and joking about my time in the trenches as I dispensed hard-earned pearls of wisdom. This crucible of failure was supposed to be the battleground for my greatness.

I never thought I'd be trudging through mud and shit just to get to being . . . okay.

"Why didn't Tavia invite me to lunch?" I ask.

"Wasn't the whole thing that you were supposed to ask for it?"

"I really thought I wouldn't have to. That the story would be so amazing—"

"The story is amazing," Thornton cuts in.

"So, then it's me." I can't look at him. "There is something fundamentally wrong with me. I'm just . . . I'm never going to be good enough."

"Joan—" Thornton sits down next to me.

"Why won't it stop?"

"What?" he asks.

"Why am I so mean to myself? I mean, Jesus, I know I may not love myself a ton, but fuck . . . does that mean I have to spend every waking moment shitting all over everything I do?"

"When you get an answer, I'd love to hear it," Thornton says, sinking back into his chair.

"I keep"—I put my hand out—out there, out there—"thinking I can earn it, work for it, that someone can give it to me. And if I get it, then all of the sudden I'll"—I take a deep breath—"be happy."

"Yeah," Thornton says, his voice faraway and haunted.

"I hate that it's—" I shake my head. Back and forth, back and forth. Getting madder and madder. "Ugh. I am my one thing." I roll my eyes. "Why . . . why can't I get that?"

"In England in the 1850s—" Thornton looks over at me and can tell right away that I'm confused. "I swear this is related. When has a story that started 'in England in the 1850s' not been what you were spiritually looking for?" I smile. "In England, in the 1850s, there was a cholera outbreak. Now stay with me. And no one could figure out the origin. Was it in the air? Germs? Interestingly, there was even this brewery in the middle of the contaminated zone, and everyone who worked there was fine. Which threw everyone off. Were they not breathing the same air? Shaking hands with the same people?" Thornton waits for me to react. I nod and lean in. "So, they finally figured out that the cholera was originating from one water source: the Broad Street Water Pump. The brewery boiled their water, so . . ." Thornton leans in and takes my hands in his. "Inside of us is the Broad Street Water Pump. But, instead of cholera, it's infecting every cell in our body with this . . ." Thornton looks up to the ceiling. He's thinking. "Bullshit." He squeezes my hands and makes eye contact with me. Makes me look at him. Makes me listen. "If we are going to live, we have to stop drinking from the Broad Street Water Pump."

"The call is coming from inside the house," I say. Thornton laughs.

"Exactly."

"I thought it would work. The story?" Thornton nods. "I thought it would make me feel like somebody." Thornton smiles, leans in, and kisses me. He pulls back mere centimeters and in the raspiest whisper, says—

"I don't know if that's how it's going to work for us, my love."

"No?"

"No." Thornton pulls me into him. I can feel him nodding.

And tucked into the crook of his neck I whisper the strongest possible thing I can think of. "But I still want to take that motherfucker down."

"Oh, yeah. He's going down."

~~~~~

Thornton and I speed up the 5 freeway. I pour handfuls of M&M's into his hand and have decided to bring a box of questions from an old Trivial Pursuit game Mom and Dad had. As we hit the outskirts of Palo Alto, Thornton has chosen Brown.

"What book ended: 'It was a curious dream, dear, certainly: but now run in to your tea; it's getting late'?" I flip the card over. I knew it.

"*Alice in Wonderland*, right? Gotta be *Alice in Wonderland*," Thornton says.

"It is none other than *Alice's Adventures in Wonderland*, yes, you are correct." I tuck the card into the back of the box, look over to the map, and guide Thornton off the freeway. Palo Alto is rainy and wet, the leaves are changing, and as usual Northern California in autumn smells of fireplaces and crisp air.

"Gimme an Orange," Thornton asks, shifting down into second gear as he makes the turn off the freeway and continues to wind through toward our destination.

"Orange it is! What's the oldest trophy competed for by professional athletes in North America?" I flip the card over. I knew it.

"Stanley Cup, my dear. Now come on, I thought you said these questions were going to be hard." Thornton floats through an intersection and I tell him to turn right at not this light but the next one. He gives me a quick nod, puts on his indicator, and gets over into the right lane. He flips on his windshield wipers and finally makes the last right turn onto the beautiful tree-lined Palo Alto street.

We find parking and pull over. Thornton turns the car off, unbuckles his seat belt, and shifts his body toward mine. I put the lid back onto the box of Trivial Pursuit questions and drop them into the Road Trip Bag o' Fun, as it's been named. It's really just a reusable bag from the Dixon Gardens that I borrowed.

"Where did they say they were going to meet you?" Thornton asks, scanning the horizon.

"Here, this is the address. We could be early, I mean maybe—"

"Breaker, breaker, this is Red Otter here with Pink Sunshine, do you read me, over?" Hani crackles through the walkie-talkie.

"Red Otter, this is Bloodhound One, we read you loud and clear, over," I say, smiling.

"We, over?" Thornton shakes his head and takes the walkie-talkie.

"Red Otter, this is Black Fox, over," Thornton says.

"Black Fox, welcome. Pink Sunshine says she saw a donut place just around the corner, over."

"Red Otter, we will obtain donuts stat, I promise, over," Thornton says.

"Black Fox, this is Red Otter. Wolf Two is among the sheep, over. I said Wolf Two is among the sheep, over."

Thornton and I look down the tree-lined street and see Chris Lawrence walking toward a sleek office building along with three other tech bros. I look over at Thornton and smile. I take the walkie-talkie back from Thornton.

"This is Bloodhound One. Wolf Two is now officially under surveillance, over."

Acknowledgments

This book was a tough one. So tough I don't think I can accurately really list . . . I'm getting choked up just . . . I am grateful to so many truly wonderful people. So endlessly grateful. Thank you.

About the Author

Liza Palmer is the internationally bestselling author of *Conversations with the Fat Girl* and several other novels. An Emmy-nominated writer, she lives in Los Angeles and works for BuzzFeed.

Recommend

The Nobodies

for your next book club!

~~~~~

Reading Group Guide available at

www.readinggroupgold.com

9/19